LOVE AND CAGES

K.J. Ersti

Other books in the Fight for Love series:

Love and Bruises

Content Warning:
This book contains heavy material including human trafficking and mention of sexual assault. Do not read if these topics are triggering to you. Your mental health matters.

For anyone who's ever felt like they were caged, I hope you find the courage to break free. And maybe find a kinky partner to help you through it.

Irish Slang

Beour - Beautiful woman

Mac - Son

Athair - Father

Máthair - Mother

A mhuirnín - Sweetheart

Bean théisiúil - Temptress

Tá tú trioblóide - You are trouble

Deartháir - Brother

Ceathrair - Cousin

1

Finn

What did you do if you thought one of your fellow cops had worked with a serial killer to kidnap your best friend's girlfriend? Get them wasted and make them spill their guts, obviously.

It had been a month since Ava had been kidnapped and since then, I had laid low, trying to move on with my life and get back to normal, but all the while, I had been plotting and planning. There was a chance that the killer had worked alone, but I didn't believe it. He was able to kill people too easily, all while evading the police. I was convinced that he had someone on the inside helping him, and I was going to use my position as a rookie cop on the force to figure out who that was.

I'd been systematically crossing people off of my suspect list and now, I had narrowed it down to a handful of people. Tonight I was going to find out just who was in on it.

Grabbing two beers from the bartender with a nod, I turned back to the corner table that I had confiscated for the night. My coworker slouched in his chair, attempting to get the last drops out of his most recent beer. I placed a fresh one in front of him as I took the chair beside him and held up my own.

"Cheers," I said, lifting my beer towards him. He grinned as he tipped his glass towards me before taking a huge gulp. He was already wasted and at the pace he was drinking, he was bound to have one hell of a hangover tomorrow. Part of me felt bad for using him like this—he was a nice guy. But I also knew he had absolutely no filter when he got drunk, and he just so happened to be close with the last people on my list. *Sorry, Greg.*

"I never knew you were such fun company," he slurred.

"I've been trying to be on my best behavior being new and all, but sometimes you just gotta let loose," I responded with a laugh.

"Ain't that the truth. How've you been adjusting to being the new guy?"

"People've been great. I was a little worried about what happened last month, but I'm glad things have died down now."

"Whatta' bout last month?" He asked with a frown.

"You know, those murders at that hotel."

His brows furrowed deeper as he took another drink. "Ya?"

"Cap started asking around after that and I was a little worried I'd be put on a short leash," I said with a shrug, attempting to appear nonchalant.

"Asking about what?"

I glanced around the bar as if I was making sure we weren't being observed. "Between you and me, they were looking into the idea that some people on the force were possibly involved with Cain," I said in a hushed tone.

Greg choked on his drink and I slapped him on the back. "You okay, man?"

"Yeah, yeah just swallowed wrong," he replied, clearing his throat.

Bullseye. I nodded as if I totally believed him and went back to my drink.

"So the captain was asking around about it?" Greg asked nervously.

"Ya and since I'm the newest guy, I think I might have been on his list." I lied.

"Shit, man." He said, rubbing the back of his neck.

"I guess someone was getting paid to look the other way." I continued. "Anyway, he finally moved on to someone else so I feel like I can finally breathe a little easier now. Sorry, gotta piss."

I abruptly stood and made my way to the bathroom, hoping my gamble was going to pay off. I stood in the hallway for a few moments, my phone to my ear. Just when I thought I was wrong, Greg's voice came through.

"Hey, man. Yeah, I was just talking to someone and they said that Captain has been asking around about the murders from last month. Yeah, well I just thought you'd want to know." A pause. "No. They didn't say." Another pause. "No. They'd been asking him if he'd done it. Yeah, Finn. No, obviously I didn't, I just wanted to let you know. Okay, okay, fine!" A longer pause. "Asshole."

My heart raced as I took a second longer before heading back to the table. I'd felt guilty about slipping a recording device into Greg's pocket, but now that he'd proved me right, all I felt was satisfaction.

I made sure my steps were loud so he heard me and didn't think I was sneaking up on him before I slid into my chair and grabbed my beer again, taking a big swig.

"How do you like working days compared to nights?" I asked, trying to act casual and turn the conversation into something safe before I freaked him out. We continued chatting for a while longer before I made a show of looking around the table and patting my pockets.

"Shit!" I exclaimed.

"Wassup?"

"I think I lost my phone. You mind if I use yours to call myself?" I asked, holding out my hand."

"Oh, sure." He passed me his phone after unlocking it and I held my breath as I swiped to his call log. *Bingo*. I copied the number, quickly texting it to myself before deleting the message thread and returning to the app to call myself.

My phone rang from under my chair where I had conveniently dropped it.

"Oh, thank God," I said, handing back his phone and grabbing my own. "I think that might be my sign to leave," I said with a laugh.

"Alright man, see ya around."

I grabbed my jacket and phone and headed for the door, excitement coursing through me. After a month of investigating, I finally got a lead.

Once in the safety of my car, I pulled up the text thread and copied the number I'd sent myself, searching to see if I had a match in my contacts—and I did. *Sam Jenkins*. "Feck yeah," I said triumphantly. He'd been on my shortlist, I knew he was close with Greg and I'd been right. I had the mole.

2

Vi

I took a final deep breath in an attempt to calm my nerves, before entering the New York ballet theater. Stepping across the threshold sent shivers up my spine and I could taste the excitement of finally fulfilling this dream.

You, a ballerina? Yeah, and I'm the king of England. I could hear my father's drunken guffaw in my head as if he was standing right in front of me and not buried six feet under.

"Here's to you, fucker," I mumbled.

"What was that?"

Face flaming, I turned to see a tall blonde standing just inside the lobby, holding her phone like she'd been responding to a text.

"Oh, sorry, just talking to myself," I said, hoping she hadn't heard what I'd said. Not a great first impression.

She gave me a warm smile as she pocketed her phone and stuck out a manicured hand, "I'm Bella, you must be new."

"Victoria, but you can call me Vi," I said, shaking her hand. "And yeah, first day."

"In that case, let me show you around." She said, before

spinning on her heel.

"How long have you been dancing here?" I asked while I did my best to memorize the rooms she pointed out as we headed towards the back of the building.

"Four years or so," she said tossing her blonde ponytail over her shoulder.

"How do you like it?"

"I can't imagine doing anything else," she said matter-of-factly as we entered a large room filled with dancers and surrounded on all sides by mirrors and ballet barres. The place was beautiful and I tried not to drool as I took in everything around me. I'd finally made it.

"Who's this?" Asked a beautiful brunette who entered behind us, looking pointedly at me.

"I'm Vi," I said, sticking out my hand. She looked at it with a curled lip before avoiding my gesture and walking past without a word.

"That's Julia, ignore her," Bella said from beside me. "She doesn't like anyone or anything, especially if you're new."

"Good to know," I said, feeling the sting of her obvious distaste.

"Dancers, welcome, come on over to the barres." Winnie, the artistic director, said as she entered from the back of the room with a flourish. She was a tall Asian woman, with a dancer's body and the first hints of gray at her temples. She looked like she was born to dance.

My heart rate quickened at her words and Bella bumped her shoulder into mine from where she stood to my left. "After all this time I still get that feeling. Honestly, we all pretty much have a girl crush on her," she admitted with a laugh.

"No kidding," I said, unable to keep the awe out of my voice. We all gathered at the center of the room and Winnie waited until everyone had taken their place in a circle.

"Happy Tuesday, my loves. I wanted to start today by welcoming our newest dancer, Victoria." She gestured to me and all eyes turned in my direction as I smiled.

"She will be taking over for Chelsea as she goes on her leave," she continued, motioning to a blonde standing right next to her. When Winnie had offered me the position, she told me that one of the members of their corps de ballet had recently gotten pregnant and was going on leave. In the meantime, they were looking to fill the hole, and that is the reason Winnie had given me a chance here.

I first met Winnie at a club I had been working at, and when I introduced myself to her I was hoping for anything— a chance at an apprenticeship, heck I'd even scrub the floors for an opportunity to get near the stage. But Winnie had been willing to watch me dance and by some miracle, had offered me a position in the company. I still felt like I needed to pinch myself every so often to make sure that this was real.

I knew I had a natural talent for ballet, and I had worked my butt off to get where I was, but a spot in the NYC ballet company was extremely competitive and now that I had this opportunity, I was not going to let anything get in my way.

"As a reminder, we are rehearsing for our fall musical. Let's start with warmups, and Victoria, I'd like to chat before you start."

The crowd broke into groups and I waited as Winnie turned in my direction.

"Victoria," Winnie said as she approached me, Chelsea following after her.

"Winnie, this is amazing," I said motioning around us.

She beamed. This theater was clearly her pride and joy. "I'm glad you're enjoying yourself so far. Hopefully, the dancers have made you feel welcome."

"Yeah, Bella was especially kind showing me around."

She looked at the girl with fondness. "Bella is one of the

best soloists we have. I'm glad she introduced herself. Speaking of introductions, this is Chelsea."

"Congrats on the baby," I said, turning towards her. She smiled back at me shyly. "Thank you. It was incredibly unexpected but we're really excited. I'm going to miss this place though," she said wistfully.

"I expect you to come on back when you're ready," Winnie said, giving her hand a squeeze. Chelsea nodded emphatically before giving me a small wave. "Good luck here, it was nice to meet you." Then she headed for the side. I turned back to Winnie who pulled out a folder that she offered to me.

"Homework," she answered my unspoken question. "For now, buddy up with someone for stretches and take the first couple days to watch and study. I expect you to be joining the routine by the end of the week."

"Of course," I said, holding the folder to my chest.

"I'm excited to have you here with us. Let me know if there's anything you need while you're settling in," she said before breezing off to catch another dancer who was stretching near us. I wondered if she ever stopped moving. She reminded me of a hummingbird, constantly flitting around.

I laughed at the mental image and walked over to the cubbies where I set down my bag and the folder on top of it before finding Bella against the far wall. She sat stretching with another dancer who looked to be her opposite, dark-skinned with short back hair. Bella made room for me as I approached, motioning between the two of us.

"Vi, this is Shelby. Shelby, Victoria."

"Hey," I said, dropping down next to them and starting my own stretches.

"Nice to meet you," Shelby said with a welcoming smile. "Is today your first day?"

"Yeah, it is."

"You'll get there, the first bit can be hard to adjust, but as long as you put in the work you'll be fine." She said encouragingly.

"Are you a soloist too?" I asked.

"I wish," she said with a laugh. "I think I've got a ways to go before I advance, but mostly I'm just happy to be here."

"Mostly?" I couldn't help but ask. She grimaced and I got the impression that she didn't want to expand.

Bella replied instead, speaking quietly. "It's great here, we love Winnie and the dancing. But— the compensation could be better."

"The pay?" I pushed and she nodded. "A lot of the dancers have to work multiple jobs just to afford the basic necessities and it can be hard to stay on top of the performances when we don't have as much time to practice."

I nodded at her words. I was used to working multiple jobs to get by, but I also knew that this job was going to be all-consuming. I could understand the frustration of trying to be the best while not having the time to do so.

"Anyway, tell us about you," Shelby said, abruptly changing the subject.

"Not much to tell, I grew up around here, got into dance when I was little, and fell in love."

"Have you ever been with a company before?"

"Nothing like this, that's for sure. I've been serving and doing odd jobs for a while but finally met Winnie and she gave me a shot. What about you guys?"

"I grew up rich, was put in every sport and recreational activity my parents could think of, and I fell in love with ballet," Bella said without hesitation.

"Little socialite," Shelby quipped affectionately.

Bella rolled her eyes with a smile as she continued. "My parents had all sorts of connections and got me in with

Winnie before my dad decided to drain our bank accounts thanks to his gambling habit."

I winced at that before turning towards Shelby. "And you?"

"I spent some time in foster homes, and one of the programs I joined offered ballet lessons, which I absolutely loved. Once I was adopted, my parents wanted to 'encourage my passion'. They're adorable. Anyway, I tried out for the company for years until they finally had an opening and here I am."

We moved to the bars as we continued to stretch and I again took in the room around me. "This place is beautiful, I can't imagine what the stage will feel like."

"Have you ever been here to see a performance?" Shelby asked, bending into a deep side stretch.

"Yeah, I've seen a couple and they were breathtaking, magical. Honestly, I probably saw you guys at one point," I said trying to remember back to the dancers I'd watched. "But I can't imagine the feeling of being the one on the stage."

"There's nothing like it," Bella agreed, her face filled with wonder. "Even after doing it for years, it seems unreal at times. The music, lights, atmosphere, it's incredible."

We fell into a comfortable silence. "Do you guys live around here?"

"Yeah, we share an apartment just down the street," Bella answered for them. "How about you?"

"I'm a little ways out but I'm right next to a subway station so it's convenient to get here."

"You have a boyfriend? Girlfriend?" Shelby inquired.

"Boyfriend," I replied, thinking about Phil. "How about you guys?"

"I don't really have time for relationships at the moment, too focused on dancing, as depressing as that sounds," Bella laughed. I turned to Shelby and she shrugged. "I'm in between relationships at the moment."

"Yeah, we don't talk about *her*," Bella said with a grimace and Shelby elbowed her. *Okay, touchy topic, don't go there*, I thought to myself.

Winnie finally called the group back together and I settled against the wall as I watched everyone line up and begin the first of several routines. I split my time between watching the dancers and reading my packet in an attempt to memorize the steps there. This was going to be a ton of work but I could already tell that this was going to be everything I had dreamed it would be and more.

3

Finn

I had to figure out what to do with the information I had now. I slept on it and the next morning, I listened to the recording that I had taken. It wasn't legal and wouldn't stand up in court, but it was very clearly suspicious. Now, I just had to decide if I trusted my captain enough to bring this to him.

Despite what I'd said to Greg, I had never actually been questioned about any involvement with the murders. I had, however, spoken to the captain about my suspicions of someone being on the inside. While he had not given me the task of finding them, he had seemed open to my suggestions.

Cain was gone. I wasn't worried about anybody on the force continuing his insane murder rampage, but I did believe that everyone involved should be prosecuted for their part.

Having made up my mind, I headed to the station to talk to Marcus Rodriguez, aka Cap.

"Morning, sir," I said as I entered his office, thankfully finding him alone.

"Sullivan," he answered warmly, using my last name as most people on the force did. "What can I do for you on your day off?"

"I have a sensitive matter that I was hoping to discuss with you."

His expression turned serious. "By all means," he said motioning to the door. I closed it before sitting in the chair opposite him.

"Do you remember our discussion from last month after the Laurie murders?" I asked.

"I do," he replied, a frown creasing his brow.

"I believe I found something indicating that there was someone here on the force working with Cain."

The look he gave me was hard. "You understand the seriousness of this accusation?"

I did my best to keep my back straight as I nodded. "Yes, sir. I'm not trying to come in here and cause division. I understand that I am the new guy and that this is absolutely stirring a pot that I don't have much to do with. But, I know that I worked with Arthur to solve that case from the inside and I truly believe that someone was helping Cain sabotage the investigation. If that is the case, I cannot just sit here doing nothing."

Marcus stared at me unblinking. I had no idea what he was thinking or how he was taking this.

"If these claims are unfounded, you understand that it is your career on the line?"

I swallowed hard. Was I willing to throw everything away for this hunch? I could ignore it, tell him I was mistaken, and go back to doing what I was doing. Ava was safe, Art's company was fine, everything was solved. But I knew I wouldn't be able to live with myself. Even if that meant jeopardizing my position here. Even if I was blacklisted from a position as a cop forever. I needed to do this.

"Yes sir," I said again.

"Alright then, what it is you would like to share?"

I took a deep breath before pulling the recorder out of my pocket. "I was out for drinks with Greg Thomas, and I took this recording without his knowledge. I told him that you were investigating people, including me, for any involvement in that case. This was a phone conversation that I recorded between him and a number belonging to Sam Jenkins." I placed the device on his desk. "I don't have any hard proof of anything, but I needed to pass it on to clear my conscious."

Marcus picked up the recorder and then looked at me under furrowed brows. "I will listen to this and be in touch."

"Thank you, sir," I said as I stood and exited the room without another word. It was out of my hands.

~ ~ ~

I spent the rest of the day catching up on errands that I saved for my days off. Grocery shopping, meal prep, the like. As I was in the kitchen finishing up my phone rang. Art.

"What's up?"

"I was calling to make sure you were coming to Ava's birthday party." My overbearing best friend said.

"Remind me when that is?" I responded, placing the last container in the fridge.

"Are you serious?" He asked, incredulously.

"I'm kidding, of course I'll be there. You are way too easy to rile up, you know that?"

He called me some choice names that I chose to ignore. Instead, I laughed at my friend and asked, "How's business?" Art had recently taken over ownership of a chain of luxury hotels after his mother's unexpected passing. He'd always had money but he'd become an instant billionaire and was now responsible for hotels all across NYC.

"Great, we officially bought our newest location and have started some updates and renovations."

"I can't wait to reserve a room. How's the change in management going?"

"Honestly, smoother than I was expecting. Tanya has been doing great and things are about as unified as I could have hoped for at this point."

"Good. You deserve some peace."

"How about you?"

Where to begin? "I talked to my captain about a possible mole." I didn't need to expand, he knew exactly what I was referring to.

"And?"

"And I think I might have found out who was involved." Silence.

"Are you sure?"

"No. But something's definitely going on."

"So where do you go from here?"

"I shared the information with Cap and he's going to look into it."

"And that's it?"

"Well if he doesn't find anything substantial, I might have just lost my career, but you know, just another Tuesday," I joked.

"Are you serious?"

"I mean, I'm coming in here accusing people of working with a known murderer, if I'm wrong, I wouldn't want me on the force either."

"I'd tell you that I don't think you shouldn't have pursued this—"

"But then you'd be lying."

He grunted his agreement. When it came to his girl, there was no lengths he wouldn't go to bring those who had a hand in her kidnapping to justice. Or even just revenge.

"I got you," I said, not needing to say more than that.

"I know. And you know if you lose your job, I'll find

something for you to do here." He replied.
   I scoffed. "Like I'd ever willingly work for you."
   "Dick."
   "Bollix."
   "See you tomorrow."
   "Absolutely."

4

Vi

I'd spent the entire evening reading and rereading, watching videos, and doing my homework until my eyes felt like they were going to bleed. I got a couple of hours of sleep and was now back at the studio. I walked in to find Shelby and Bella already stretching together, deep in what looked like a serious discussion. I was tempted to give them space, but I didn't want to just stand there awkwardly, and I did need to stretch, so I finally joined them. I glanced over as I settled in and asked, "Am I interrupting something?"

"No," Shelby replied without hesitation and Bella bit her lip as she looked at her friend.

Now I really felt awkward.

"Bella is just being her overbearing self," Shelby finally said.

"I'm trying to look out for you. If it seems too good to be true, it probably is." Bella retorted.

"I can leave if you guys need to continue this," I said.

"It's fine," Shelby said with a sigh. "Some of us just don't have the freedom to play it safe."

"Shelby was approached by a group that wants her to dance for them for cash," Bella said, plowing ahead.

"Like…stripping?" I asked cautiously.

"No," Shelby said quickly but Bella continued to look at her pointedly.

"They said it was nothing like that," Shelby argued.

"Well then why else would they be willing to pay you? There's no way they just want to watch you perform Swan Lake."

"They said," Shelby interrupted Bella. "That they want us to help some young girls who don't have the ability to take official ballet lessons."

"Yeah, that doesn't sound shady at all." Bella scoffed.

"If you're going to be such a freaking downer you can just leave it alone," Shelby snapped.

"When are they wanting you to do this?" I asked, trying to smooth some of the tension in the room.

"We're going out for dinner tonight to talk details. If I don't like it, I can just say no." Shelby replied.

"I'm coming with you," Bella said. "I'm not letting you go alone."

"Great, then maybe you'll see that it's fine. They said they'd pay as many of us who wanted to join. You could come too, Vi."

"Tonight? I can't, I have my best friend's birthday party. I agree though, I definitely think it would be smart not to go alone, even if it will be in public."

Shelby rolled her eyes. "Not you too."

"Hey, I completely understand the need for some side gigs and have no problem even if it does turn out to be stripping, I've done my fair share of side dancing, but I still think you should be smart about it. How did you hear about them anyway?"

"They reached out to me. I'm assuming they saw my

information on the website or something. Regardless, beggars can't be choosers," she said with a shrug.

Just then a large group of dancers entered, including Julia who's eyes immediately filled with disdain when they landed on me.

"I really don't get why she hates me," I muttered.

"Ignore her," they both said in unison. I laughed and shook my head. "Easier said than done."

We continued stretching and Bella brought us back to the previous conversation. "Don't you think it's weird timing with all the creepy shit going on lately?"

"I think you're paranoid," Shelby retorted.

"What creepy shit?" I asked.

"Don't encourage her," Shelby grumbled but Bella turned towards me. "Multiple dancers have admitted to feeling some weird vibes around the theater. And no, I'm not super witchy or anything, but when multiple people feel like they're being followed or watched I do tend to believe that something is going on."

"So what, you think people are stalking the theater and now are trying to get me to meet up with them? Why would they do that?" Shelby asked her friend.

"I don't know," Bella said with a shake of her head. "I'm just saying it's weird and I don't like it."

"Has anything been done about it?" I asked.

"There's nothing concrete to really pursue," Bella responded. "A random shadow here, a maybe suspicious car there, doors that are unlocked that should have been locked, that kind of stuff."

"Yeah, that's creepy." I agreed. "This place is beautiful, but it's huge. If there's someone messing around in here I can't imagine how unnerving that would be."

"See, now you've got her all creeped out too," Shelby sighed.

Bella shrugged. "Maybe it's just the cautious person in me, but I'm just saying, keep an extra eye out and if you see anything weird, tell someone."

"Got it," I reassured her.

Winnie came in and the group moved to the middle of the room again. I found my place by the wall and settled in to memorize more of the routine, putting the girls' concerns out of my mind for the moment.

5

Finn

"Sully."

I glanced up from my cubicle where I was currently standing putting on my gear.

"Yeah?"

"Cap wants to see you." My coworker said. Well, here it was.

I'd spent all evening stressing about what he would say when I saw him next and how it would turn out. Honestly, after the anxiety of the last twenty-four hours, part of me was glad to get this over with.

I finished dressing for my shift, before heading to hear my future—even though I might end up packing it all back up.

"You wanted to see me?" I asked as I entered my boss' office.

"Yeah, close the door behind you and sit please." He said, his face serious.

I did and could feel my hands start sweating even as I placed them on my legs.

"I'm going to cut to the chase." He began. "I knew you had

expressed concern over the Laurie case and how it might have been handled, but I was still completely taken aback to hear that you had been doing your own investigating." I nodded but didn't speak as he appeared to contemplate his next words.

"The idea that there are people on my force here who would stoop so low to work with a murderer and kidnapper is appalling, insulting, and horrifying. I pride myself in creating a trusting and safe environment here, a group of people that I trust to serve and protect. Anything less than that is unacceptable."

Another pause.

"I looked over the information you gave me and did some investigating of my own." I took in the dark circles under his eyes and his slightly more disheveled appearance than normal. Had he even slept last night?

"It turns out that you were right. Jenkins and Thomas are no longer employed here due to the information that connects them to Cain. The investigation is ongoing and I cannot share anymore, but I did feel like I owed it to you to let you know."

I sat in stunned silence. I had been sure they had something to do with it. I'd looked into them and was confident enough to bring it forward, but hearing him say it aloud, I couldn't believe it was actually true. Cain hadn't worked alone. Jenkins and Thomas had played a part in Ava's capture, however small. I clenched my hands in my lap and nodded. It was over.

"The ongoing investigation includes a thorough investigation to make sure that they were the only ones involved. This entire unit will have a complete overhaul, if needed, to make sure that everyone receives justice. Part of that includes you."

My head shot up as I tore myself from my thoughts.

"Sir?"

"That was ballsy. Risky, you pursued something above your clearance and chased a tail without permission or direction. You took the initiative and it paid off. I would like to promote you to a detective position. We need guts and the confidence to take risks like you did. I can sense your passion, your drive to see justice served, even at the expense of your career, and I applaud you for that. I would really like to promote you if that is something you are interested in."

"Yes, absolutely," I answered without hesitation.

Marcus laughed, "You don't need to answer right away, it would be a big change. Feel free to take some time."

"Not necessary, sir. Don't get me wrong, I enjoy what I do, but my goal has always been to someday work as a detective."

"Good, I was hoping you'd say that. Now, enjoy your shift on the street, I will have HR begin the paperwork and let you know the next steps regarding training."

"Thank you, sir, truly, it means a lot."

He waved his hand dismissively and I stood to exit.

"One more thing, Sullivan."

I turned back around.

"I know that I said I appreciate your guts, but I also value your life. If you keep going the way that you are, one day it might just get you in some deep shit."

"Yes, sir."

With that, I exited and headed to my squad car, double-checking that I had everything before radioing in the start of my shift.

Immediately I was dispatched to a noise complaint. My mind spun as I buckled and drove towards the address. I enjoyed what I did, some days more than others, but I'd always wanted to work on the detective side of things. I'd been expecting to have to put in years before I was promoted, never had I imagined that it could happen so soon.

When I'd started investigating Jenkins and Thomas it truly had been for selfless reasons. I wanted to make sure anyone involved in Ava's disappearance was brought to justice. And I didn't feel right letting it go when there could be something deeper involved. But the fact that Marcus had seen me and I was getting rewarded for it? Excitement coursed through me at the thought.

Focusing back on the call at hand, I parked in front of the address I'd been given and knocked on the door. An older woman opened it as if she'd been waiting for me to arrive, which she probably had been.

"My name is Officer Sullivan, I'm here about the noise complaint."

"Yes, thank God you finally got here."

I resisted the urge to roll my eyes as I nodded solemnly. "What seems to be the problem?"

"The problem? The problem..." She exclaimed, her voice rising. "Is that the new couple down the street will not keep their dog in check. All hours of the day, he's outside howling and here I am just trying to enjoy my morning coffee and he is going absolute nuts next door. I can't even concentrate on reading the paper. You'd think they run an animal shelter with all the noise coming from there—"

I continued to nod and jot notes as she talked and complained. "Which house is it?" I asked when she paused for a breath. She sighed in exasperation before pointing across the street. All was quiet at the moment and I took a deep breath as I nodded. "Okay, I'll be sure to write a report on this."

"Are you not going to go talk to them?" She asked in shock.

"Ma'am, right now I don't hear anything—"

"That's because you took so long to get here! If you'd come when I first called it in, you would have heard it."

"I understand ma'am, and you can feel free to call it in again if it happens."

"So my word means nothing?"

"It does, which is why I will be writing this up so we have it on record for when it happens again."

She huffed but seemed marginally satisfied. I finished up and made my way back to my car. I drove down the street so that Karen, as I'd affectionately named her, couldn't think of some other reason to need me, and then I finished my case notes before putting myself back in service.

I was driving towards a local breakfast spot when dispatch radioed me for another call. This one was a medical and my heart sped up as it always did when I had one of these. I only had basic medical training—EMR was the highest level I needed as a cop—so I didn't know much, but I did have first aid and CPR training, which I honestly had to use frequently since I was usually the first responder on scene.

An hour later, I wrapped up at the hospital after riding with the paramedics to help apply pressure to a massive bleed from a knife wound. Never too early to start knifing each other. Thankfully, I hadn't been first on the scene, so I didn't have the massive headache of paperwork to deal with now.

My clothes were dirty and I caught a ride back to the station where someone had dropped off my car. I changed clothes, taking a quick shower before heading back out.

By the end of my shift, I'd also dealt with a lift assist and a domestic call. Thankfully Karen hadn't called back and I felt bad for whichever one of my coworkers had to deal with her again tomorrow morning.

I took another shower at the station before changing into my casual clothes and clocking out for the day. I'd completely forgotten to get Ava anything for her birthday and, thankfully I had a little bit of time, so I stopped by her favorite café to buy a gift certificate. Not the most meaningful gift, but I had never claimed to be sentimental.

As I checked out, I thought about the fact that Vi would be there and anxiety bubbled in my gut. I'd been enthralled with her basically from the moment I'd met her, and that attraction had only grown the more we'd hung out and gotten to know each other. Our best friends were dating each other and it seemed only natural for us to go out as well.

Unfortunately, she'd turned me down when I asked her out, stating she had a boyfriend who Ava conveniently told me afterwards was a massive dick. Today would be the first time I'd seen her since and I was already dreading the awkwardness of this next encounter. *You can do this, Finn. You're not a prepubescent boy,* I berated myself. People got turned down all the time, but I could handle it maturely without making things awkward.

If only the knowledge that she was taken would lessen the desire growing inside of me.

6

Vi

By the time practice was over, I was thoroughly exhausted. I'd stayed back against the wall while they practiced, still not ready to join them, but I had done the routine as best as I could while watching. I was getting the hang of it, and all of my homework the last couple of days was paying off. I was confident that by the end of the week, I'd be able to follow along through the whole thing like Winnie had hoped.

I used the theater bathrooms to shower before I needed to leave for the club for Ava's party since I didn't have time to run home first. As I was finishing up, I heard voices in the stall next door which I couldn't help but listen to.

"It's a camera, I freaking told you."

"There's no way it's a camera, who would do that?"

"I don't know, but I swear that's what it is."

I wrapped myself in a towel before stepping out to join the two girls who were arguing.

"What's wrong?" I asked, looking towards the wall where they were staring intently. One of them turned towards me and motioned inside the stall.

"I found a camera inside the stall. Someone is watching us shower."

"What?!"

"We don't know that for sure. How would someone even get it inside here?" The second dancer interjected.

Just then the bathroom door opened and Winnie and a third dancer entered.

"Where is it?" Winnie asked as she approached.

The first girl who was convinced that it was a camera showed her where it was and I noticed a small lens stuck in the corner of the shower stall. Winnie scratched at it and it came off and fell into her palm. She stared down at it with a frown. "I will have to have this assessed, but for the moment, I think we should close the showers temporarily as I figure out what it is and where it came from."

I tightened my towel around myself and glanced around cautiously, half expecting to find another camera somewhere nearby. Why on earth would there be a camera in the bathroom? Was it related to the other strange things that Bella had mentioned feeling?

Goosebumps prickled my arms. Well, I'd definitely not be comfortable showering in here for a very long time now.

The group left and I dressed as quickly as I could before exiting the bathroom. Winnie stood in the hall on the phone with someone. "Are you the last one in there?" She asked me.

"Yeah, I think everyone else left."

"Okay. I'm going to be closing the area for the moment." She frowned and shook her head. "As if I don't have enough on my plate already."

"Are you okay?" I asked, noting the shadows under her eyes.

She sighed. "Nothing you need to worry about. But thank you for asking. I'll see you tomorrow, Victoria."

I waved before making my way out of the theater and onto

the subway toward the club where Art had reserved an entire VIP area for Ava. I found her seated on a bench with a half-full glass of rum if I had to guess.

"Starting without me, bitch?"

She glanced up at my voice and jumped to her feet, giving me a big hug. "Ahh, I'm so glad you're here."

"You know I wouldn't miss it," I said squeezing her before settling into the plush cushion next to her.

"How's the ballet?" She asked excitedly. While it was true that we technically still lived together, she was spending more and more time at Art's and we hadn't had time to properly catch up since I started.

"A dream," I said, accepting the drink that mysteriously appeared in front of me. "Seriously, Winnie is a goddess and I've already made a couple friends with some of the other girls, they've been so kind." Well all except Julia but we didn't need to mention her.

"Well obviously, everyone loves you, I knew you'd fit right in."

"I met the dancer who I'm replacing, she's going on maternity leave and was super nice about me replacing her, at least to my face. How's work been for you?"

Ava made a pained face in response.

"Uh oh."

She rubbed the back of her neck. "I've been looking elsewhere, but I really don't want to get a different position just because of my connection to Art," she said motioning to her billionaire boyfriend who stood against the far wall giving us 'space.' "I just don't know how long I can work with Kim knowing the part she played in everything. I'm trying not to think about it, but it's been kind of slow right now so it's easier said than done."

"Well if you want to investigate a weird group who's been trying to recruit the ballerinas, I have a story for you," I said with a laugh.

Her face grew serious. "What do you mean?"

I instantly regretted saying anything. I didn't want to worry her, and, honestly, I had no idea if there was anything to be worried about to begin with. I had no idea if the bathroom incident was related in any way to Shelby's strange group.

"It's probably nothing, but two of the dancers I've made friends with were talking about how there's been some weird stuff going on at the theater, and then one of them was approached by these people offering them cash to dance. One of the soloists, Bella, seemed really concerned about it. I was going to go see what it was all about but it was tonight and obviously—" I motioned around us to the room that was slowly filling with people.

"Promise me you won't go." She said as soon as I paused.

"What?" I said, turning back to her.

"I don't like that. Promise me you won't go alone, not without someone like Art or Finn with you."

"I don't need a man to accompany me A," I said indignantly.

"Do it for me, call it my birthday present. I don't want you getting into anything shady without some backup."

I rolled my eyes but relented. "Fine, I promise."

She nodded but didn't look relieved.

"Okay, can we change the topic? Like about how old you're getting or the fact that your boyfriend spent a bajillion dollars for your birthday party?"

She laughed and looked towards Art. As if he could sense her, his gaze swung to hers and they stared into each other's eyes, lost to the world. *Barf.*

I tore my eyes from the couple, feeling that familiar ache of jealousy at their love. My eyes fell on the man who had just entered, muscular build and an orange mop of curls that bounced as he walked. Without meaning to, my thoughts drifted back to the conversation we'd had the last time I'd seen him.

"I know it might not be great timing, but I've been thinking about it for a while and I was wondering if you wanted to go out with me sometime?"

"—I have a boyfriend," I'd had to answer with.

Guilt hit me. Had to. Who thought of their relationship status as a reason that they *had* to turn someone down? I knew it wasn't right, I just didn't know what to do about it.

Phil was great, he was a computer geek and we'd met at one of the restaurants that I waitressed at. He'd been funny, and straight to the point and had asked me out the first time he saw me. I'd loved how he went for it and we'd gone out that week. Our chemistry was fine, nothing like the fireworks that Ava and Art exuded, but, like I'd told Ava, not all love stories were like that.

Love. Did I love Phil? Absolutely not. I mean, not right now. We had our own lives, we were busy. Did I sometimes feel like his accessory? Yes. But when he *did* make time for me it was nice. He was a great boyfriend when he wanted to be. *And when he didn't?*

I pushed that thought out of my mind. It didn't matter. I was busy, I was mostly fine with the lack of attention. Plus, I didn't want to be suffocated like Ava was when Art was around. I was just fine, even if a pair of green eyes and a mop of orange curls took up a little too much space in my thoughts.

7

Finn

The first thing I noticed when I entered the party was Vi and Ava lost in conversation on the couch. Art was at his usual spot playing guard dog to his girl. Possessive gobshite.

"You made it," he said clapping me on the shoulder and tearing my gaze from the olive-skinned goddess on the couch. I swear every time I saw her she got more beautiful.

"Of course, any chance to spend your money," I said with a grin. He rolled his eyes at me but fell into step beside me as I approached the birthday girl.

"Happy birthday, gorgeous," I said, pulling her to her feet and kissing her hand for an exaggerated moment. I swear Art growled in response.

"Thanks, Finn," she said giving me a wide smile before tucking herself into Art. I plopped down into her vacated seat, draping my arm over the backrest—maybe or maybe not —intentionally brushing Vi's shoulder as I did. She shivered against my touch and I had to refrain from smiling. She was spoken for. She'd already told me she had a boyfriend, I was a dick for doing anything even as simple as a brief touch. But

I couldn't help it, her skin had a magnetic draw to it and it took everything in me not to get lost in her.

"What did my bestie do to spoil you on this special day?" I asked, attempting to break the growing tension between me and the brunette seated beside me.

Ava launched into an elaborate explanation of their day and I laughed and joked but couldn't quite tear my thoughts from Vi.

"How's work?" Ava asked when she finished her story.

"Good. Actually, I just got a promotion."

"Oh my gosh, that's awesome!" Ava exclaimed.

"Congrats," Vi said and I finally let myself look towards her.

"Thanks," I said with a genuine smile.

"What are you doing now then?" She asked.

"I'm getting promoted to detective."

"Detective?" Vi's eyes widened and I smiled at the surprise there.

"It's not that impressive but yeah, a little more training."

"Come with me to get a drink?" Ava said from beside me and I looked over to see Art nod before the two of them headed towards the bar.

"How's the ballet?" I asked Vi.

"Good," she said, her face lighting up at the mention. "I'm not really participating in the choreography so far, but just getting to be there in the environment is amazing."

"I'm happy for you," I said sincerely. "I'll be front row at your first performance," I said with a grin.

Her smile faltered. Damnit. I'd pushed too far.

"How's Phil?" I said, trying to change the subject. "That's your boyfriend, right? That's what Ava said."

"He's fine. Good." She said shortly. *Feckin eejit*, I berated myself. *You can come back from this. Play it cool, play it cool.*

"How's it been living alone?" I asked. She cocked an

eyebrow and I motioned to our friends. "You know with the love birds basically moved in together."

She laughed. "Yeah, they're kind of insane."

"Believe it or not, he was even worse before he met Ava."

She laughed again and I could get lost in the sound forever.

"I kind of hated him at first," she admitted softly.

"Really?" I asked, turning in her direction again. I knew I gave him crap all the time but he was a great guy.

"Yeah, when they were still figuring stuff out and had a fight, Ava mentioned some of the stuff he said and I kind of decided I'd never forgive him."

"And did you?"

"Yeah," she said sheepishly. "It only took a couple times watching them together to see how absolutely in love he is with her. Plus, all the stuff he did to get her back—"

Silence fell between us as we both thought back to that time. Not wanting to stay in this serious place I tried to change the subject.

"I'm glad you forgave him. Guys can be dicks but he has a good heart."

"You can say that again, the part about guys being dicks," she laughed.

"Tell me about it," I said with a dramatic sigh. "I've been living with one my entire life."

She laughed again and I smiled, staring at her. The moment stretched on and my eyes dropped to her lips for the briefest moment. Her tongue peeked out to wet those goddamn lips and I could feel myself getting hard imagining that tongue doing other things.

I forced my gaze back up to meet her eyes and she was staring at me in a way that I could almost convince myself was reflecting the attraction that I felt. I leaned towards her just the slightest bit and her breath stuttered. It would be so easy to close the last bit of distance between us…

Someone nearby laughed loudly and she jerked back, the spell broken. I cleared my throat and stood, "Do you need something else from the bar?" I asked.

"I'm okay, but thank you," she responded with a smile.

I made my way to the bar calling myself all sorts of names. She'd turned me down. It was fine. It was her right. I needed to stop making things awkward and get back to just being friends. I was not going to ruin this friend group because I was horny.

"Finn."

Art walked up to me, looking abnormally serious.

"What's up?"

"Victoria. Ava said she mentioned to her that there's some weird things going on with the ballet. Girls getting suspicious invites. Ava's worried, said she wants you to keep an eye on Victoria, make sure nothing weird is going on."

"Of course. What exactly is happening?"

"Apparently Victoria didn't want to talk much about it, but there's a group of people offering to pay the girls to come dance for them and it sounded off. They were going to go out tonight to meet them, but Victoria came here instead. Ava said she made her promise not to go out without one of us, but she said she's not too confident she'll listen if the other girls are going."

"I'll see what I can find out," I said.

"Thanks, man. She's her best friend, if something happened to her—"

"You don't need to explain. I'll keep an eye on her. I know your whole alpha thing extends beyond Ava to her friend," I said with a wink. He shoved my shoulder but didn't respond. He had no good comeback. He and I both knew he was absolutely whipped.

"Love looks good on you, man," I said seriously.

His face softened in that way that only Ava could bring

out. "She's the best thing to ever happen to me."

"Besides me of course."

"Whatever you say, Sullivan," he laughed as he walked back to his girl.

Envy ate at me as I watched them together. I was man enough to admit that I was lonely. I wanted what he had. Maybe after I settled into the new position and figured out what was going on with Vi I'd start genuinely looking for a relationship. Life was too short to spend it alone.

8

Vi

"What was that about?"

I glanced over at Ava as she sat back down beside me in Finn's vacated spot.

"What do you mean?" I asked as innocently as I could.

"I mean the fact that you guys looked like you were about to start the room on fire from the heat emanating between you."

I felt my face warm at her comment. I truly didn't know what it was. I was attracted to him, yes, but I knew I was in a relationship, he knew I was in a relationship, and yet somehow that didn't seem to matter when we got lost in conversation.

"Nothing, I don't know what you're talking about," I replied instead. There was no use admitting it when I knew it was wrong and couldn't go anywhere.

"Mhm," she said, totally unconvinced.

"Here," I said, changing the subject by placing a package in my bestie's lap.

"Ooh, I'm excited," she said as she began to open the

present. The boys appeared out of nowhere and I did my best to ignore Finn's presence even as I felt him beside me as we watched Ava.

She unwrapped the small box and opened it to find a silver tennis bracelet with half of a heart inside. She looked up with a smile and I held up my wrist to show off the matching bracelet that completed the heart. "I thought it was time to replace the ones we lost years ago."

"I love it so much," she said, pulling me into a hug. We'd had similar bracelets years ago but Ava had lost hers in a move when her parents divorced and I had promptly gotten rid of mine because I felt bad having only half a heart.

"You two are disgustingly adorable," Finn said, pulling me from my thoughts. We laughed as we sat back and Ava raised an eyebrow at him. "You're just jealous that Art won't get you guys matching best friend bracelets."

"Is that true, Arthur?" Finn said, turning towards him, looking utterly offended.

"Send me your wrist size and I'll get one made for you for your birthday," Art responded, rolling his eyes.

"Well it only counts if you have a matching one that you wear," Finn retorted.

Ava laughed, wrapping an arm around me and grabbing Art's hand on her other side. "Thank you guys for the best birthday ever. Seriously, this last year was insane, but I'm so thankful to celebrate stepping into the new year with you all. I couldn't ask for anything better."

I felt tears prick my eyes and I squeezed her tight. "Cheers to a better year with less psycho kidnappers."

"Cheers!"

9

Finn

I entered the station the next day, my stomach a knot of both excitement and nerves. Here I was about to fulfill my childhood dream.

My goal had always been to advance to detective, but with how competitive of a field it was, I hadn't assumed it would be so soon. Working the streets was meaningful and I wasn't complaining, but the idea of more, of getting to investigate and solve puzzles, I loved it.

"Sully," one of my coworkers said as we grabbed our equipment together.

"Anders."

"I heard about the promotion, congrats man."

"Thanks," I said, unable to keep the smile off of my face.

"Not gonna lie, I'm totally jealous."

I held up my hands, "Hey, I didn't do it. Take it up with Cap."

He continued to grumble and I pointed to the picture inside his locker. "How are the girls?"

His demeanor instantly changed as he grinned like a

lunatic, "They're amazing. Still not sleeping through the night, but Carrie's a saint, and God, they're perfect."

This man was head over heels. I stepped closer to the picture of him and his wife each holding a baby girl who appeared only a couple of months old. They were identical, dressed in pink and purple matching outfits.

"They're adorable," I said truthfully.

Pride filled his face as he nodded. "Yeah, I'm so lucky."

I finished strapping on my equipment and he headed for the break room while I walked towards Cap's office. I entered to find one of my coworkers, Libby Brown inside. "Cap, Brown."

"Come on in, Sullivan. You know Detective Brown?"

I nodded. "Yes, sir."

"She's going to be your FTO as you learn the ropes. You've got some online training to complete, but you'll be shadowing her once you get that done. Consider her your partner for the next couple months."

"Awesome. Homicide, right?" I asked, turning to the short, dark-skinned woman in front of me.

"Yep," she answered with a smile. "Also, I prefer if you call me Libby. You're the one who helped take down those two involved in the Laurie, right?"

Marcus coughed and she shrugged. "Everyone knows, boss."

"Yeah," I responded. "Art, the CEO of Laurie, and I grew up together."

"Ahh. Well, welcome aboard, it'll be nice to have you."

"Feel free to use one of the offices for today, you can start shadowing Brown after you get through the initial courses," Marcus said.

"Yes, sir."

"You guys already have similar shifts so your schedule shouldn't have to change too much. I already sent you a revised calendar. Let me know if any of those days don't work for you."

I checked my phone to confirm that I had received his email before I gave Libby another nod and walked over to my office for the day. I slid into the leather chair and pulled up Vi's contact as I waited for the computer screen in front of me to load. I hadn't talked to her about the situation at the ballet yet, but I hadn't been able to stop thinking about it since Art told me. I sent off a text before I could stop myself.

Me: Good morning, I was hoping we could chat about something when you get a chance.

I knew she was an early riser, but as far as I knew practice didn't start quite this early so I wasn't surprised when her text came through a moment later.

Beour: That doesn't sound ominous at all.

I sent back an image with sealed lips.

Beour: I have a little time before I leave for the ballet, what's up?

How to go about this. 'Your best friend's boyfriend is worried about you and told me I had to check in' was true but seemed a little too direct.

Me: Ava mentioned something weird might be going on at the ballet and now that I'm training to be a fancy detective she thought I should check it out.

Beour: Ughhh of course she did.

I waited for her to expand as I logged in and maneuvered to the training Marcus wanted me to complete.

Beour: There's not really anything to tell. Some of the girls were approached by someone who wanted to pay cash for them to dance for them. I don't know much more. They were going to go out last night with the group so maybe I'll hear from them today how that went.

Me: I can stop by after work to talk to ya'll if you want.

Beour: That's really not necessary. But thanks.

Well, that couldn't be any clearer of an answer.

Me: No problem, let me know if you change your mind Beour.
Beour: ???
Me: It means girl.

Beautiful girl, but I didn't need to add that. It wasn't flirting if it was true, right? *You're being a dick, Sullivan. Stop trying to infringe on their relationship. You're not a home wrecker,* I chastised myself.

I was tempted to text back and apologize when she responded.

Beour: Okay, el hombre.

I laughed as I put my phone down. She was fine, it's not like I was asking her to break up with Phil for me.

I settled back and clicked on the first training video.

10

Vi

Did he really think I wasn't going to look up the meaning? Google was free.

I shook my head as I finished dressing and left my house, walking towards the subway station. I could hear his voice as I read his text and the way that I read his nickname sent butterflies to my stomach. He was a flirt. I'd seen it firsthand with Ava, and yet somehow when he made those comments to me it felt different. More sincere.

I tried to push those thoughts out of my mind as I entered the theater. I was irritated, but also not surprised, to hear that Ava had told Finn what I had said. It really was my fault for telling her in the first place, but maybe I'd talk to the girls today and be able to tell her that it turned out to be nothing.

Shelby was already stretching when I entered and I joined her in what was becoming our usual spot along the wall. The group was split up into multiple rooms and times for the majority of these practices so far. Once we got closer to performing we would start rehearsing altogether, but in the meantime, it was easier to spread out the number of dancers.

"Morning Shel. How was last night?" We had a group chat, but I'd been busy last night and they hadn't volunteered anything about their evening.

"Good," she said, smiling up at me from her spot on the floor. "There were a couple people there, both men and women, and they seemed really interested in our talent and experience. I think it could honestly be a great thing."

I dropped down next to her to start my own warmups. "That's amazing. And the pay is good?"

"Amazing. It's through some nonprofit, I think, but they have grants or something to pay us with. It will go a long way in helping me cover my bills."

"What did Bella think?"

"Yeah, what did I think?"

I glanced up to see her dropping her bag down next to us with raised brows. I turned back to Shelby who rolled her eyes.

"She's less than thrilled about the situation, but no one is forcing her to go along with it. I'm relieved to see that they aren't a bunch of old, creepy, men wanting me to twerk for them and that's good enough for me."

I laughed. "I'm also relieved to hear that."

Bella grunted in response but didn't say much else so I took that as a good sign. Maybe they wouldn't be outright fighting today.

I was getting so much better at dancing and by our lunch break, I had a huge smile on my face along with the sweat. I'd been able to keep up with Bella and Shelby and, while I might not be as polished yet as they were, I was close. It had been a little while since I'd danced this much and I definitely felt like I was dusting off cobwebs, and at the same time, my body felt like it was coming home.

My phone rang as I was filling my water during our break and I answered when I saw it was Ava.

"Hey, babe."

"Vi, sorry I didn't know for sure if you'd have a break for lunch."

"Yeah, you called me at a great time."

"Good. Did your friends let you know about the dinner from last night?"

I rolled my eyes. Here was journalist Ava. Like a dog with a bone anytime she sensed a possible story.

"Yes, and you will be pleased to hear that Shelby said they seemed perfectly normal. It's part of some nonprofit with grants for low-income kids, not some creepy, old, men wanting a strip tease."

"Did she mention what nonprofit?"

"No."

"Vi—"

My phone buzzed, interrupting her. "Hey, sorry, I promise I'm not trying to ignore you but Phil's calling me."

The line went quiet for a second. "Okay, we'll talk later. I'm going to be at Art's tonight, but I'll be home tomorrow, maybe we can do a movie or just drinks and girl time."

"I'd love that. See you then."

I hung up and answered after a deep breath. "Hey."

"Victoria, how are you."

"I'm good, how are you?"

"Good, good," he said, almost absentmindedly. It had been several weeks since I'd seen him last, he hadn't come to the celebration breakfast that Ava had thrown me but, let's be real, that was more of a casual thing over coffee. I knew he'd been busy with work, but it was still a little frustrating to have only gotten a text here and there. He must have been experiencing a lull at the office if he had time to call me now.

"I wanted to know if you wanted to meet me for lunch."

"Phil, it's already 1230."

"And?"

"And it's a little short notice for lunch, plus I'm busy."

"Oh, what are you doing?"

I could feel my irritation grow. "I'm at the theater until five."

"The theater?"

I tried not to grind my teeth. "Yes, the ballet theater, dancing, at practice."

"Since when did you start there?"

Anger pulsed through me. I knew he'd been busy recently, but I had told him as soon as I had gotten the call from Winnie with my acceptance. I'd even seen him after my audition with Winnie and told him all about it. Did I matter so little to him that he couldn't even remember any of that? *No big deal, you know, just finally achieving my dreams here and you can't even care less*, I silently berated him.

"I started this week, I told you about it already," I said, unable to keep the bite out of my voice.

"Hey, don't get upset, I spaced it. Yeah, of course, the ballet. Well, we could do dinner after you get done if you want. Scratch that, I have something tonight. Tomorrow? Yeah, I could make that work."

Not even an *Oh shit yeah how's your dancing going?* No, just straight to trying to find time for a booty call.

"I'm busy tomorrow," I said, letting the irritation come through.

"Babe, don't be like that. I've been busy, you know I've been swamped at work."

"I've been busy too, Phil, working multiple jobs, auditioning for the ballet, and all the training and practice I've had since starting."

"I know, I know. But I just haven't had time to think about your dancing—"

The way he said it made it sound like I was trying out to be in a garage band, not that there was anything wrong with that, but it pissed me off how condescending he sounded.

"Phil? Go fuck yourself." I hung up and dropped my phone into my bag.

Was that my most mature response? No. But it did make me feel better. I knew ballet wasn't going to save anyone's life or change the world, but the way he completely diminished it was ridiculous. It wasn't like he was out saving lives either.

I angrily recapped my water bottle. Maybe he'd call back and leave a voicemail apologizing, maybe he'd be pissed. Honestly, at the moment, I was too angry to care. I was at the perfect place to release my anger anyway. Might as well use this energy for something good.

I left the water fountain and walked back toward the main room, passing several doors along the way. I stopped when something flashed in the corner of my eye. I turned towards my right where there was an empty hallway. It was dimly lit and I stared into the darkened space. What had I seen? It almost seemed like a camera flash, but I didn't see anything now. What would have caused that?

The bathroom incident came to mind as I stood frozen in place. I hadn't yet heard if the device they'd found had truly been a camera, but the showers were still closed as they investigated.

The hair on the back of my neck stood up and I swiveled around to look behind me. I had the creepiest feeling that I was being watched. But had someone really escalated from placing cameras in the bathrooms to breaking and entering?

Turning back towards the practice room, I walked a little faster than I needed to until I reentered the occupied room. I felt my shoulders relax when I was once again surrounded by people. It was probably just my imagination after everything that had been going on the last couple of days.

The rest of the day was uneventful, I got to watch Bella perform her solo and it was everything I'd imagined it would be. I kept up with the corps de ballet, and satisfaction filled me with a day well spent. I was really here, practicing with the rest of the theater, for a show that we would be performing in just a few short months. Nothing could ruin this.

As practice came to a close, Winnie gathered everyone together for an announcement. "I'm sure you've all heard by now, but there was a device found in the girls' bathroom the other day. We immediately closed the showers, but I have recently been notified that it was indeed a camera that we found."

Gasps rang out through the room and Bella turned towards Shelby and me with worry lining her face.

"We are having a security company come and do a thorough investigation of the theater, but in the meantime, I do suggest that everyone buddy up when leaving the building after dark just as a precaution. I take your safety extremely seriously, and I do not want any of you to feel like you are at risk."

"You hear that?" Bella asked, grabbing our hands. "We don't leave without each other."

Neither Shelby nor I argued. A camera in the shower was more than a little unnerving. Whatever was going on, I didn't want any part of it.

11

Finn

After a day of PowerPoints, quizzes, and employee videos, I felt like I was about to lose my mind and was second-guessing my decision to move up in the company. I knew it was necessary for the company to prove I'd been *adequately trained,*' but did the higher-ups really think that we learned anything from these things?

By the time I was clocking out, I was dreaming of an ice-cold beer and trashy TV. My phone rang as I slipped into my car and I answered it after seeing Ava's name pop up.

"Hey girl, what's up?"

"Are you home yet? I was hoping to catch you before you left work."

"Well, you have impeccable timing 'cause I'm just getting in my car now." I turned on my vehicle and let the call transfer to the car speakers.

"Oh, awesome. Sorry to be obnoxious, but I'm really worried."

My anxiety instantly rose. "What's wrong? Are you okay?"

"Me? Oh, yeah, totally. It's Vi I'm worried about."

I felt a moment of relief before the anxiety came back in full force. "What happened?"

"Nothing yet, but I'm concerned she's going to do something dumb. Art said he told you about the whole dance thing, right? I called her today and it sounds like her friends feel confident in meeting with this random group and I don't like it. I was hoping I could be really annoying and ask you to swing by there to talk some sense into her on your way home?"

I pulled out of the parking lot and drove towards downtown. "It's no problem at all, but you have a lot of faith in my persuasion skills."

"I figured maybe hearing the concerns from a cop might help since I don't think she's taking me too seriously."

"It's no problem," I said again.

"I know it might seem like I'm freaking out over nothing but I was looking into it and I don't like it."

"What do you mean?"

"I did some digging and it doesn't seem like this is the first time girls from the NYC ballet have mentioned being pursued by a group of people like this."

"And?"

She blew out a breath. "The NYC ballet is extremely competitive. Generally, if you're lucky enough to get a spot there, you stay for a long time. Well, there's been a suspiciously high turnover rate for the last couple of years, and several years ago one of the main soloists mysteriously disappeared. Nobody ever figured out what happened to her, but her family did a bunch of interviews saying they thought something bad happened to her, she wouldn't just up and leave without telling anyone, etc."

Goosebumps rose on my arms. I prided myself on my intuition and judgment, and Ava's story was sending blaring warning bells throughout my head.

"What's the name of the missing dancer?"

"Rosie Sanchez."

"I'll look into it."

"Thanks, Finn, I know I'm using you for your position but —"

"That's what friends are for A. I have no problem checking it out. And I'm on my way now to the theater, I'll check in with her before I head home."

"You're the best." There was muffled talking and then her voice again. "Art says you need to come over for drinks on your next day off."

"Count on it."

I hung up after a brief goodbye and spent the rest of my drive contemplating what Ava had told me. I didn't like the sound of it one bit.

I pulled into the employee parking lot for the theater and had just parked when the backdoor opened and dancers began to spill out. After a couple of minutes, I caught sight of Vi walking with two other dancers. I exited and strolled towards them. Vi looked up as I approached and I didn't miss the smile that lit her face at seeing me. I really shouldn't be that affected by a smile.

"Finn, hey." She said.

"Hey back," I responded, not quite sure how to tell her that her best friend had sent me over. I suddenly noticed the silence and questioning looks being sent between us by her friends.

"I'm Finn," I said, sticking my hand out towards the blonde standing closest to me.

"Bella," she said shaking my hand. "This is Shelby," she said motioning to the other girl who gave me a small smile and a wave. "We were going to go grab a bite to eat if you wanted to join us?" Bella asked.

I could have just pulled Vi aside to chat about what Ava

told me, but honestly, I was starving after work and the thought of hanging out with Vi and her friends sounded much more appealing. "I don't want to intrude, but sure, I'd love that."

"Definitely *not* intruding," Bella said with a smile and I caught the hint of flirtation in her voice. "Thai food okay with everyone?"

Nobody objected and with that settled, she nodded to Vi. "I'll send you the address if you want to ride with him."

"Do you not have your car here?" I asked Vi.

"No, it's a straight shot on the subway."

"See you guys there," Bella said before she and Shelby headed for the parking lot.

"I like your friends," I said as we started towards my car.

"They're amazing. Bella was the first person I met when I got here and she pretty much pulled me in and introduced me to Shelby. Bella's kind of the self-proclaimed mother hen of the group."

"She seems really nice but yeah, definitely the ring leader." I laughed.

I opened the door for her and went around to the driver's side after she was seated.

"Not that I'm not happy to see you, but why are you here?" She asked.

"Ava called me," I said, starting the car. She groaned in response but I continued. "She's really worried about you and I'm not sure she's wrong to be."

"Not you too."

I held up my hands, "I'm not saying it's anything serious yet, but yeah, from what she's found about the previous dancers going missing, I'm pretty concerned."

"Dancers going missing? She didn't say anything about that. Although—" she didn't finish whatever else she was going to say. "I haven't even met the group, and from what

Bella and Shelby said they seem innocent enough."

"So you're saying you wouldn't go meet them if your friends went?"

When she didn't answer I nodded. "Exactly."

"I'll be careful, it's not like I'm going to go signing my life away to someone random for the promise of extra cash."

"Well, I'm relieved to hear it."

We rode in comfortable silence and I parked outside the restaurant that Bella sent us. I looked towards Vi and saw her staring unseeing out the window. She seemed a little quieter today than usual and I wasn't sure if it was because of what I'd said.

"You okay?" I asked.

She glanced back at me. "Yeah, why?"

"You just look—troubled."

She laughed but it didn't hold any humor. "It's just been a long day. Let's go get something to eat."

We entered the restaurant and I was surprised by how cozy it was. Definitely a mom-and-pop shop, the kind that probably went unnoticed unless you knew about it. We settled at a table where Bella and Shelby were already seated.

"So, how did you guys meet?" Bella said, jumping right into it.

I laughed and, when Vi didn't immediately answer, I took the lead. "Our best friends are dating. We met through them."

"And what do you do, Finn?"

"I work for the NYPD."

"A cop?" This time from Shelby.

"Yes, ma'am."

"Oooh," Bella said throwing a not-so-subtle look toward Vi who ignored her. *Interesting. Did they know about Phil? Or just not care? And why didn't Vi correct them?* I tried to ignore how happy that fact made me and turned my attention back to the girls.

The waiter appeared and, after we ordered, I asked Vi's friends. "How long have you guys been dancing?"

"Years," they answered in unison.

"And you like it?"

"There's nothing else like it," Bella said, her face lighting up in the same way that Vi's did when she talked about ballet.

"So I'll see both of you on stage at your next performance?"

Bella sent another look towards Vi who was all but guzzling the beer the waiter had just dropped off.

"We'll save you a front-row spot," Bella said with a beaming smile.

Our food was delicious, conversation was fun, and by the time we left my stomach was bursting and I felt a low buzz from the alcohol I'd consumed. Vi on the other hand hadn't stopped drinking all night and her eyes had a glassy sheen to them. She finally looked untroubled by whatever had been bothering her, however, so I chose not to comment on the amount of liquor.

I drove us to her flat and parked in one of the visitor spots. I didn't currently trust her to get inside without falling into a bush, regardless of how graceful she normally was.

"I'm fine," she muttered as I took her arm and helped her towards the front door.

"Oh, I can tell. I'm just doing my gentlemanly duty walking you to your door."

"I's not like we're 'n a date or something." She mumbled and I tried not to acknowledge how much that stung. I must not have done a good job though because she patted my arm as we stopped so that I could unlock her door.

"Sorry."

"You've got nothing to apologize for," I said stiffly before opening the door and helping her inside.

"Ida be nice if it was a date though. I haven't been on a date in so long." She said as she stumbled down her hallway.

I chose to ignore that comment, instead leading her towards her room, grateful that I'd helped the girls move in so I knew my way through the place. We made it to her bed and I helped her sit on the edge before turning towards the door. "I'll go get some water."

I made my way to the kitchen, rummaging around in the cupboards until I found some aspirin and filled a glass with water. I made my way back to her room to find her staring out the window. Guess she wasn't ready for bed yet. I set the glass and pills on the bedside table, pulling back the comforter before turning around and almost falling over. Vi was bent over in the process of taking her leggings off. *Fecking hell.*

She stood with one leg up as she struggled to get the pant leg over her ankle. Her ass was gloriously out, her thong doing nothing to cover it. *Fuck, fuck, fuck.* I should not be looking. I needed to get out of there, she wasn't even aware that I was there. This was *wrong*.

I went to pass her to leave the bedroom when she stumbled, falling headfirst towards the dresser.

"Woah there," I said, jumping forward and catching her before she could hit anything. Her ass pressed straight against my growing erection and I carefully helped her to her feet before stepping backward. She turned, having freed her legs from her clothes and I couldn't help my wayward eyes that dropped, taking in those beautiful, long legs. My gaze finally met hers and she smiled sheepishly.

"Thanks for catching me, I guess I drank a little more than I meant to."

"It's fine," I said through a tight throat. "Let's just get you to bed before you end up hurting yourself.

"You're so sweet," she said as she took a step towards me

and the bed. How had I ended up in Victoria's room with her pantsless and drunk? Ava was going to kill me. Art was going to kill me. Phil was going to kill me. Wow, my future did not look great.

"Okay, bedtime," I said before I could do something even more stupid.

"I don't want to go to bed," she said, stopping in front of me.

"Trust me, you do," I replied, trying not to breathe too deeply and risk smelling more of her intoxicating scent or feeling her body brush against mine. I was already rock hard just seeing her in her underwear and the feel of her ass pressed against me even for that brief moment? Yeah, I was definitely going to think about that later in the shower.

"Thanks for bringing me home," she said, wrapping her arms around my neck. She was tall, not much shorter than me, and her head fit perfectly in the crook of my neck when she nestled herself in. I needed to untangle myself from her, I really did, but how many times had I dreamed of being this close to her? Plus, friends hugged right? It's not like I was doing anything wrong.

My conscious laughed at that but I ignored it as I wrapped my arms around her back in a gentle embrace, making sure to keep my arms over her shirt and away from that delicious ass that I was never going to get out of my head.

"You really need to get to bed," I murmured into her hair, feeling my restraint pulling taught.

She mumbled something I couldn't understand and I gently pushed her back enough so that I could hear. "What was that?"

"I said you're so bossy," she grumbled and I grinned.

"I'll take that as a compliment," I winked. She reached up her hand and wrapped one of my curls around her finger.

"I've always wanted to do this," she whispered, weaving

her hands along my scalp. Fecking hell, I was in so much shite.

"Vi," I warned, but she didn't take the hint. Her fingers kept their exploration and god did it feel amazing. I wanted her to trace every single inch of my body. I wanted to be completely at her mercy as she did exactly what she wanted to me, touching me, feeling me, tasting me.

I groaned at the thought and an evil smile lit her face at the sound as her hands dropped to my waist, finding themselves under my shirt. Her touch felt like a brand against my bare skin and it took everything in me not to strip down naked in front of her and let her fulfill every desire in that pretty little head of hers.

"Victoria," I said, trying desperately to stop this before it went somewhere we'd both regret in the morning. Well, she'd for sure regret it. I don't know if I could manage to, even knowing that she was in a relationship. Fuck. I'd never been a cheater, I hated cheating, and I would not do that to another person, regardless of how much Ava said she deserved better.

I grabbed her wrists to stop her. I opened my mouth to explain all of the reasons we couldn't do this, but all at once she closed the distance between us and her mouth was on mine. All of my reservations melted away at the feel of her soft lips, the taste of the beer on her tongue, and the way she kissed as if she were trying to consume my very essence.

I groaned into her mouth and it only seemed to spur her on as she pressed closer. My hands left her wrists, moving into her hair and angling her head so that I could get better access to her mouth. She was the best thing I'd ever tasted. Soft, and firm, warm, and when her tongue parted my lips I knew she was damning me. I was about to rip off her shirt and throw her onto her bed when the alcohol on her breath brought me back to reality.

This wasn't her. She wasn't in any position to be making

this decision. She was way too drunk, she didn't have the ability to consent, and she was surely going to regret this in the morning.

I pulled back, both of our chests heaving. I pressed my forehead to hers as I grabbed her hands again. "I can't. Not right now. Not like this." I pressed a kiss to her forehead before forcing myself to exit her room. I didn't look back as I locked up and finally made it to my car. Once seated I dropped my head against the back of my headrest and cursed myself out with every name I could think of. How could I have been so stupid?

It didn't matter that she was the one coming on to me. She was drunk. She was in a relationship. She'd already told me no while she was sober. There was no way she actually wanted this. And now, I might very well have messed up our entire friendship. *Fecking eejit.*

I arrived home, still smelling Vi all over me. I needed to get this off of me. I turned the shower as hot as it would go before stepping into the scalding water. I flinched at the burn and began scrubbing at my skin, punishing myself for the lack of self-control. I may not have initiated anything, but I sure as hell didn't do enough to stop it from happening either.

The memory of her perfect ass pressing into me, her flowery smell wafting up. My cock jerked, not carrying that the moment had been entirely wrong. And then when she'd pressed her lips to mine—

I groaned as I fisted my aching cock. She tasted so good, felt like heaven. I stroked myself from base to tip, thinking about her hands sliding under my shirt. If I hadn't stopped her she would have pulled my shirt up and off, hands sliding across my abs. Her hands would have traced the top of my jeans before pulling them down to expose my dick.

I closed my eyes as I continued to rub my hand up and

down, picturing her standing there in front of me instead. The desire in her gaze, those perfect lips. I imagined her dropping to her knees in front of me, wrapping her mouth around my cock and—

I came so hard, spurting myself into my hand as I groaned out my release. *Fuck.* I didn't deserve to find release to her. Another man's girl. But there was no way my dick was listening to that.

I finished showering and climbed into bed, feeling the guilt and regret and *if onlys* fill my mind.

~ ~ ~

The next morning came with a headache and so much guilt. I half expected to have a text waiting for me when I woke up, from Vi or Ava or Art or maybe even Phil. I didn't know whether to be concerned or relieved when that wasn't the case.

I made it to work, stopping to pick up coffee with an extra shot. I needed all the help I could get to make it through today.

I checked in with Marcus to start my shift.

"Sullivan, good morning."

"Good morning, sir. I wanted to get my orders for today."

"How were your training modules yesterday?"

"Exhilarating," I deadpanned.

"I see they haven't changed since when I went through it," he said with a laugh. "You have a couple more things to finish up today, HR sent over some things that need extra signatures as well, so it looks like another day in the office. Your next shift you can start shadowing Officer Brown."

"Alright," I said, feeling excitement at the prospect of starting so soon. "Oh, Cap, I had a weird request."

"Shoot."

"I have a friend who recently started at the NYC ballet company. There's been some weird interactions with a strange group and some mention of missing persons. While I'm still getting office work done anyway, I was wondering if I could take a more official look into it. It could very well be nothing but—" I trailed off, not exactly sure how to explain why I wanted to pursue this.

Marcus looked thoughtful and then finally nodded. "Sure, if you want to look into it by all means you can go through whatever we have about it. I'm not going to sanction you going and investigating on sight there or anything, but feel free to do your own digging."

"Thank you, sir." With that, I exited, making my way back to the office to see what exactly I could find on the missing ballerinas. Vi may never speak to me again after last night, but that didn't mean I was going to stop making sure that she was safe.

12

Vi

What had I done?

I woke up with a pounding head and rolled over to find aspirin and a glass of water on my nightstand. My alarm was blaring and I inwardly cursed myself for having drank so much last night as I turned it off and downed my water. I'd been pissed at Phil so I had figured drinking would be a nice temporary fix. Given my pounding head and the fuzzy details from last night, that had been a terrible idea.

I remembered Finn driving me home and— *FUCK*. Images from last night flashed through my mind unbidden. I'd tried to fuck him. I'd kissed him, tried to unclothe him. Oh my god. He was going to hate me. Phil was going to hate me. *Phil.*

I dropped back down to my bed and covered my face with my hands. It was an accident. I hadn't meant to do anything with Finn. But I had. Regardless of how far we'd gone, how drunk I was, or how mad I was at Phil, I had cheated on him with Finn.

Guilt hit me like a freight train. I wasn't a cheater. I'd never been one. So many of my friends had been cheated on and I had always scoffed saying just break up with your partner if you couldn't stay faithful. And then I'd done that very thing.

It wasn't fair to Phil. It wasn't fair to Finn. It just wasn't fucking fair.

I groaned into my hands. How bad would it be if I called in sick today? *Bad.* While I was happy with the progress I was making, I couldn't afford to miss out on a day of practice. Plus, I had just started. It would look horrible if I were to call in already.

That decided, I attempted to push thoughts of my relationship and last night out of my head as I pulled on a pair of leggings and a T-shirt and quickly brushed my teeth.

My resolve didn't last long when I walked into the studio to find Shelby and Bella grinning at me. I made my way towards them and was stopped by Julia.

"Late after less than a week, great look," she sniffed. Embarrassment heated my cheeks. She was right, but also what did it have to do with her?

"Knock it off, Julia," came Bella's voice.

I used that as my excuse, mumbling something as I slipped past her and plopped onto the ground.

"You look like hell," Shelby remarked.

"How's Finn?" Bella asked with a mischievous grin.

"Thanks, and he's fine I'm sure," I muttered.

"Mhm." She responded with a raised eyebrow.

"You know I'm in a relationship right?"

"Oh yeah, you've told us all about this Phil guy. What you had failed to mention was that you have a cute Irish man who shows up after work to make sure you're alright." She waggled her eyebrows at me.

I groaned as images of him from last night flashed through my mind. "Doubt he'll do it again," I muttered.

"Why? What happened?" She asked, leaning forward and

abandoning her stretch. Shit. I should not have said anything. But it was too late and I could tell she was not about to let it go.

"I may or may not have drunkenly tried to seduce him last night."

"Victoria," Shelby said.

"You did not!" Bella squealed and I glared at her, glancing around to see people looking our way.

"It's horrible, I cheated on my boyfriend last night, Bella."

She shrugged as if it wasn't a big deal. "Was it good?"

"No, I mean yes…but no…we didn't do anything. I mean we kissed but that was it. He stopped and left."

"Ooh, so he's hot *and* a gentleman."

I groaned again as I rubbed a hand across my face. "He's never going to want to see me again but he's best friend with my best friend's boyfriend, so we're absolutely going to run into each other whether we like it or not."

She shrugged again. "I wouldn't count on it. I saw the way he was looking at you. He must have really had some self-control if he stopped things last night. That guy is smitten with you."

"He asked me out in the past and I turned him down because *I'm in a relationship*," I enunciated the last part.

"Dancers, to the center please," Winnie interrupted any further discussion and I could not be more grateful as I stood, followed the group, and we began our routines.

Despite Bella's clear disregard for my cheating actions, I had to say something to Phil. I had to admit what I'd done. Or maybe I'd just end things with him.

It was the coward's way out, not telling him I'd been unfaithful, and guilt gnawed at me at the thought. But then I pictured Finn's swollen lips and the way his hands had held me close, and desire slowly replaced some of the guilt. I was a horrible person, and I was so royally screwed.

After a sweaty day of practice I was really missing the theater showers, the thought of riding a crowded subway smelling like body odor didn't hold any appeal. But neither did the thought of some strange man watching me from a camera in his basement.

The girls and I walked out together like we had been doing every day since Winnie's announcement, before I waved goodbye and walked towards the subway station. As I was waiting for the subway to arrive, I finally pulled out my phone, taking a deep breath. I needed to do this, but that knowledge didn't make it any easier. Part of me worried that he wouldn't even answer given our last conversation, but I had to try.

"Victoria," Phil's voice came through when he picked up on the third ring.

"Hey, sorry I know you said you were busy tonight, I was wondering if you have a minute."

I heard muffled voices and then I assumed he stepped into an empty area. "Yeah, I have a couple minutes, what's up?"

Damnit. Guess this was happening now. "I know life's been crazy for both of us lately and it's been hard to find time to connect."

"Yeah," he said, sounding distracted.

"Well I was thinking about it and—"

"Phil," I heard a feminine voice laugh near him.

My irritation at being interrupted rose and I tried to stay calm, knowing he was busy, probably with something for work.

"Hey, Victoria, now's not a great time." He said, still sounding incredibly distracted. Fuck this.

"Phil, I want to break up."

A pause. "What do you mean?"

"I don't think this is working anymore, I know we had a great time, but I think whatever this is is over."

"Victoria, we can talk about this later." I wanted to laugh at his response. I couldn't get him to pay attention to me, even when trying to break up with him.

"Phil, I kissed someone else." This finally seemed to get his attention.

"Who?" He asked in a steely voice.

"It doesn't matter. It was wrong, and I'm sorry, but I think we need to end this."

"Fine. Good luck whoring yourself out."

"Are you fucking serious?" But he'd already hung up. Well, if anything, that was confirmation that this was the right choice. He had every right to be mad about Finn and I, but what the fuck.

I put my phone in my pocket and breathed out a deep breath. The train finally arrived and I got on, taking a seat.

The train made several stops on the way towards my house. At the first stop, quite a few people exited, leaving only a few others riding with me. We had gotten out early today due to the weekend so it wasn't as busy as it normally was when I left for the day.

I glanced down at my phone only to have the same feeling from the theater come over me. I was being watched.

I looked around the car but didn't see anything suspicious. Nobody seemed to be overtly staring a me, but that feeling didn't go away. I kept my eyes up and off my phone, glancing around every so often. I probably looked like the creep now, but I couldn't shake this feeling.

More people came and went as the ride continued and the train began to fill. Part of me felt better at the crowd, but another part whispered that it would be easier for someone to hide in a group if they truly were following me.

Making a split decision, I decided to switch my destination. Instead of getting off at the stop for my house, I quickly mapped where I'd need to exit for Finn's. If there truly was someone following me and I wasn't just being paranoid, I didn't want to bring them to my address. Instead, going to a cop's house felt like a much safer idea.

We finally reached his stop and I exited, throwing a glance behind me at the others who followed me off. There were several people heading in the same direction and I noted a couple of men wearing hoodies. It was fall so that wasn't unusual, but all I could think about was how it hid their faces from view and how they could be hiding weapons under their sweatshirts.

I began to jog towards his house in the fading light, feeling my heart rate and adrenaline spike as I veered off the main road and headed towards the residential area. Anyone could jump me now and get away with it easily. Fuck, fuck, fuck, this was such a bad idea.

I wanted to pull out my phone and call Ava but I was also terrified of looking down even for a second. So instead I kept my head up and grabbed my keys from my pocket, putting one between my knuckles so that I was ready to stab someone if they grabbed me.

I finally reached his house and I broke into a full-out sprint, running towards his door and the safety that I knew existed beyond. I reached the front step and pounded on the door before putting my back to the house, making sure no one could come up behind me. I heard footsteps and then the door swung open, revealing a tall man with short-cropped brown hair.

"Hey," he said, with one eyebrow raised.

"Hey, sorry I'm here for Finn. This is his place, right?"

"Oh, yeah. I'm his roommate Jake. He's not home yet but he should be anytime now if you want to come inside to wait for him."

I moved forward without a word, entering the house. Jake closed the front door and I finally let myself relax and breathe for the first time since getting on the subway. I'm sure I looked like a freak but frankly, I was too relieved to care.

"I'm getting ready to head to work but like I said, he should be home anytime now," Jake said from behind me and I turned to see him staring at me from the front door.

"Oh, yeah, totally. I'm Victoria by the way."

"Ahh Victoria. Nice to meet you," he said reaching out a hand to shake mine. "Can I get you anything while you wait?"

"No, I'm fine, thanks though."

"Okay, well feel free to make yourself at home."

"Thanks," I said, awkwardly taking a seat on the couch that he motioned to. Now that I was safely inside of his house I started feeling extremely foolish. Why had I let my imagination run away with me? Maybe I should just leave now before Finn got home and I had to explain everything. Or maybe it was time to tell him about what had been happening at the theater. I hadn't wanted to mention it in case it amounted to nothing, and I already knew Ava had been abusing her friend privileges asking him to look into things. But if I was now convinced that people were following me, it was probably time to tell him.

Jake left after a few minutes and I settled onto the couch to wait for the awkward confrontation.

13

Finn

The educational modules provided a nice background noise as I began to search what I could find on Rosie Sanchez. She'd been a single mother and an amazing dancer. She'd moved up quickly at the company and had become a principal which, according to what I could find, was the highest level of dancer one could reach. According to reports from her family, dancing had been her pride and joy, only second to her son. Then one day, she mysteriously disappeared without a trace.

I scrolled through the information we had. Most of the interviews had taken place with her mother who it appeared had gotten custody of Rosie's toddler. My heart broke reading the document. To lose a daughter and mother so suddenly and with no closure.

The NYPD had followed what few leads they could, but nothing concrete had been found, and it was still an open missing persons case.

I skimmed more of the article, looking for anything I could possibly use. My heart stopped when I saw a familiar name.

Cillian Sullivan. I scrolled back up to the beginning of that section. Rosie had apparently been seen with him in the weeks leading up to her disappearance and he had been questioned, but nothing had come of it. My blood ran hot and I had to work to take deep breaths so as not to punch a hole straight through the computer screen. There was no way. It had to be a coincidence.

But even as I thought it, I knew in my gut it wasn't. He was involved in her disappearance. He'd done this. And now, there was a chance he or the people he worked with were involved in what was happening with Vi and the other dancers.

I pushed back from the chair and began to pace. I had to do something. I had to go back there.

I'd spent so long trying to forget. So long distancing myself and swearing that I would never reopen that part of my life. And here it was. A viper comes back to strike right where it hurt the most.

I could feel the anger and fear, all those familiar emotions bubbling back up to the surface from the deep dark hole that I had stuffed them in. I took slow breath after breath until I was once again able to think. There was no point rushing off right now. It would just lead to more problems. I'd finish out my shift, find everything I possibly could on Rosie, and then tonight, I would once again enter the lion's den. I wasn't a child anymore. This time, I would come out victorious.

By the end of my shift, I hadn't found much more concerning Rosie. Like I'd imagined, the trail had abruptly gone cold, no one had talked, no one had seen anything, and there was nothing more for the police to pursue.

I hadn't come up with much more of a plan but I knew what I had to do.

I stopped by Cap's office on my way out to let him know I'd finished the modules and he gave me the green light to shadow Libby on her next shift in two days. In the meantime, I had some time off to do what I needed to.

I pulled my car into my neighborhood, still thinking about what this night would entail. I would grab a few things and then I planned to head straight back out.

I let myself in and stopped dead in my tracks when I saw Vi sitting on my couch.

"Hey," she said sheepishly.

I'd been so distracted with what I'd found and what I had to do that I hadn't thought about last night since the shame this morning.

"Hey back," I said. Uncertainty hung in the air and I had no idea what to say.

"Jake let me in," she said motioning to the couch where she sat.

"You're off early," I replied, noting the time.

"We have the next two days off so Winnie gave us an early break today."

I nodded. This was so awkward. I had to say something. "About last night—"

"I was scared that I was being followed from the theater so I came here," she rushed out, interrupting me.

"What?" I asked, turning to look out my window as if I would see a person standing there.

"I'm sure I was just overreacting, but with the weird shit that's been going on at the theater and then on the subway, I felt like someone was watching me and—"

"What weird shit at the theater?" I asked, dropping down onto the couch next to her.

She let out a pained sigh.

"Victoria." I pressed.

"They found a camera in the girls' showers," she said with a wince.

"They what?" I asked, my voice rising. "When?"

"A couple days ago. Winnie said she reported it and they don't know how it got there, but we've been told to leave in pairs now and the other day I thought I saw a camera flash in the hallway when I was getting water."

"Victoria," I said again, my anger rising.

"I know, I know, I should have told you but I didn't want you to worry and—"

"Consider me fecking worried," I said, reaching over and grabbing her hand. Immediately I let it go as if it had burned me. "Fuck, sorry," I said, putting more space between us. An awkward moment passed between us and then she spoke.

"I broke up with Phil."

"Oh." That was not what I'd been expecting her to say.

"I just thought you should know. Given, what happened last night." She said with another wince. Welp, there went my pride.

"Okay," I said. Normally I'd be thrilled, I mean I still was, but I was also guilt-ridden that I might have just ended her relationship. Plus, I was way too distracted with what I'd found at work to think of much else. And now this shite at the theater?

"Anyway, how was work?" She asked, standing.

"It was— enlightening." I finally managed, pushing to my feet to join her. She cocked her head to the side and her long chestnut hair fell over her shoulder. My hand itched to brush it off, remembering the feeling of my hand in her hair last night as her lips covered mine.

"What does that mean?" She asked, appearing oblivious to where my thoughts were heading.

"Ava found something about a missing person, one of the previous dancers from the NYC ballet company. She asked me to look into it and I found something that might be worth pursuing. And now with what you just told me I'm even more determined to get to the bottom of it."

"Oh, damn," She said, chewing her bottom lip.

"Yeah, I'm actually taking off to go ask some questions now."

"I'll come with."

"Absolutely not," I said before she had even finished talking.

"If it involves the ballet I deserve to know."

"Not about this, you don't. This is police business."

"Oh, so you're going to question someone in official police capacity?" She asked but the look in her eyes told me she already knew I wasn't.

I ground my teeth. "No, but—"

"Then I'm coming with."

"Over my dead body."

"Fine," she said, suddenly relenting. I was going to get whiplash from her constant mood swings.

She walked towards the door. "If you won't let me come with I'll just ask Ava to do some of her own digging and go there on my own."

My hand reached out to snatch her wrist before I could even contemplate the action. Her answering grin told me she knew exactly what she was doing.

"It's not safe." I argued, not releasing her wrist.

"Then why are you going?"

I had no answer for her.

"If you're going to put yourself at risk, at least let me come with you so that I can call for backup or something if you need it."

Backup. Yeah, like that would work. But maybe it would. Would they really do anything to her? I didn't trust them, but also they wouldn't go around making her disappear just like that. Plus, if they truly were involved in this, she was already in massive danger.

"Fine," I relented, finally releasing my grip on her. She

might just be stubborn enough to go herself if I didn't bring her with and I couldn't take that risk.

She beamed and I swear she did a little dance. That did not help my dick behave itself as thoughts of her perfect bare ass filled my head once again.

"I was planning on taking my bike," I said, one last attempt to convince her to stay.

"Well, do you have an extra helmet?"

I nodded reluctantly.

"Then I don't see the problem," she said, the light in her eyes telling me that this was about to be a big mistake.

14

Vi

Finn came back from his room and I swear my knees almost buckled at the sight. He'd changed into a pair of jeans and a black t-shirt that hugged his muscles like a glove, carrying two helmets and an extra hoodie. I swear, my ovaries danced. Did I have a thing for bikers?

"In case you get cold," he said handing me the sweatshirt. I took it willingly, slipping it over my workout tank. It smelled delicious, his cologne all over it. Had he sprayed it on his shirt before bringing it to me?

"What about you?" I asked, referring to his bare arms.

"I ride hot," he replied.

Oh god. Yeah, he did. *Get it together Vi.*

I took the offered helmet and followed him to the garage. I'd wanted to face the awkward tension of last night head-on and I wasn't sure how I'd expected it to go, but jumping on the back of his motorcycle definitely wasn't it.

My thoughts drifted to my previous relationship. Despite how shitty Phil had taken the breakup, I was so relieved that it was over. Ava had been right, he didn't really seem invested and now I kicked myself for all the time I'd spent saving myself from doing anything out of respect for him. Well until last night of course.

The guilt threatened to come back but all thoughts vanished when I turned to see Finn wearing his reflective motorcycle helmet. He was something out of a thirst trap damnit. I had always loved his curls and would never want them gone, but there was something about him hidden behind his helmet that made me want to do insanely nasty things to him. The way his muscles bunched, his veins popped, his shirt hugged his toned body and his jeans put his ass on display— I was absolutely ogling him.

"Need some help?" He asked, motioning to my helmet and bringing me back to earth. I had to be ovulating, there was no other explanation for this lust that was consuming me.

"Oh, uh yeah," I said, not exactly sure how to put the helmet on. He lifted the visor before slipping it over my head. I tiled my chin when he tapped on the bottom of the helmet and he deftly tightened the chin strap. I couldn't see his eyes through his reflective visor and somehow that made this ten times hotter as I imagined what was going on behind the glass.

"There you go." He said, closing my visor. "Have you ever ridden before?"

"Yeah, once or twice."

He nodded. "Hold on tight, don't let go, and let me do the rest."

Yes sir, I could do that.

I nodded and he turned to his bike, sliding his leg over it. He turned it on and kicked the kickstand up. I waited until he twisted towards me before I came up behind him and slid on, wrapping my hands around his waist. Fuck. From this position, I could feel his toned abs under my hands and smell him so strongly. I scooted a little closer and felt him stiffen as my front molded to his back. Okay, I could already tell this was going to be one of the highlights of my life.

"Ready?" he murmured above the purr of the engine.

"Yeah," I said back, my voice coming out huskier than intended.

And with that, we were off.

Adrenaline filled me as we rode, weaving through the dark streets. His solid back kept my front warm, but I was grateful for the sweatshirt he'd loaned me as I felt the wind whip against me. I had no idea how long we'd be riding because I had no idea where we were going. Maybe I should have asked more questions before demanding he take me with him, but it was a little too late for that.

And honestly, I didn't care. It had been a long week, and between my nasty hangover and my breakup, I just wanted a distraction. This, this is what I needed. I felt free in a way that I hadn't in a long time. Maybe ever, except when I was dancing.

We finally pulled up in front of a warehouse after what seemed like an hour or so. I slid off of the bike and he turned to me as I took in our surroundings.

"No chance I can convince you to stay here while I go inside?" He asked halfheartedly.

"Nope," I said giving him an innocent smile even though he couldn't see me. He grunted and reached up to pull his helmet off, setting it on the bike. I went to follow suit before his hands settled on mine, causing me to stop with a jerk.

"You forgot your strap," he said quietly.

"Oh, yeah, thanks."

I tipped my chin up and let him release the strap and lift the helmet off. I took a deep breath of the cool air and ran my fingers through my now tangled strands. *Mental note: braid your hair next time you get on his bike.* If there was a next time.

"Once inside, stay next to me and let me do all the

talking," he said, more serious than I'd ever seen him before.

What were we about to get into? Part of me wanted to back out now but my pride wouldn't allow me to. Plus, I didn't want him going in alone to whatever this was. So I straightened my shoulders and replied, "Got it."

He sighed and grabbed my hand, tugging me along beside him. Despite my jittery nerves, the feel of his hand on mine sent butterflies through me. There were a million things I'd rather be doing with him right now besides walking into an ominous-looking building. Bad Vi.

He used his free hand to rap his knuckles on the door in front of us. The door opened a few seconds later as if whoever it was had been expecting us. The entrance was too dark to see much and I almost jumped when a deep voice spoke from within.

"Finn, welcome home, mac. It's been too long."

I looked at Finn in confusion as his hand tightened on mine. "Hello, athair."

15

Finn

My dad stood on the other side of the door, larger than life, as always. He'd used the Irish term for son and I'd hated how completely natural it felt to respond in kind. He ushered me in and only when I stepped through the door, tugging a quiet Victoria did he seem to notice that I was not alone.

"Well, hello. I didn't realize my son brought company."

Just seeing my dad talk to Vi had my anger rising and I put my hand on her lower back protectively as we stepped inside. The interior of the warehouse looked pristine with expensive leather couches and a coffee table in the center. I could see Vi's surprise and internally cussed myself out for bringing her here.

"I assume you would like to go to my office to chat?" Brady asked, gesturing behind us. I nodded wordlessly and we followed after him. I saw two of my cousins peer at us from several other rooms as we passed and my hand tightened on Vi's waist.

We stepped into Brady's office and Vi let out a small breath. The room was beautiful, covered in expensive art, sculptures, and a large oak desk right in the center that my father went to lean against.

"Can I get you something to drink?" He asked.

"We're fine," I answered for the both of us.

"Alright then, let's cut to the chase. To what do I owe this unexpected and long overdue visit?"

I ground my molars together, determined not to let him rile me up so easily. Vi squeezed my hand and I held on tightly, thankful for the support.

"I work for the NYPD now."

"I am aware," he said with a nod. Of course, he was. I hadn't imagined anything different.

"I am investigating a missing person's case and came across something rather interesting."

He crossed his arms and lifted an eyebrow, waiting for me to go on. Smug bastard.

"One of the people who was interviewed was Cillian Sullivan." Something that looked like surprise flashed in his eyes and I pressed on. "He was one of the main suspects, but they conveniently never found enough evidence to pin it to him."

"And you're telling me this, why?"

"He's your goddamn brother, you've been working together forever."

"I have not seen nor worked alongside him for over ten years, something you would know if you had deigned to show your face every once in a while."

"Oh, so this is my fault?" I bit out, that familiar anger rising up as it always did around him.

He shrugged. "You made it very clear when you left that you didn't want us to contact you. If you wanted to talk to us you've always known where to find us."

"I *don't* want to talk to you."

"And yet here you are."

"Yes, because your little business ventures apparently include abducting women."

For the first time tonight, his face screwed up in something other than cold indifference and I was suddenly exceedingly grateful that I had sent Art our location and all of the information I had in case this did not end well.

"I do not appreciate the accusation, especially when it is completely unfounded." My father said firmly.

"So you're saying you had nothing to do with Rosie Sanchez's abduction?"

"Or any other woman you might be investigating, yes," he responded without a moment's hesitation.

I knew he wouldn't just openly admit to it, but I hadn't been expecting this outright denial.

"There is proof that Cillian was one of the last people to see her before she disappeared." I tried again.

"And that may be so, but neither I nor my organization had anything to do with that."

"And I'm supposed to just believe you?" I almost laughed.

He shrugged. "Whether you do or not is not my concern. If you decide to bring the whole police force here to question us, they will find that we indeed had nothing to do with it."

He knew I wouldn't. If I had enough to warrant that I wouldn't be here with Vi. Anger surged inside me like a living being as I worked to stay as calm as possible. None of this had gone the way I had hoped.

"Is that all?" He asked, bringing my attention back to him.

"For now, maybe I'll take your advice and come back with more people."

"Well in the meantime, you could stay for dinner." He said as if I hadn't just threatened to bring the police to his doorstep.

"I'm not hungry."

"Well, maybe your friend here is."

"She's fine," I answered sharply.

"Is she not able to answer for herself?" He asked with a cocked brow. I clenched my jaw so hard it ached but turned towards her. She looked between the two of us and finally shook her head. "I'm fine, thank you."

He gave her a small nod before looking back towards me. "At least stay until your mother can get here. I know she would love to see you."

I laughed aloud at that but bit back the retort on the tip of my tongue. He must have taken that as encouragement because he left his office and barked out orders to one of my cousins.

Vi turned towards me, still holding my hand. "Your parents?" She whispered.

I blew out a breath. "It's a long story."

"Do you want to stay?" She asked

Did I? Absolutely not. I already felt the past pressing down on me from the short time I'd spent in my dad's presence. All those old feelings were right below the surface ready to break free. And yet— it had been over ten years since I'd seen my mom. What did she look like? Did she ever think about me?

Vi must have sensed the internal war going on because she squeezed my hand again. "We can stay if you want. We can leave whenever you need."

I nodded. "Maybe just for a moment."

I took a deep breath and finally left the office to join my father.

"Conor is going to grab something to eat, are you sure I can't get you guys anything to drink while we wait?"

"No," I said without hesitation.

"I'll take a water, thank you," Victoria spoke from my side. I had half a mind to warn her that it might be poisoned, but now I was just being dramatic.

"A water for the lady," Brady said, returning a moment

later. She took it with a thank you and he turned his attention back to me.

"How has work been?"

"Fine," I said.

"And what about you? Do you for for the NYPD as well?" He asked Vi. She laughed and I hated the fact that he was hearing her genuine amusement.

"No, I'm a dancer actually. Ballet," she quickly amended.

"Ahh, how wonderful. We'll have to come watch you sometime."

She smiled graciously at him but I could see the apprehension in her gaze. Good. She wasn't completely letting her guard down.

Several minutes of uncomfortable silence later, my mom entered the room in a flurry. My breath caught as I took in her appearance. She looked exactly the same as she had when she'd dropped me off at boarding school for the last time. My gut hollowed out as so many memories threatened to overwhelm me.

"Finnian," she said in that gentle tone of hers.

"Máthair," I said tightly. She looked like she wanted to come give me a hug but she held back and instead came to stand next to my father.

"It's been too long," she replied.

I laughed in response. "As if that's not exactly how you wanted it."

"You know that's not true..." she said, sounding hurt.

"Really? I didn't get that impression when you were leaving me for years in that fecking school."

I'd told myself I wouldn't go here but apparently, my inner child was not passing up this opportunity to let the hurt out after all these years.

"You know we only wanted the best for you, that school could provide for you in ways that we couldn't. Plus, we didn't want you stuck in the middle of this world—"

"Yet that didn't stop you from taking over the business and immersing yourselves in *this world* did it?" I interrupted her, not willing to listen to any more excuses.

"That's enough," my father said in his discussion-ending tone, but my mother waved him off as she stepped closer and took my hands. "I know we made mistakes with you, but we never wanted to hurt you or go years without seeing you." I refrained from telling her that's exactly what she did when they dropped me off at boarding school. I shook off her hands and the hurt on her face almost made me feel guilty. *Almost.*

"If you really feel that way you never should have gotten involved in this business."

She shrugged as she stepped back to stand next to my father. "I am sorry if we hurt you." *'If'* we hurt you. Always the same song and dance.

Conor entered carrying several bags of takeout and I put my hand on Vi's back and ushered her towards the door. "We're leaving."

"Mac—"

I didn't wait to hear what else they had to say as I marched us out of the building and towards my bike. I helped Vi with her helmet, put my own on, and took off back towards my house.

We had to stop for gas on the way back to the house and when I stopped Vi slid off to wait by the pump. I stared out at the dark sky, trying to process what the hell had just happened. I couldn't believe after all these years I'd finally seen my parents again. And Vi had met them. And they'd claimed they weren't working with Cillian anymore.

I sighed as I tried to wrap my mind around all that had happened. Vi's voice broke through my thoughts.

"Well this was definitely not what I was expecting when I came by your house today," she said drily. I chuckled as I turned my gaze to her. I hadn't had a chance to really admire her and holy shite did she look good in my hoodie and helmet. I would absolutely need to invite her on another ride, next time somewhere that didn't involve meeting my estranged parents.

"It's almost like there's a reason I didn't want you coming with," I said with a pointed look.

She shrugged. "Sorry, I've never been good at following directions." I narrowed my eyes at her sass but before I could say anything else the gas finished and I returned it to the pump before getting back on the bike.

"Come on, let's get you home."

16

Vi

The ride back to Finn's was loaded with tension. I could feel the tension in the muscles of his back as I held on. He was going to have a massive stress headache by the end of the ride with the way he was holding himself.

I didn't know much about his family or history, but from the brief glimpses I had gotten tonight, it wasn't good. He clearly hadn't seen them in years. They'd apparently dropped him off at boarding school for a while, and they kept referring to "this life." From the looks of the warehouse, I had an idea just what that might be.

Knowing what I did now, I was kind of surprised that he had relented and agreed to let me come with him. Then again, I had threatened to go by myself if he didn't.

We arrived back at his house and he parked in the garage, taking off his helmet without a word. I undid my own and set it next to his on the seat. He entered the house and I stood in indecision for a moment. Was I supposed to follow him or just see myself out?

He turned back to me in the doorway and motioned inside.

"I have a frozen pizza or something I can heat up if you're hungry."

I was, but I also didn't want to burden him with my presence if he just wanted to decompress on his own. And yet, he didn't seem in a hurry to kick me out.

In the time since I had known Finn, he'd always been laughing, lighthearted, and smirking. Right now he was grim, quiet, and subdued. I'd never seen him like this before and maybe he needed the company.

I followed him into the kitchen and sat down on a barstool as he began to rummage around in the freezer.

"Well, that was— something."

He grunted in response. Okay so maybe he didn't want the company. I was about to see myself out when he broke the silence.

"As you probably deduced, my parents are in the mob. Or more like they *are* the mob." I stayed quiet, unsure what to say to that. He placed the pizza in the preheating oven and finally turned to me.

"We left Ireland when I was really little. We came here looking for a better life. My parents worked hard, taking odd jobs, and doing whatever they could to keep us afloat. I was really young so I don't remember much, but I do remember when my dad started being gone for long periods of time and then we started having random visitors at all hours of the day. At first, I didn't mind because it meant more time for my mom and I to spend together. But then she began to stay out with them and I was expected to lock myself in my room and keep to myself.

Then one day, my parents came to me telling me I was starting a new school. I wasn't particularly attached to the one I was attending, so I was kind of excited at the prospect of meeting new friends. I started going to this boarding school and it was fine, I met new friends and enjoyed not being locked up in my bedroom for hours on end. And then they missed a holiday. I was told they weren't coming to pick me up and I'd be staying at the school over break. And then it was another holiday. And then summer break."

My heart broke at the pain in his voice as he recounted his past. I could imagine a little Finn, excitedly waiting with the other kids for his parents, only to learn that they weren't coming.

"Eventually I stopped waiting for them, expecting them to come. There were a couple other kids, like Art who happened to be my roommate, that also stayed over breaks and we created our own little club. When I finally graduated I swore I'd leave and never contact them again. Tonight was the first time I've seen them since then."

"That's— a lot." I finally said after a moment of silence. He let out a bitter laugh.

"Yeah."

"And your uncle?"

"He came over with my family. He and my dad were connected at the hip, involved in the same stuff, and grew their business together."

"And you said that you found a connection between him and the ballet?"

"Yeah, he was questioned in the disappearance of one of the dancers, Rosie. Nothing came of it and I have every belief that it was because of his connection with the mob."

"And you think your dad had something to do with it?"

"Yes. No, I don't know." He said, sighing deeply. "My father is many things, but a liar is not one of them. Or at least didn't used to be. He always stubbornly backed up his decisions, regardless of how ridiculous or illegal."

"Was he maybe lying to protect himself because he knows you're a cop and could have been recording him?"

"No. Their place has special equipment, if you'd tried to

use your phone or any sort of electronic device while inside you would have found that it didn't work. He's always been extremely mistrustful of the government and paranoid about any listening or tracking devices. I sent Art our location and everything before we entered 'cause I knew everything would be blocked once we were inside."

"I'm sorry," I said softly.

"What for?"

"That you've had to live this, that you know this so well you just plan for it."

One side of his mouth lifted in a small smile. "Thanks."

"So what now?"

"Now I'm back to square one. I'll continue looking at what little information we have, maybe I'll see if I can redo some interviews with Rosie's family and people from the theater. If Cillian has anything to do with the disappearances though, and maybe even this group trying to reach out to the dancers, I really don't want you involved in it. I don't want Bella or Shelby involved either but please, stay far away."

I nodded. "Believe me, I'm not trying to get involved in anything like that."

He pulled out the pizza as the timer went off, setting it on the stove.

"I could help though," I said, my words causing him to swivel and look at me.

"What?"

"If you truly think this group has something to do with dancers disappearing, I could help you investigate."

He was already shaking his head but I pressed on. "I'm serious, I could go meet them, get some information from them, be your in."

"Absolutely not."

I held up my hands. "It was just an offer."

He shook his head at me but a small smile played on his

lips. I was relieved to see some of that stoic Finn gone.

"So…you ended things with Phil, huh?" He asked, setting a few slices of pizza on a plate in front of me.

"Yes," I said staring at his profile as he turned back towards the stove.

"How are you doing?" He asked, not looking at me.

"Fine. It was a long time coming, honestly."

"So it had nothing to do with— last night?"

"You mean when I drunkenly tried to bang you?" I offered.

He choked on a bite of his pizza and I laughed as he coughed, trying to clear his airway.

"Yes and no. I felt guilty and knew I couldn't keep things going with him if I was tempted to get you into my bed. But honestly, after our last fight, I knew I would probably need to end things sooner rather than later. Last night just meant it was sooner."

He finished off his slice of pizza without another choking incident and I watched him stare out the window as I ate my own pizza. I stifled a yawn and he glanced back towards me with a smile. "It's late. Based on a lack of car I'm assuming you took the subway?"

I nodded.

"Thought so." He set his dishes in the sink. "I don't want you leaving at this time of night. You can have my bed, I'll take the couch."

"It's fine—" I protested.

"Nope. Not gonna argue about this. You, my bed, end of discussion."

"I don't think I've ever been ordered to someone's bed like that before."

He smirked and rolled his eyes. "Come on, Vi. I'm sure you're exhausted. I can put some fresh sheets on there before you go in if you want."

"It's fine." Honestly, the thought of sleeping enveloped in

his scent was extremely appealing.

"Okay then."

He led me towards his room and I followed, taking in the rest of the house as we went.

"I can get you a fresh toothbrush and a t-shirt to wear if you want."

"That would be awesome, thank you."

He nodded and went to his closet for a shirt. This wasn't exactly how I'd pictured the first time staying at Finn's place. Not that I'd imagined it often or anything. Given how last night went I would have expected a little more intimacy tonight with me staying over. Then again, he'd stopped things from happening last night. I'd been the one to turn him down when he tried to ask me out and then he'd stopped me last night. Maybe he wasn't interested anymore.

The thought hurt but was also fair. I didn't expect him to just be sitting here pining for me after I rejected him. There had been no denying the desire in his gaze last night, but then again he was a guy and I was a half-dressed woman throwing myself at him. Of course he'd have a knee-jerk reaction like that.

Feeling foolish and a little embarrassed, I determined to stop trying to force something that wasn't there. And maybe I felt a little angry that these feelings were now one-sided because when he left the room to get a toothbrush I stripped off my clothes, sliding his t-shirt over me. Given the fact that he wasn't much taller than me, the shirt did little to hide my underwear and maybe I got some satisfaction from that.

"Here's a new one—"

I turned to face him when I heard his voice cut off.

"Thanks," I said, walking towards him to grab the offered item. His gaze lingered on my bare legs and a satisfied warmth spread through me at the heat in his gaze.

"Vi—" he said in a low voice.

"Yeah?" I asked, as innocently as I could manage.

"Is there a reason you are not wearing any pants right now?"

"I'm getting ready for bed?" I said with a shrug. "You should be glad that I'm still wearing a shirt, I usually sleep naked."

A pained groan came from him and he stalked towards me, forcing me backward towards his bed.

"And why exactly would that make me glad?"

I shrugged again, trying and failing to slow my racing heart. "I don't know, you're the one determined to sleep on the couch."

"Yeah, out of respect for you. You're the one who just ended a relationship."

"What if I don't want you to respect me?"

"Vi—" he groaned again and I felt my legs hit the edge of the bed. "You can't say things like that and expect me to not do something about it."

I glanced down at his crotch where his dick was straining against his jeans between us. I licked my lips and looked back up to meet his gaze. "Then do something about it."

He stared at me for a long moment and I thought that maybe he'd refuse the bait and leave. But then his restraint broke and he was on top of me. He shoved me to the bed and my back hit the soft comforter a moment before his weight pressed on top of me, his lips capturing mine. One hand cupped the back of my neck while the other dove under my shirt, sliding up and feeling every inch of my bare skin.

I moaned into his mouth as his touch ignited me. His hand roamed my stomach, coming up to tweak my nipple. I gasped at the sensation and plunged my tongue into his mouth, our tongues tangling for dominance. The act only spurred him on and his hand moved to the other nipple, tweaking it even harder. The mix of pain and pleasure sent a wave of heat straight to my core and I could feel my panties dampen as I gasped, my hands coming up to grip his hair and tug.

Our mouths were clashing, fingers pulling. Nothing about this was soft and sweet, it was rough and explosive, a match that was igniting after being close to the flames for too long.

His hand slid down to cup my crotch and I pulled away to let out a whimper.

"You're exquisite," he said, rubbing his thumb over my underwear-clothed clit.

"Finn—" I moaned at the touch. He grinned and it felt like a challenge. No way was I letting him have all of the control here.

I reached for him, grabbing his shirt and tugging. He let me lift it over his head and my mouth watered at the muscles staring back at me. A deep v pointed towards his zipper and as much as I wanted to run my hands and tongue all over his chest, that would have to wait.

I reached for his zipper and his grin widened. "So impatient."

I ignored him as I undid the button and unzipped him. I reached for his waistband and popped him free. My mouth dropped open at the sight and his smile was so big that I was concerned it might break his face.

"What? First time you've seen a pierced dick, or is it the size that has your mind blown?"

I licked my lips in response and his gaze went feral. Before he could do anything else, I reached down and gave him a hard tug.

17

Finn

Holy shite, I was going to die. This woman was going to be the death of me. From her habit of stripping down to her underwear in front of me, egging me on to go rough on her, to the way her long fingers were expertly stroking my dick. Everything about her was perfection.

She tugged and squeezed and I felt heat build at the base of my spine. No way was I going to let her get me off before I'd even fully undressed her. I gritted my teeth against the pleasure building inside as I slid my hand into her underwear. It was a mistake because as soon as I felt just how wet she was my cock threatened to explode.

"You're fecking soaked," I murmured and she laughed.

"I love it when your accent comes out."

"How long exactly have you been dreaming of getting me naked?" I asked as her touch became frenzied.

"Probably as long as you've been coming in your pants to thoughts of me." She replied.

"So since the moment I laid eyes on you," I said, eliciting a moan from her sweet lips. That fecking mouth. I was going to do sinful things to it. But for the moment, I really needed to be inside her. The way she was stroking me, I wasn't going to last much longer.

"Are you on birth control?" I grunted.

"Yeah," she replied, her words turning into another moan as I plunged a finger inside her wet heat.

"Good, 'cause I'm going to fuck you raw if you don't tell me no right now."

She didn't say a word and that's all the permission I needed. I reached down to rip her underwear off before using one hand to grab her wrists, pulling them up above her head. I used the other hand to push my pants down even further before positioning myself at her entrance. I locked my gaze with hers and when I saw no hesitation there I plunged inside her.

"Oh my god."

"Finn—"

We moaned in unison as I rocked my hips against hers. She was so tight, so warm and her pussy clenched around me, threatening to end it right there. I pulled almost all the way out, trying to slow this down and savor the feeling of her.

"Finn—" she whined and I smirked at her desperation. "I'm trying to make this last, Beour."

"I don't care if it lasts, I need you now."

I grunted at her admission and pistoned my hips against hers, plunging in and out, deep, hard, and fast.

"Yes, oh god, yes." She cried and I gritted my teeth again, willing myself to hold on just a little longer. I reached one hand down to the space between us and began to circle her clit. Her moans grew in pitch and I captured a nipple with my mouth, tugging slightly with my teeth. She arched into me and I moved to the other nipple, biting down at the same time as I flicked her clit and thrust as deep as I could go. All at once she broke, her hands sliding from my grasp as she reached around to claw at my back, her legs wrapping around my hips as she held on for dear life. Finally, I let myself go and I pumped once more before shooting deep inside her.

Her pussy milked me dry as I pulsed into her and then we were both limp as I propped an elbow on the bed to keep from placing all of my weight on top of her.

"Holy fuck," she said nuzzling into my neck.

"Mmm," I murmured back, feeling more content than I had in a long time.

Finally, reluctantly, I rolled off of her, propping my head on my hand and letting my gaze trail over her. She still had my shirt on, although it was bunched around her neck. Her hair was splayed over the comforter in the most beautiful mess and I reached a hand forward to stroke a soft strand.

"I meant what I said, you truly are exquisite."

She smiled as she reached a hand to trace my face. "So are you, Finn."

I turned my head to kiss her palm. "You gonna be opposed to me sharing the bed with you tonight?"

"I mean, it is your bed," she laughed. "But no, you can share as long as you don't snore."

I reached up to tweak her nose. "Back at you."

18

Vi

I woke to a soft snore and turned to see Finn splayed out on his back, one hand over his eyes as if to block the morning light streaming in through the window. So much for him not snoring.

He was attractive all the time, but he looked especially boyish as he slept, his forehead screwed up just enough to make me think he was dreaming of something. Maybe the meeting from last night.

I still couldn't believe that his parents were in the mob. Or that Finn's uncle could have something to do with a dancer disappearing.

I also wasn't totally convinced that the two things were related, the missing person and the current group reaching out to dancers. But if Ava and Finn were worried about it, I wouldn't stop them from trying to figure it out.

Ava. I'd need to tell her about Finn. I groaned softly as I rolled to my back. She would be thrilled to hear about Phil. I couldn't believe I hadn't told her yet. But I'd gone straight to Finn's after and then all of that had ensued. Would she be mad that I was messing around with Art's best friend? Based on comments she'd made before I didn't think so, but there was always the risk of us making everything uncomfortable if things got awkward between us. It's not like we had the option to just stop running into each other, at least in groups.

"Good morning," came Finn's sleep-laden voice. I turned back to see him staring at me from his side of the bed.

"Morning," I said with a smile. "You snore, for future reference."

"I do not," he said indignantly.

I rolled my eyes in response and he stretched before bringing his hand down to trace the bottom of my shirt, leaving goosebumps in his wake. "You look good in my clothes."

"I do need more t-shirts, you might not get it back."

"What were you thinking about before I interrupted you?"

"What?" I asked, surprised at his sudden subject change.

"You looked concerned about something when you were lying here."

"Oh." I sighed. "I was just thinking about Ava and how she's gonna react when I tell her I slept with you."

He quirked a brow. "Oh, so now we're gonna kiss and tell?"

"Like you weren't planning on telling Art."

He shrugged. "Honestly, hadn't really thought about it."

"Well, unlike you, I actually talk to my best friend and she's gonna be pissed if I don't tell her."

"Why does it matter?"

"It's like your sister having sex with your best friend's brother."

"First off, I don't have a sister, so I don't know anything about that." I swatted his arm as I rolled my eyes at him again. "And secondly, I think you're making it way more complicated than it needs to be," he said as he reached over and tugged me closer.

I came to him willingly and nodded, "Maybe. I have a habit of doing that."

"Well, I think you should stop and move on to other activities." He murmured into my neck before pressing a kiss to the skin beneath my ear. I shivered at the touch.

"Mmm, and what exactly did you have in mind?"

"They say actions speak louder than words," he said as he lifted my shirt and pressed a soft kiss between my breasts.

"Hmm," I said as I arched into his touch.

He continued his trail of kisses, moving lower and lower until he reached the top of my underwear, which I had somehow managed to find after last night's activities. He tucked a finger under the band and slowly, so slowly trailed it down.

"You know, I generally skip breakfast," he said out of the blue, pulling my gaze to his. "But today, I'd like to make an exception."

I rolled my eyes again, something I was starting to do quite often around him, and then suddenly his mouth was on me and I gasped as his hot breath tickled my entrance before those delicious lips were true to his word and he began to feast.

Moans and intelligible words tumbled out of me as he continued his ministrations and I felt my orgasm start low in my belly. He felt so good, but I needed more, I needed him exactly where I wanted him. I reached down and tangled my fingers into his hair, tugging his head to where I needed it before I undulated myself against him. He went willingly and let me use him as I rode his face, getting closer and closer to that high. I was so close to falling over that cliff, so full of ecstasy. I removed one hand from his hair and used it to rub my clit and that was all it took to send me over the edge. I came with a cry that tore through me. His tongue didn't stop until I collapsed boneless on the bed. Finally, he sat up and made a show of slowly licking his lips.

"You have no idea how hot it is to watch you take control and get exactly what you want from me." He said, heat simmering in his gaze.

"You're quite the amazing toy," I replied, still a little breathless.

"You can't just say things like that," he said as he crawled up me, intent on closing in. Instead, I pushed him until he was lying flat on his back. He propped his arms behind his head in a cocky manner and I grinned. I would quite enjoy wiping that look off of his face.

I inched forward and rubbed my hand over his dick which was straining against his underwear. His face instantly changed as he realized my intent. I made quick work of pulling his underwear down and I looked up at him before spitting on his cock. He grunted in surprise and I grinned before sliding my hand up and down him once before dropping down and taking him into my mouth.

"Fuckkk," he said, drawing out the syllable.

"Mmm," I murmured against him as I pulled off him with a pop.

"Victoria," he breathed before I sucked him back in and began to bob up and down on him in time with my hand that squeezed his base. His moans and groans spurred me on, encouraging my movements and reigniting the throbbing between my legs. I reveled in his salty taste and the feeling of his piercing on my tongue before I took him as deep as I could, gagging when he hit the back of my throat. I pulled back enough to take a breath before doing it again, this time cupping his balls as I did so.

He jerked in my mouth and I could tell he was close. I did the move a third time, intending on finishing him, but as soon as I pulled back he sat up, swinging around and pushing me onto all fours.

"You've had enough fun in charge. My turn," he said before placing one hand in my hair and thrusting inside me from behind. I moaned at the sweet intrusion, loving the delicious feel of just how deep he could get at this angle. He thrust again and I gasped when I felt his piercing rub against a sensitive spot. I had never had sex with someone with a pierced dick before, and last night I hadn't noticed much difference. In this position, however, it added an amazing friction that I hadn't even known was possible.

I was already strung tight from listening to his sounds of pleasure and, when he reached down and swirled his hand on my clit, I ground my ass into him, chasing my orgasm. He grunted and pumped into me one more time before I felt his hot cum fill me. That was all it took and I found my own release, rocking against him as his hand continued to rub me exactly where I needed him. I finally pulled away when the sensation became too much for my overstimulated clit. I rolled to my side and he followed suit, pulling me close against him as I caught my breath.

"I love starting my day inside of you," he murmured, trailing a finger down my arm and I grinned.

"I could get used to this." *Shit. Didn't mean to say that.* "Do you have any coffee?"

He sat up, thankfully ignoring my previous comment. "Absolutely. I would suggest putting on some pants before leaving the room, however, Jake will be home anytime."

"Well, that would have been a lovely surprise for him to walk into."

"Wouldn't be the first time," he replied with a smirk.

I found my leggings from last night and took them into the bathroom with me to get cleaned up. By the time I joined him in the kitchen, he was already making a pot of coffee.

"What's your day look like today?" I asked as I joined him

at the bar.

"I have the day off, but I think I'm going to try to do more research on Rosie and my family's potential involvement. How about you?"

"Ava and I have been trying to hang out for the last week but something keeps coming up. I think I'm going to try to actually see her while I've got a day off."

He smiled as he set a mug in front of me. "You should. I'm sure she needs a break from Art. I don't know how she manages to spend that much time with him."

I laughed. "Honestly, I'm just waiting for her to tell me that she's officially moving out. I have no idea what I'll do with my lease but I know it's coming."

"Oh, I'm sure Art will just buy out the building and give it to you as an 'I'm sorry I stole your roommate' present."

I laughed but he looked dead serious. "You're kidding."

"Nope. He has a habit of doing things like that," he said with a shrug.

My mouth popped open. What would I do if he actually offered to give me the house? Say yes, obviously. Feel slightly guilty, but absolutely I would take it.

Before I had a chance to respond the front door opened and Jake came through, dropping his bag by the door before kicking off his shoes.

"Hey," he said to Finn.

"Hey, man."

"Oh, hey," he said seeing me.

"Morning," I said with a self-conscious smile. I wasn't sure if he'd imagined I'd still be here in the morning when he let me stay yesterday, but he didn't seem bothered by my presence.

"I'm gonna go crash," he said before heading towards his room.

"I should head out," I said sliding off my stool.

"You want a ride?"

"No, I'm good. I like taking the subway," I said when he looked unsure.

"Okay. Tell Ava I said hi."

"Will do," I said, heading for the door. "Bye, Finn."

"Bye, Vi," he said with a smile.

19

Finn

After Vi left I took my coffee back to my room to get ready for the day. I had just stepped out of the shower when I saw an email come through from an unknown email address. I knew enough not to open suspicious links in emails, but my curiosity got the best of me and I opened the email when I read the subject line: Finnian.

Unknown: This is all I could find on C's involvement. I don't expect you to believe me, but I swear everything I said was the truth. Fifi misses you. B.

An encrypted file stared back at me for a long moment while I processed my father's message. Was it a trap somehow? I couldn't figure out how. I honestly didn't care what he thought of me and I wouldn't assume he cared what I thought of him. So why go to all of this trouble if it was a lie? He had nothing to prove to me. He knew I didn't have anything on him to bring him in. And what was in the message?

I got up to pace for a moment before finally sitting back on my bed and clicking on the attachment before I could talk myself out of it.

The first part of the message contained all of the information I could want on Cillian. Legal name, known aliases, birthday, government ID.

I scanned downward and it was a comprehensive timeline of the last known locations and people associated with my uncle. If this was true, this was a goldmine.

I spent a few more minutes looking over it before setting my phone down. What was I going to do with this?

I had just been promoted to detective, but that didn't give me permission to hunt down and investigate whatever caught my eye. I'd need to bring it to Marcus, but how on earth would I approach that? I hadn't even completed a single shift shadowing in my new role.

I had all of this information and felt utterly stuck. In my gut, I knew something was off. But I didn't have any concrete proof to turn this into a case, diverting resources and pursuing leads based on what? Someone suspicious talking to the girl I liked?

I really just wished I had someone in my corner that I could talk to about this.

Libby, the thought came to me. I didn't know her well, but I was about to spend the foreseeable future as her partner. If there was anyone I could or should talk to about something like this it was her.

Feeling like I finally had some sort of direction, I picked up my phone again.

It was Libby's day off too so I didn't want to disturb her, but I also knew if she was sleeping or busy she should hopefully have her phone off. I called, unsure if she'd pick up, but she did after several rings.

"This is Libby."

"Hey, Libby. This is Finn Sullivan."

"Hey, what's up?"

"I have a weird request for you, and feel free to tell me to fuck off since I know it's your day off."

She laughed. "Okay, now I'm intrigued. Go on."

"Okay, bear with me. A friend of mine recently started working at the NYC ballet. There's been some weird things happening there including a group of people soliciting some of the girls to dance for them, and someone finding a camera in the girls' bathroom. I started looking into it and found a case involving a missing ballerina from a couple years ago. The case is still technically open, nothing ever came of it, and they never found her, but I read some of the reports and one of the suspects has some strong ties to the mob. I honestly think it was brushed under the rug and forgotten about. And now with this group trying to single out some of the women, I'm concerned it's going to happen again."

Silence rang through the phone. I didn't know how she'd respond. Call me crazy, laugh, tell me to take it up with the captain, ask why on earth I thought I should be investigating this.

"Have you talked to the captain?"

"Briefly. I shared some of my concerns and he told me I could look into what we had. I did and what I found just made me more nervous."

Another moment of silence. "I don't know you well, but I've heard about your work on the Laurie case. You clearly have some good instincts, and if this is that concerning for you, I'm willing to back you up in looking into it."

That was honestly a better reaction than I could have hoped for.

"Thank you. I know I don't have a lot to go on right now, but something feels really wrong."

"Okay. I'm busy this morning but if you have some time this afternoon I could meet you at the station to talk to Cap. I know we have the next couple days off, but if it's that concerning to you, I think it's worth mentioning to him."

"Absolutely. Just tell me the time and I'll be there. Seriously, I appreciate you sticking your neck out like this for me, Libby."

"Don't mention it. I'll see you in a couple hours."

20

Vi

I took the bus back towards my place, stopping at Ava's favorite coffee shop to get her an apology treat for bailing on her last night. I'd felt bad, but I had known that I wouldn't be able to breathe properly again until I had cleared the air with Finn, and then last night happened.

I unlocked our front door, knocking it open with my hip as I carried in the goods. "Honey, I'm home," I called as I entered. I heard a laugh from inside and smiled when I saw Ava lounging in the living room.

"You're scaring me," she said, taking the offered bag.

"Why?"

"First, you bail on me last night, and then you show up with apology muffins?"

"These aren't apology muffins," I scoffed. "These, are regular muffins with an apology attached."

She laughed and rolled her eyes. "Seriously though, are you going to tell me where you were? I was going to check your location, but I was trying to be a good friend and give you privacy."

"You have more self-control than me," I said, plopping down next to her. "And I'll tell you, but only if you promise not to freak out."

"Nope, not a chance. I'm not promising anything about my reaction to whatever scandalous thing you were getting yourself into."

"You make me sound awful."

"You know I love you, and would never *openly* judge your decisions. But you do make some shitty decisions sometimes, Vi," she laughed.

"Okay, I can't argue with that. However, I don't think last night was a shitty decision."

"I'm listening," she said, leaning forward.

I covered my face, afraid to see her reaction but she peeled my hands off. "Spit it out."

"I slept over at Finn's."

"Okay… like you slept over because you were so wasted that you couldn't safely drive home?"

Guilt hit me as I thought of all I hadn't told her yet. "Not quite," I answered. She cocked an eyebrow and motioned for me to go on. "A couple nights ago, I *did* get wasted and he drove me home. I ended up kissing him and yesterday, I went to his place to, I don't really know honestly, clear the air? Tell him I broke up with Phil?" I left out the part of me being terrified that someone had been following me on the subway. In the light of day that sounded ridiculous now.

Ava's mouth popped open but I hurried on before she could interrupt. "So I was over there last night and then— well, it got late and he didn't want me driving home and then we might have ended up hooking up and I stayed over."

"You broke up with Phil?"

I nodded.

"You slept with Finn? Like naked, body parts intertwined, not getting much actual sleep?"

"To be honest, I was never fully naked but yeah, other than that—"

Ava squealed and lunged for me, pulling me into a tight embrace. "I'm so fucking happy for you! Both of you. I knew this would happen, I could tell from the minute I saw you two interact."

"Okay Ms. Matchmaker, it was just one night."

"Even still, you guys are perfect for each other."

Now it was my turn to roll my eyes. Then I sobered as I remembered my earlier concerns about how she'd react. "You're honestly not mad?"

Ava's brow wrinkled in confusion. "Why on earth would I be?"

I shrugged. "It could complicate things with the four of us and our friend group."

"I trust that all of us are mature enough to handle whatever happens. Now," she said, gripping my hands. "You've got to tell me all about it. Wait, but first, when did you break up with Phil? And why exactly did you not tell me?"

I groaned as I slid deeper into the couch. "So Finn went out to dinner with me and some of the other girls from the theater after work. I had a bad fight with Phil, just the usual stuff, fighting about the lack of time and him not taking my dancing seriously, but I was pissed and had a couple more drinks than I should have." I paused to take a breath and Ava waited quietly for me to go on. "Finn drove me home and I was a total whore and tried to get him to have sex with me." Ava's eyes widened but she remained silent. "We didn't. We kissed and then he left, but the next day, I felt so shitty. Phil might not have been the greatest boyfriend, but even still, he deserves someone who's faithful to him."

Ava looked like she wanted to argue but she refrained. "So I decided enough was enough and broke up with him over the phone," I said, wincing.

"How did he take it? Did he even remember you guys were still together?"

"Considering he called me a whore I think he remembered."

"That piece of shit."

I put my hand on hers. "It's fine. He was hurt, I *was* wrong to kiss Finn, but it's over now."

"And Finn?"

"What about him?"

"Was it good?"

I laughed as I felt an unusual blush climb my cheeks.

"Oh my god," Ava exclaimed.

"What?" I asked, trying to play it off.

"You totally like him. You're blushing. You never blush."

"Of course, I like him, I had sex with him after all."

"No, but you *like him* like him."

"Yes, we've established that, can we move on?"

She laughed and pulled me into another hug. "I'm just saying. I'm so excited for you. When are you seeing him next?"

"Not sure, we don't have anything planned yet."

"Oh my god, we can totally go on double dates now!"

I laughed. "I can't believe you want someone else to crash you and Art's time."

"Of course I do, it's you." She relaxed against the couch and I could see her mind already planning future outings for the four of us.

"So what are we watching today?" I asked, bringing her back to the present.

"Ooh, I saw something the other day that I thought would be perfect. Let me find it," she said as she reached for the remote. I smiled as I settled back with my muffin. The possibility of something with Finn, girl time with Ava, and the opportunity to dance with my dream company. Life was pretty damn good.

21

Finn

I met Libby in the parking lot and we entered the station together, heading for Cap's office. She'd already called him to make sure he had some time for us to come by and chat. When we entered his office he was on the phone but he waved for us to sit down. We took our seats and I contemplated how I would present my request to work this case. He ended his call and after a few moments of typing on his computer, he turned his full attention to us.

"Sorry about that, what can I do for you two? I was a bit surprised to hear you needed to see me already as you haven't even started together yet," he said with a perplexed look. Libby nodded to me and I jumped right in.

"I know I talked to you briefly about a case regarding the NYC ballet company and a missing ballerina." He nodded but didn't interrupt so I continued. "I looked into it and I'm concerned that it was never solved due to some of the suspects' ties with the mob. There is one person in particular that I believe may have played a part in her disappearance. And now with the suspicious events surrounding some of the current ballerinas, I'm concerned that it is happening again."

"What would you like from me?"

I took a deep breath. "I am requesting to formally open the case again and work this new angle involving the ballerinas and this group that is reaching out to them." Marcus' face showed no emotion and I didn't have a clue what he thought of my request.

"What is your plan?"

"I have a connection to one of the ballerinas and she said that this group has already met with them once. I propose we mic up some of the dancers when they meet with this group again and see if we can get any information on them."

"You're suggesting we send untrained civilians on an undercover operation?"

"No. Not technically. I'm not expecting to get anything incriminating on the group, necessarily, but if they're going to meet with them anyway to discuss the details, I figured it wouldn't be that much harder to record the conversation if you were okay with it."

Marcus turned to Libby. "And you're on board with this?"

"Truthfully, I have no idea if anything will come of it and I don't have much information about this case that he is talking about. But he's proven he has a good intuition and I am willing to work this angle with him if he is that concerned."

Marcus looked thoughtful as he nodded. "After you asked me about it I did some digging of my own since I couldn't remember that case. It was from before I was captain, but I vaguely remember hearing about it from some of the other detectives. It's very sad how nothing came of it. If there's a chance that this is related, I am willing to let you investigate."

Relief washed through me at his declaration.

He continued. "You can use our recording technology, and try to record the meeting. I want to hear a detailed report afterward, and from there I will determine if this is something you should continue to pursue."

"Thank you, Cap."

"When do you plan to have this meeting?"

"I will reach out to the dancers and see what they can make work, but I'm hoping within the week."

He nodded. "Let me know. And Brown, I think it's pretty obvious, but I want you working this case with him.

"Yes, sir."

We talked a moment more about logistics before leaving his office and I turned to Libby. "I'll call Victoria and let you know as soon as I have a timeline."

"Alright. I'll wait for your call." We walked out together and I waited until I was settled into my car to call Vi. The phone rang to voicemail so I left a message.

"Hey Vi, I just got done talking with Marcus, my police captain. He said he's okay with us investigating the group that is contacting your dance company. If you're serious about helping with the investigation, Cap agrees that we could possibly mic one of you when you meet up with the group next. My partner and I would be right outside, nothing dangerous and if you're not comfortable, you don't have to. Now I'm rambling. Anyway, when you get this message let me know your thoughts so we can plan something. Thanks."

22

Vi

Ava and I were leaving the mall when I felt my phone buzz. I looked down to see a missed call and a voicemail from Finn. My heart did a weird little skip of anticipation at the sight.

"Who's that?" Ava asked from beside me where I had stopped.

"Finn."

"I knew it! Your face, man you are smitten."

"I am not," I argued but it was halfhearted. It had been a while since I had felt this excited over a guy and it didn't hurt that the physical chemistry was amazing. Still, the fact that we were stuck together in this friend group made me nervous for the long term.

"What does he want?" Ava prodded and I laughed but sobered as I listened to the message.

"What?" She asked again, more serious this time. Part of me wanted to lie to her or just to avoid telling her, but I couldn't do that to Ava. Not after everything we'd been through.

"His boss agreed to let him officially start working the

ballet case."

"That's great," Ava said with pinched brows.

"Last night I told him I'd be willing to help out with the investigation and he said they can give me a mic to listen in on the conversation."

Ava went still. "Well, I'm glad he's taking it seriously. I don't like the idea of you participating, however."

"I know. Believe me, I'm not planning on playing hero or anything. If I do this it's going to be with the other girls and we're just going to be meeting to chat. Nothing's going to happen to me in the middle of a crowd."

Ava looked unconvinced but nodded. "You'll keep me updated on what's happening?"

"Absolutely," I said as I pulled her into a hug.

We walked towards Ava's car and I took the opportunity to call Bella. She answered on the first ring.

"Hey girl, what's up?"

Hey, sorry to bother you on your day off—"

"Oh, don't even start. I'm just catching up on stuff today but Shelby and I were thinking of going out tonight if you wanted to join us."

"I'd love to." I moved the phone from my ear for a second. "You wanna go out tonight with some of the dancers?" I asked Ava.

"Absolutely."

"I'm in," I told Bella. "And I'm bringing my bestie with me."

"Amazing! I'm assuming that wasn't the reason you called."

"It's not, no, but it can wait until tonight."

Bella gave me the name of the new restaurant she wanted to try before I hung up and turned to Ava. "I'm so excited that you're coming with me. You need to make some more friends here in the city so it's perfect."

"I'm excited to meet the girls you hang out with every day. Gotta scope out the competition," she said with a laugh.

We spent the rest of the day relaxing at home before getting ready to meet Bella and Shelby. We arrived at the restaurant and Ava grinned happily. "One of my favorite things since moving to the city is definitely how there will always be new restaurants and clubs to try."

I looped my arm with hers. "And it's much more fun to try them out when you're here."

We found Bella and Shelby in the back of the restaurant, already settled into a booth. I gave both girls a hug before we took our seats.

"Girls, this is my best friend and soul sister Ava, Ava this is Bella and Shelby. They're been lifesavers as I've tried to get caught up on everything."

"Are you the best friend who's dating Finn's friend?" Bella started and my mouth dropped open. Thank god I had already told Ava about my recent interactions with Finn. Ava just laughed.

"Yep, my boyfriend is Art, and he and Finn have been friends forever. I take it you've already met him?"

"Yeah, he came by the theater this week to 'check on Vi' and went out with us for dinner afterward."

"You guys know I'm right here," I interjected and they both gave me a pointed look.

"He seems like a sweetheart," Shelby piped up and I sent a betrayed look her way. "Way to gang up on me."

She shrugged. "It's true, and you look so cute when flustered," she said with a wink.

The waitress arrived to take our orders and after she left I changed the subject. "Not that I want to spoil this great conversation we're having—" the three girls just grinned at me. "But speaking of Finn, you know he's a cop." They nodded so I continued. "Well, he's started investigating a missing person's case involving a ballerina from our company. He thinks her disappearance might be connected to the group that's been trying to solicit you guys, and he asked if I'd be willing to wear a mic and attend your next meetup with them."

I was unsure how they'd take it, and based on the faces staring back at me, it wasn't well.

"I wasn't really planning on doing anything else with them," Bella started.

"I don't know if I feel comfortable using a meeting with them as an opportunity to try to investigate them," Shelby replied. "I know you guys have suspicions about them, but I really need the extra cash," she said, her voice cracking. She cleared her throat before continuing. "I don't want to jeopardize an opportunity with them."

I reached across and grabbed her hand, squeezing it. "I swear I'm not trying to jeopardize anything. I'm not sure how I feel about the whole situation, I honestly don't know enough to feel strongly about whether or not they have ulterior motives. If I do this I'm not going to be trying to dig up dirt on them, it would just be a regular meeting where I can ask them questions about their organization and what they want from us like I'm assuming you did when they first reached out." I turned to Bella. "And I am not going to force you to come with. If you're not comfortable with it, I'm definitely not gonna drag you into it."

"If you guys are going, I'm going," she said stubbornly. I turned back to Shelby who was still looking contemplative.

"You don't have to decide right now," I said but she shook her head.

"If we're going to do this I'd rather get it over with. I was tentatively planning on meeting them again the day after tomorrow if you wanted to come."

"Let's do it, I'll just give Finn the information later. Now, enough of this, since we're ganging up on people about their relationship I want to hear about this mysterious person people keep referring to," I said with a pointed look at Shelby.

Bella laughed and Shelby glared at us both. "And who exactly is gossiping about me?"

"Umm, just about everyone at the company," I replied.

She sighed, looking exasperated. "Her name is Sara," she said and looked at me as if waiting for a reaction. When I didn't respond she continued. "We auditioned for the company at the same time, and, unfortunately, she didn't make it. Somehow we still managed to make it work, but, I don't know, things kept coming up causing little fights here and there and it always led back to the ballet. I tried to be there for her in her disappointment about not getting in, but it's like she always resented me that I did."

Shelby stopped and started guzzling her beverage so Bella picked up. "She's still not over her," she said pointing to Shelby. "But Sara couldn't come to terms with the fact that her girlfriend was living her dream. She wanted nothing to do with the ballet after, and, well, ballet is kind of Shelby's life."

"She basically asked me to choose her or the ballet and when I didn't immediately choose her, she left."

"Damn. I'm so sorry. That's awful."

Shelby shrugged. "It sucks. I feel like she was my one true love, you know? But what do I know, I'm young, I'm sure there's a girl or guy out there who'll change my mind."

I reached over and squeezed her hand. "I'm sure there is."

"What's your story?" Shelby said, turning her attention to Ava.

"I work here in the city as a journalist, been best friends with Vi forever." She said with a smile.

"And how did you land Mr. Billionaire?" Bella asked.

Ava laughed. "It's a very long story, but I was actually

interviewing him for a story and somehow we ended up falling in love."

I snorted at her simplified version and she elbowed me. "No one has time or interest in the long story right now, Vi."

"The more pressing question is, does he have a brother?" Bella asked, her hand on her chin.

"Nope, only child I'm afraid," Ava said with a smile.

"Damnit."

"I thought you didn't have time to date?" I asked Bella.

"You can bet your ass I would make time if I met a man with some money," Bella retorted and we all laughed. It was so nice to have my two lives interconnected, Ava and the girls. I felt so incredibly lucky to be surrounded by such amazing friendships. I could get used to this.

23

Finn

Art and I had just finished up a late night at the shooting range when I got Vi's text.

Beour: The girls are in. Planning for a meetup day after tomorrow if that works for you.

Me: Perfect. Are you free to come by in the afternoon so we can go over some stuff beforehand?

Beour: I'll be there :)

"You good?" Art asked as we left the building. Somehow I'd managed to not bring up Vi the whole time we'd been hanging out today. Now was as good a time as any.

"Yeah. I'm assuming Ava told you about me investigating the ballet company?"

"Yeah."

"I asked Vi to help out by wearing a mic tomorrow while they meet with the group so that my partner and I can gather some information."

"And she's willing to help you out?" He asked, surprise thick in his voice.

I gave him a hard look. "This is the girl who came barging

into your flat to find her kidnapped best friend."

"Good point, good point," he held up his hands in surrender. "I'm just saying, it seems like a lot for her to be willing to help out with your investigation."

"She's selfless like that." Pause. "Also, we might have hooked up last night." And again this morning but I wasn't keen on sharing all the details.

"You what?"

"You know, the birds and the bees. When a man loves a woman—"

"Dick," he said elbowing me. "I'm just shocked that you went there. Wait, doesn't she have a boyfriend? Ava keeps talking about him."

"She *did*. Not anymore."

"Really, poaching women again? Back to your old ways, huh, Sully."

"Fuck off," I laughed as I shoved him, forcing him to catch himself before he fell on his ass. "I didn't tell her to break up with him. I asked her out before and she told me she was in a relationship. I backed off, and, well she broke up with her boyfriend and then we hooked up. Not my business what was going on in their relationship."

"Well, I'm happy if you're happy. And as long as you don't do something stupid to upset Ava."

I rolled my eyes. "Overprotective dick."

He left and I settled into my car, pulling up my text exchange with Vi again. Now that I'd finally gotten a taste of her, I felt addicted. I knew she was busy, but there was no hurt in trying so I sent off another text.

Me: You free tomorrow to hangout?

I got a response a moment later. *Beour: What do you have in mind?*

Me: I'd love to take you out for dinner if you're free.

Beour: It's your lucky day Sullivan, cause I'm free.

Me: The luckiest. I'll do some research and text you the details.
Beour: Okay :)

~ ~ ~

I picked her up at her condo with my bike. I honked when I parked in her driveway and a moment later she came out the front door, locking it behind her.

"A bike date, huh?" She asked.

"I could tell how much you liked it last time," I said with a smirk.

She mock glared at me but she couldn't refute it because we both knew it was true. Instead, she came up to me, taking the helmet I offered her. She put it over her head and damn was it hot watching her get ready. I whistled and she swatted my arm.

"Hey, last time we rode I was trying to be respectful," I said.

"And you're not today?"

"Not a chance," I said, smiling at her wickedly.

"I am suddenly *very* excited for our date," she said as she climbed onto the back of my bike and molded her body to mine.

I laughed as I took off towards the restaurant, excitement pulsing through me.

We had brunch on a cute patio where she ordered a turkey sandwich and I discovered that she hated breakfast food, well, primarily eggs, but she didn't discriminate when she lumped them all into the 'disgusting' category. We held hands and laughed and talked about the dumbest things.

I checked the time and then waved toward our waitress. "Time to head out."

"Are you going to tell me where we're going next?" She asked with a raised brow.

"Not a chance, I didn't plan out this whole date to ruin it by telling you now."

She shook her head at me. "Of course not, gotta keep it a huge secret."

"I mean it is pretty big, but I appreciate you saying that," I said, touching my chest in gratitude. She stared at me for a moment before rolling her eyes and I couldn't help but laugh, something I felt like I did constantly in her presence.

"You seriously have the humor of a middle school boy."

I shrugged. "Maybe true, but I have yet to hear you complain about my performance," I said matter of factly. She glared at me, tipping her head at our waitress who was clearly within earshot.

"I'm not ashamed," I said and she laughed before pushing her chair back. "I'm going to use the bathroom before we head out."

I waited for her at the exit and, when she joined me, I held out my outstretched hand. She linked her hand with mine, and I led her out to my bike.

"I like this, having brunch with you and listening to your inappropriate jokes," she said.

"Me too," I said, squeezing her hand. We took the short ride to the movie theater and I parked before bowing elaborately. "M'lady."

"What are we seeing?" She asked as she handed me her helmet and attempted to tame her hair.

I shrugged. "Whatever was available at this time."

Her mouth popped open. "You don't actually know?"

"I did when I purchased the tickets, but unlike some people," I gave her a pointed look, "I'm not a movie snob."

"I am not," she argued, "I just choose to actually know which movie I am about to see."

"But isn't that half the fun?" I asked.

"I can tell you honestly, the idea of being surprised at the movie theater has never crossed my mind."

"Well, there's a first for everything."

We made our way to the kiosk, I entered my order number and the tickets printed. Vi had decided that since she didn't know the movie yet, she wanted to be completely surprised when it finally started. I loved that she was embracing the experience, so I didn't show her the tickets. We made our way to the theater and settled into the seats. I'd picked spots right in the middle and we kicked out the recliners.

"I haven't been to a movie in so long," she whispered as the commercials played.

"If I've had a really bad day I like to come and watch whatever is playing," I replied, getting comfortable.

"By yourself?"

"Yeah," I shrugged. "It's actually kind of fun."

"Why don't you just stream something at home?"

"The experience, obviously," I said, clicking my tongue at her. We sat back in silence to watch the rest of the commercials and finally, the movie started. It was a romantic movie set in outer space and, to be completely honest, I didn't care about the plot one bit. Vi dutifully watched the screen, however, and I took the opportunity to stare at her in the dim light. As the movie played, the screen would flash, illuminating her profile. She was seriously the most beautiful person I'd ever laid eyes on.

Finally, she noticed my staring and she turned towards me. "Movie not catching your interest?" She whispered.

"Not nearly as much as you are." She squirmed at the praise and I loved how flustered she got. I reached for her lap and she went to hold my hand but I gently pushed it away and continued my path. She gasped and stared at me wide-eyed as I slid my hand up her dress. When she'd asked what to wear I'd told her a casual dress. It had nothing to do with the fanciness of the restaurant and everything to do with the easy access.

"Finn," she whispered and I raised an eyebrow at her in mock innocence. "Watch the movie, Beour."

She gave me another glare before turning her attention back to the screen. I slid closer to her, wrapping an hour around her shoulders to pull her into my chest, continuing my other hand's descent under her dress. She twitched as I touched her panties and I smirked at the reaction. This was going to be so incredibly fun.

I traced wide circles on the front of her underwear, her breath hitching every time I got close to her center. I never went far down though, just brushing low enough to cause a gasp before moving back upwards. It didn't take long before she began to squirm under my touch, attempting to move my hand lower. Having teased her long enough, I let her push my fingers down to her center and she gasped as I touched her entrance. I immediately stopped and pulled my hand back. Her gaze shot to mine and I leaned down to whisper into her ear.

"You've got to stay quiet or I'll stop. Do you understand?" She nodded. "Do you think you can be a good girl for me and keep quiet while I finger you?"

She bit her lip but nodded in silence.

"I knew you could, you're such a good girl, you take my fingers so well."

I could tell she was biting hard onto her lip and I guessed it was to keep any sound inside. Fuck, she was perfect. As a reward, I slipped my hand under her panties and began my slow trek downward again. As promised, she kept quiet but when I reached her folds, her hand shot out to grip my wrist. I thought for a second she was pushing me away and I almost stopped, but then I felt her tug me towards herself and I smiled. Greedy, greedy, girl.

I made one last slow circle before I gave her exactly what

she wanted, plunging my fingers inside of her. Her entire body stiffened and she held my wrist in a chokehold, almost cutting off my circulation, but like the good girl that she was, she made no sound. I swirled my fingers inside of her, in and out, curving them to hit the spot I knew drove her insane. Her hips thrust up and she let out a squeak. I immediately stilled.

She turned her face towards me, burying her mouth in my neck. "Please, Finn, please."

"I said to keep quiet," I whispered back.

"I know, I'm sorry, I will, I promise. Just, please don't stop." She begged desperately.

I pressed a kiss to her temple before I began to move my fingers again, circling my thumb on her clit. She bit down hard on my neck and I jerked but she remained dutifully silent so I rewarded her by continuing the motion. My fingers plunged, my thumb circled and then she was coming, her hips jerking as her pussy clenched around my fingers and she clung to my neck. I was absolutely going to have a bruise tomorrow, but fuck if this wasn't the hottest thing that had ever happened to me.

When her body finally relaxed I removed my fingers, bringing them up to my mouth to suck them off. I had to work not to moan myself at the taste and she stared at me with pure adoration.

"You taste incredible," I murmured to her and she reached towards my crotch. I put my hand on hers, stilling her. "Later," I whispered.

And later she did. After the movie, I drove her back to her house and, when we found it empty, she gave me the best handjob of my life before I ended the date buried inside of her. As we lay cuddling naked in her bed, she smiled shyly at me. "I don't want to jinx anything, but this may have been the best first date of my life."

"You mean to tell me that none of your past boyfriends have fingered you during a movie about an alien invasion?" I asked, incredulously.

She laughed as she shook her head. "I can't say that they have."

I leaned forward to press a kiss to her collarbone. "Definitely the best first date I've ever been on," I confirmed.

We heard the front door open and I jerked up as if I'd been caught. "She knows about us," Vi said, watching me.

"Be that as it may, I don't relish the idea of getting caught with my pants down," I said motioning to my nakedness and beginning to search the floor for my clothes. We dressed in a comfortable silence and when we exited her room Ava had already gone to her own room. We stopped by the front door where I pulled her in for another kiss. "Thanks for today, Vi."

"Anytime, Finn."

"I'll hold you to that," I said with a promise and she smiled.

"Good. See you tomorrow?"

"Absolutely," I said before heading towards my bike. I waved at her before taking off and I could feel her eyes on me until I was out of sight. I had really hit the jackpot with her, and I had no intention of letting anything fuck it up.

24

Finn

The next morning I began planning for the stakeout tonight. I'd filled Libby in, and she was planning on meeting me at my place before we drove to the club the girls had picked.

In the meantime, Vi was going to head over and we'd talk logistics. She wouldn't need to do much besides wear the piece so there wasn't a lot to go over, but I'd take any excuse to see her.

I was sitting on the couch in my living room when she arrived and knocked on my door. I couldn't keep the smile off my face as I let her in.

"Hey, thanks for coming by. What was the girls' reaction to doing this?" Somehow yesterday we had managed to avoid talking about the investigation and I realized I'd never asked how that initial conversation had gone.

She followed me to the couch and took a seat next to me. "They were a little hesitant. I told them there was no obligation and I could do it by myself if they didn't want to, but of course Bella jumped in all 'I'm going if you are.'"

"Do they understand it's not going to be a huge operation?

I'm going to be nearby so I can listen in, but this isn't going to be us coming in guns blazing, serving a warrant type of thing. It should be just a regular conversation with the addition of your inconspicuous microphone."

She nodded. "I think Shelby feels bad about spying on them, but if this turns out to be anything shady like you guys think it is, then obviously that feeling won't last long."

"True. You wanna see the device?" I asked, changing the subject. "It's in my room."

"I mean if you want to get me to your room you could just ask, Finnian."

I glared at her. "Hey now, just 'cause you happened to be part of my secret family reunion doesn't mean you get to take advantage of me like that."

She laughed as she motioned to the bedroom. "I happen to think it's a very nice name. Very proper."

"I'll show you proper," I muttered as I led the way to my bedroom, her laughter echoing behind me.

Once in the bedroom, I grabbed a phone from my dresser, holding it out to her. "Meet the Phantom."

Vi looked at it with raised brows before turning her attention back to me. "Your cellphone?"

"Well, it's technically the department's, but yes."

"I'm going to be recording the conversation on your phone?"

"There's an app downloaded on this phone that records and broadcasts the conversation to where I'll be listening in from my car. All you need to do is keep the phone on you, in your pocket or something, and I'll be able to listen in."

"So you're telling me I don't get to wear a fancy wire hidden in my shirt?"

"I mean, I can still stick some things down your shirt if you want," I offered with a grin. She rolled her eyes as she shoved my shoulder. "So that's it? I just need to keep the phone in my pocket and you'll do the rest?"

"Yep. I'll make sure the app is up and running before you go in, but otherwise there's nothing special you need to do. Just be your charming self and ask them about their organization, what they want from you etc."

"Sounds easy enough."

"Easy peasy," I said, placing the phone back on my dresser.

"Is there any specific information you want me to try to get from them?" She asked with a furrowed brow.

"Names would be helpful, although I imagine they'll probably be fake. Otherwise, who is running the company? How many people are involved? What's the purpose? Locations, where you'd be meeting. How often? Basically any and all details you can get."

"And you think they'll just give up some incriminating information?"

"No. Honestly, I'm not expecting to get much helpful information." She looked startled at this and I winced as I continued. "If they truly are involved in what we think they are, they aren't going to be broadcasting it."

"So then what's the point of this?"

"If they are a real organization we should be able to look them up based on the information that they provide and verify that. Today isn't really about finding dirt on them, but more so to establish that we believe they are not the innocent group that they claim to be."

She nodded slowly. "At least then we'll be able to tell Shelby if she's good to continue or not."

"Exactly."

"So, that's it?"

"Pretty much?" I answered with a shrug.

"And you asked me to come to your house early just for this?"

I cocked an eyebrow. "You had something else in mind,

Beour?"

Her mouth turned up in a smirk that sent a rush of blood to my cock.

"Uh oh," I replied warily.

She laughed as she dropped her purse onto my bed and rummaged around in it before pulling out a pair of pink fluffy handcuffs. My mouth dropped open at the sight.

"I figured we could get in the mood by practicing some other police skills," she said innocently.

"If you expect me to role-play arresting you, you're shit out of luck. I do that too much in the real world to want to bring it into the bedroom."

"Who said I'd be the one wearing them?" She countered. *Fuck.* My dick was now fully awake as she twirled the toy in her hand. "If you're too scared, I can put them away. We're done here so I can leave—" she said the threat so casually.

"Not a chance," I answered as I stepped forward and captured her lips with mine. She laughed against me which turned into a soft moan as her free hand came up to tangle in my hair. Even though we'd just been together yesterday, I'd missed her. The feeling, the taste, the smell, everything about her intoxicated me.

I pushed her backward towards my bed until her legs hit the mattress. I reached down to grasp her ass before picking her up and depositing her onto my comforter. She laughed as she bounced a little and the hunger I saw reflected in her eyes made my cock twitch. "You're perfect a mhuirnín," I said, devouring her with my eyes.

"You're not so bad yourself, Finnian," she said as she pulled me back to her and our lips met in an explosive kiss. I could kiss her all day long. Her lips were soft and warm and she tasted amazing. No one should be allowed to taste as good as she did. Her hands roamed my back, finding the bottom of my t-shirt and lifting it over my head. I helped her by shimmying out of it and the appreciation I saw in her gaze as she took in my bare skin warmed me from the inside out. Her fingers dusted over my chest and down to the trail of hair above my waistband.

"I love this," she murmured.

"Good, 'cause this fair-skinned boy worked hard on that," I replied and she giggled. The sound ignited all sorts of cravings inside of me. I had been honest when I said I'd never had the desire to handcuff my partners. It really lost the sexual appeal when I had to do it at work, but for the first time, I actually wanted to. Remembering the smirk on her face when she pulled them out of her purse, the fact that she had thought and planned ahead for this—

I reached up and plucked the cuffs from her grip, meeting her gaze as I rose up, straddling her body. She licked her lips, sending a fresh wave of desire straight to my already aching dick. I secured one of her hands in the pink cuff before reaching down and lifting her shirt up and over her head, leaving her in a lacy pink bra that didn't quite match the cuffs, but had clearly been planned.

"All this for me?" I asked teasingly. She squirmed underneath me, rubbing against my rock-hard erection, eliciting a groan from me.

"Naughty," I said, grabbing her other hand and securing it to the first above her head. She lay in her bra and leggings below me and I scooted backward, climbing off of the bed to stand above her, taking in every curve and line. She stared back at me, a light pink tinge on her cheeks. God, I wanted to do depraved things to this woman.

I reached down, grabbed the waistband of her leggings, and pulled them down and off. Like I had been beginning to suspect, a matching pink pair of panties stared back at me. "Were you hoping to cancel tonight? Because wearing this, I don't know if I will be able to let you leave."

She shrugged in her cuffs. "If we have to reschedule so be it."

"Bean théisiúil," I murmured before climbing back up and claiming her mouth with my own. She opened for me so willingly, seeming every bit as desperate for me as I was for her. I ravaged her mouth before sinking lower, leaving a trail of kisses along her collarbone and towards her chest. Remembering how crazy she went when I pinched her nipples, I used one hand to hold her secured hands to the bed and the other to pull down her bra, exposing one breast and then the other. I stopped right above her nipple, letting my breath fan across her and watching her skin pebble and her nipples harden. Finally, I closed the distance, sucking one of the stiff peaks into my mouth. We moaned in unison and I took my time before moving to the other side. She writhed underneath me, attempting to rub her thinly clothed crotch against me.

"Nuh, uh," I said, bringing my hand from her chest to press her hips into the bed. "I'm not done with you yet."

She let out a sound very similar to a whine and I smiled in amusement. "You came to play, baby, let me play."

She relaxed obediently and I stroked my hand against her hip towards her core, "Good girl."

She whimpered and I had to force myself not to grind against her at the sound. How could she simply breathe in my direction and I was already ready to explode?

Finally, satisfied with my treatment of her nipples, I released my grip on her enough to pull her underwear off.

"Ahem," she said nodding towards my jean-clad legs.

"So antsy to get me naked, huh?" I asked.

"It's only fair."

"I never promised to be fair, but I will oblige this time." I removed my pants and underwear in one smooth motion, noting how Vi's gaze didn't leave my body once. Finally, I kneeled on the bed again. "You're going to keep your hands above your head or I will secure them up there, understood?"

She nodded and I smiled before trailing a hand down her thigh. "You're such a good girl, so good at following directions." She squirmed at the praise but did indeed keep her hands above her head. I rewarded her with a kiss to her inner thigh.

"Finn," she breathed and I did it again, higher this time, getting closer and closer to that perfect pussy that I just knew was aching for my touch. I continued kissing and nipping at her skin, watching her face scrunch in concentration as she worked to keep herself still. Finally, I moved up and pressed a gentle kiss to her clit. She was soaked and I couldn't help the moan that left me at her perfect taste.

"I could feast on your perfect cunt for the rest of my life," I said before plunging my tongue deep inside.

25

Vi

Finn's tongue entering me was the most perfect intrusion. I did my best to obey him as I kept my hands up, but I couldn't help rocking against his face. His tongue was the most magical thing I'd ever experienced, and I felt like I could die happy in this moment. He worked me skillfully and I felt the tension coil tighter and tighter in my core as my orgasm loomed ahead. I was so close and it was a mix of wanting this feeling to last forever and also needing to fall over the edge. I moaned his name louder as my pussy clenched and—

He pulled back at the last second and I wanted to cry out at the loss of his mouth. I opened my mouth to tell him he was bad at this, when I saw the evil smirk on his lips. He knew exactly what he was doing. *Oh no he didn't.*

"Something wrong?" He asked in what I was sure was his attempt at an innocent voice. It came off as an evil purr instead.

"Asshole," I grunted.

"Oh, I'm sorry, did you not come?"

I glared at him but shook my head.

"Well then, I better remedy that," he said before diving back between my legs. This time the orgasm rocketed even higher and I chased that high, desperate for the feeling of euphoria that I knew was just around the corner. I thrust my hips toward him and he matched my rhythm, his tongue caressing my inner walls before pressing back against that perfect spot that sent sparks against the back of my eyelids. Just when I felt like I was about to explode he pulled back again, my pussy clenching against empty air painfully.

"Finn," I said, the sound coming out as a sob in my desperation.

"Shhh," he said crawling up to kiss my forehead tenderly as if he wasn't the one torturing me. "Do you want to come?"

"Yes," I begged, past the point of caring.

"Ask me nicely to let you come," he said pressing a kiss to my throat.

"Please Finn, please let me come."

He reached down and dipped his fingers inside me, swirling over my clit before plunging them in and out, filling me so deliciously. I rocked my hips against his hand, chasing the high that only he had the power over, and, like before, just as my body was about to clench around him, he withdrew. "I'm going to need to hear a little more desperation than that, baby." He crooned.

"Finn, please," I sobbed, desperate, willing to do anything, give anything to find my release. "I need you, I need you to make me come, please—"

"Spread your legs." He commanded.

I did so willingly and he ran a finger through my soaked entrance before positioning his cock against me and plunging deep inside. I groaned at the perfect stretch and the added friction of his piercing inside me. He reached up and gently wrapped a large hand around my throat, squeezing gently. At the same time, he reached down with his other hand and pressed his thumb against my clit. "Come for me, baby girl."

And I did, exploding in one of the biggest orgasms of my life. I cried and whimpered, making sounds I'd never heard come from my mouth before.

He continued to thrust inside of me and then I felt him too find his release as my orgasm finally faded and I panted in the aftermath. He pressed one last kiss to my mouth before reaching up to open the cuffs. With my hands released, I brought them down to trail against his bare back.

"You're cruel, and amazing and perfect," I murmured against him.

"You're the one who brought the cuffs," he said tweaking my nose. "How was I supposed to know that you weren't prepared for what that would mean?"

"How was I supposed to know that you were such a sadist?" I volleyed back.

He laughed but then leaned forward to press another kiss to my neck. "You were such a good girl, I'm so proud of how well you came for me."

The praise filled me with warmth and just like that I was ready for round two. Before I could say anything else, however, Finn stood up. "I need to shower before we head out, wanna join me?"

I wasn't usually the biggest fan of shower sex, but I couldn't help following him to the bathroom, unashamedly taking the opportunity to watch his ass as he walked ahead of me.

He turned the shower to a comfortable temperature and we stepped inside. He gave me the spot in the direct stream of water and I took the opportunity to borrow some of his shampoo to lather in my hair. I closed my eyes as I rinsed the suds out when suddenly I felt something soft against me. I opened my eyes to see Finn gently caressing my skin with a soapy washcloth. He moved it leisurely over my shoulder, across one breast and to the other. I hummed in appreciation but his eyes didn't meet my gaze as he continued to stare at my body and meticulously washed me. When he brought the cloth to the space between my legs I opened them and sucked in a sharp breath.

"I heard something that I want confirmed," he said, distracting me from his ministrations.

"Hmm?" I murmured.

"Detachable shower heads," he said, finally looking up to meet my gaze.

Somehow, despite the intimacy we'd already shared, I felt a blush creep into my cheeks. "Yes?"

"I just figured I could experiment," he said, cocking an eyebrow.

I opened my mouth to reply but he was already reaching past me to grab the shower head from the wall and remove it. The spray pointed to the wall before he twisted it, adjusting the settings as he went.

"What exactly is your experiment?" I asked breathlessly.

He didn't answer, instead trailing the gentle stream over my buzzing skin until it hit my already sensitive center. I jerked at the feeling and he pulled it away to meet my gaze. "Is it okay?"

"Yes," I said shakily.

He grinned and pushed me back towards the wall of the shower. I felt my back hit the tile and he used one hand to grip my hip before bringing the stream back to my crotch.

"Finn," I gasped as the water hit my clit again and he smirked as he began to swivel the shower head, causing me to twitch and gasp. The water continued its gentle assault and I felt my orgasm begin to build again.

"Oh my god," I said, squirming and tilting my hips back further for a better angle. He adjusted with me and my toes curled at the feeling of the water pounding into me. "Finn," I moaned, reaching for his wrist, needing more. He twisted the dial on the shower head and the stream grew more forceful.

"Fuck, fuck," I said as my body began to jerk, desperate to be filled. He dropped the shower head and plunged his fingers inside me, filling me while I rocked against him. He continued to plunge inside of me until I finally stilled, going limp against the shower wall.

"Hmm, it seems the rumors were true." He said with a smirk.

"You're insane," I said, leaning forward to kiss him as he laughed against me.

26

Vi

We finished up in the shower and, after exiting and dressing, Finn offered me some coffee which I was learning he drank copious amounts of every day. Despite his reassurances that there wasn't anything to worry about, I knew tonight would be a long night so I took him up on an offered cup. I was sitting on the couch, scrolling on my phone while he got ready in his room when his doorbell rang.

"Can you get that? It should be Libby," he called from his bedroom.

"Yep." I opened the door to find a petite woman in plain clothes and a gun on her hip. "You must be Libby," I stuck out my hand which she took with a smile.

"Yeah, and you are?"

"Oh, sorry," I felt a blush creep up my neck. "I'm Victoria, a friend of Finn's."

"Ahh, very nice to meet you. You're one of the ballerinas, right?"

"Yeah. Come on in, he's finishing getting ready."

She followed me into the living room and we settled onto

the couch to wait. Thankfully, before the silence could become uncomfortable, Finn joined us.

"Thanks for swinging by, I was hoping we could talk logistics before heading over." He said.

"No problem."

"I'm going to use the bathroom," I said as a way of excusing myself. I wasn't sure what they needed to discuss, but I knew I didn't want to intrude. I settled in at the bar while they chatted, trying to keep my nerves at bay.

I pulled up my phone and texted Ava in an attempt to distract myself.

Me: Tell me about the dirtiest thing you and Art have done.

She sent back a laughing emoji a minute later. *A: I'm scared. What's up?*

Me: Just feeling the nerves. I know you aren't a cop but you still do the investigating stuff all the time, how do you not freak out?

A: I do feel nervous but I just channel it into productivity and excitement.

Me: Yeah that's not happening.

A: Are you okay? Finn will be there the whole time. I can come too if you need backup.

Me: No, that would probably mess up the whole thing.

A: You don't think I could pass as a dancer? I'm offended.

I laughed and she sent another message. *A: Seriously though, are you okay?*

Me: Yeah, I'm okay. I'm just not cut out for this life. Once this is over I will happily go back to only worrying about dancing.

A: And screwing a certain redhead, she sent back with a winking emoji.

Me: About that…

"You ready?" Finn said, making me jump in my chair and hide my phone. He looked at me with raised brows and I laughed.

"Yeah, sorry, just texting Ava."

"Mhm," he said. "You can ride with me and then I can drop you off at your place tonight if you want."

"That'd be perfect, thanks." I sent a quick last text to Ava.

Me: Sorry, boss man said it's go time.

A: Okay, but I expect a detailed explanation of whatever you were about to say later. I'll be at Art's tonight but tomorrow night.

Me: You got it. Love you babe.

A: Love you back.

I hopped down from my stool and turned to Finn. "Sorry," I said again. "I'm ready."

I followed him out to his car, giving an appreciative glance at his motorcycle as we passed. Definitely needed to take another ride on that with him. He slid behind the wheel as I buckled up and took a deep breath.

"Nervous?" He asked as he backed out.

"A little," I said, downplaying the nest of butterflies currently taking residence in my gut.

"I'll be right outside the whole time, promise. At the slightest hint of something going wrong, Libby and I will be inside. She may be small, but I've heard some very intense things about Libby's fighting skills."

I laughed, picturing that. "Oh, I have no doubt she could take down anyone she wanted to."

"Even me?" He asked in mock offense.

"Oh, *especially* you."

"Mean," he said. "I thought ballerinas were supposed to be sweet and docile."

"I don't know where you heard that, but whoever said it was lying through their teeth."

We both chuckled before falling into a comfortable silence.

"How long have you had your bike?" I asked as we approached the restaurant.

"I learned to ride in high school. A bike was one of the first things I ever purchased for myself once I started working.

Something about riding really helps me clear my mind. There's nothing like it."

"I can see that," I said. "Maybe I'll have to get one someday."

"My ballerina biker, I like that." He said smugly.

"We go on one date and I'm suddenly yours now, huh?"

His face tinged pink and my mouth opened in surprise. I'd meant it as a joke but— "Did I just embarrass you?" I asked. "Honestly, I didn't think that was possible."

"Shut up," he said in an uncharacteristically self-conscious tone.

I reached over and grabbed his hand, squeezing, "Keep fucking me like you have, let me ride your bike, and you can call me whatever you want."

He rolled his eyes as he muttered, "Tá tú trioblóide."

I let go of his hand with a laugh, then sobered when I realized we were parking.

"Deep breaths, A mhuirnín, deep breaths."

I did just that and he handed me the phone. "I made sure it's up and running. Just keep it in your pocket and go have fun with your friends. Libby and I will take care of the rest."

As he spoke she approached my side of his car and I got out, watching her slip into the seat. I nodded towards them, took another deep breath, and headed towards the restaurant.

I entered, scanning the lobby as I went. Shelby was already inside, waiting by the hostess stand.

"Hey girl," I said giving her a hug.

She squeezed me back with a smile. "I'm glad this is where we're meeting 'cause I'm absolutely craving their apricot salad."

"You and apricots," Bella laughed from behind us and we turned to watch her saunter in. "Let's do this."

We gave our names to the hostess who led us back to a corner booth where two men and a woman sat with— Julia.

"Hey Jules," Bella said in what I could tell was her best attempt at a polite voice.

"What's she doing here?" Julia responded, motioning to me.

"Not sure what you mean, we were all invited to come," Shelby shot back.

"I didn't realize this opportunity was so *inclusive*."

"Get over yourself," Bella spoke, and I turned to her in shock, but she only smiled sweetly, a saccharine edge to her expression.

"Ladies, welcome," said one of the men as if he hadn't heard the exchange. I took a moment to look at him and his companions as I settled in. They were clean-cut and normal-looking. I don't know what I had been expecting, maybe for them to look like they were in a secret society or the mob, whatever that meant. Instead, they looked like an average person you'd meet on the street.

"Thanks for having us," Shelby said with a smile. "As you can see we brought another friend who is interested in the opportunity as well, hope that's okay."

"Of course, the more the merrier," the woman said. She had long black hair and a nice-looking smile.

I smiled back, "Thanks. Like most people these days I could definitely use some extra income and I've heard bits and pieces from the girls here, but I'd love to hear more about the opportunity from you."

"Of course, as you should." The guy who seemed to be in charge replied. "I'm Marvin, this is Andrea and Nate," he motioned to the people sitting beside him. "We'd be happy to explain more about the company. We work for a nonprofit that believes the arts should be accessible to everyone, regardless of their financial status. Our goal is to provide no-cost dance classes to underprivileged children in some of the poorer communities. We have several financial backers who are passionate about this work and are able to pay several dance teachers. That's where you come in. We would love to have some experienced dancers like yourselves to come teach a class once or twice a week depending on how many people we have. We will compensate your time," he said handing me a folder. I opened it and saw a list of figures, names, and contact information. I scanned it before looking towards Shelby who had an excited smile on her face.

"This sounds awesome," I replied.

He smiled and dipped his head, "We are all passionate about this idea and so grateful that you guys would be willing to consider working with some of these children who deserve the same opportunities as everyone else, regardless of financial status."

I could tell this was the perfect opportunity for Shelby, and I was suddenly hoping that all of this checked out for her sake. I'd give Finn the packet that I received and let him verify everything. And if it did indeed check out, I would love to be a part of something like this.

"How do we get involved in this?"

"If everything looks good, we'll just take your phone numbers so that we can send out all the details once the number of participants is finalized."

I nodded and he passed me an information sheet. I wrote my name and phone number but left the rest blank. In case they weren't who they claimed to be, I didn't want to give too much information. Finn might be irritated that I gave them those two things in the first place.

"Now, we'd love to just hear more about you guys, your dreams, and your passions. And please, order whatever you'd like, it's on us."

27

Finn

It sounded way too good to be true. From what I could hear through the mic, Vi had been handed papers with more information. I didn't catch any company names to start pursuing while they were inside, so I'd have to wait until she came out with the details to begin my research.

"There's no way it's legit, right?" I asked Libby from beside me. "People don't just offer free services and paid teaching gigs out of the goodness of their hearts."

"I do wish they had actually mentioned anything that we could look into," Libby said, echoing my thoughts. "But yeah, I am hesitant to believe everything they've claimed so far. Have you found anything else about the missing dancer?"

"Nothing. After this, I'm hoping to maybe revisit some of those interviews and eyewitnesses. But so far she just vanished."

Libby nodded thoughtfully as we continued to listen in. The group had moved on to other topics, their love of dance, and some of their previous performances. While I hated that Vi was involved in this investigation in any way, it was fun to hear how close she was already with some of the other dancers. Except that Jules person. She sounded downright disgusted to have seen Vi there. I tucked that away as something to ask her about later.

The rest of the evening was uneventful and uninformative. Libby was fun to talk to and she told me all about her family, her husband, and two girls. It was cool to hear about her experience at the NYPD and, before long, we heard the girls wrapping up their meeting. They said goodbye to the group before heading out to say their own goodbyes.

Libby opened her door and slid out as we saw them exit the restaurant. "We'll plan to meet up tomorrow if that works?"

"Absolutely. Thanks, Libby."

"Of course, have a good night."

She passed Victoria on her way to my car and I smiled as she settled into the front seat, holding a folder.

"Well that went better than I expected," she said, handing the packet my way. I opened it and briefly skimmed it. There was definitely enough information here that I should be able to determine if this was a real organization or not.

"Thanks again for doing this, I really appreciate it," I told her as I pulled onto the road.

"You're welcome. I have to say, after meeting them I'm really hoping this is legit. Shelby is so excited and, honestly, it's something that I would be totally interested in doing too."

I took the offered cellphone from her. "I hope so too. Ava seems especially hesitant, but it shouldn't take much for us to figure out if it's shady or not."

"Good."

I drove towards her house and she turned to look at me. "You'll let me know as soon as you find out something?"

"You can count on it."

We fell into a comfortable silence that she finally broke.

"You know what sounds really good right now?"

"What's that?"

"One of those head-clearing motorcycle rides." She said with a laugh.

"You want to go back to my place now? Little late-night spin?"

She seemed to contemplate it but finally shook her head. "It's been a couple too many late nights. I really need to get some sleep before work this next week. But I really do want to. Raincheck?"

"I'd love that."

I parked in front of her house and she paused with her hand on the door. "I'm not sure exactly what this is," she said motioning between us. "But I like it. And I know I turned you down before, but I'm glad you gave me another chance."

My smile felt like it was going to split my face in two. I reached across the car and grabbed her hand, intertwining our fingers. "You have no idea how happy that makes me. I know the next couple days are busy for both of us, but this week, you, me, my bike, and a nice restaurant."

"I'd love that," she said with a soft smile.

I couldn't help myself, I leaned forward and gently kissed her. Every kiss we shared was amazing, but something about this felt different. Fresh, new. Full of hope and promise. She kissed back softly and when we broke apart I rested my forehead against hers. "Good night, a mhuirnín."

"Goodnight, Finn," she breathed.

Reluctantly I let her go and watched her exit and unlock her front door. She gave a small wave before disappearing into her house. I backed out of her driveway and drove towards my house, my chest bubbling with excitement. I couldn't believe I was lucky enough to get her, but I planned on showing her every reason she should be mine.

28

After Finn dropped me off, I undressed and slipped into my freshly made bed. I had practice tomorrow, and, despite my anxieties concerning what Finn was going to find, I fell asleep quickly.

I awoke to an unnatural squeak, something out of place. I rolled over to glance at my phone. *2:15.* I was disoriented and half-asleep as I pushed up onto an elbow, trying to figure out what had woken me. I listened again but heard nothing. Maybe I was imagining it.

I rolled over to tuck myself back into my cocoon of blankets when I heard something else, causing me to sit straight up. There was definitely something wrong. My eyes were more adjusted to the dim light now and I watched as my bedroom door was pushed open. A scream caught in my throat as I saw a masked man walk through my door like he owned the place. I scrambled away from the door, realizing too late that I had left my phone on the nightstand on the opposite side. Shit. But it was too late. I wouldn't have time to get it before he was on me.

He didn't even break his stride as he changed direction to follow me to the other side of the bed. I tried to lunge in the other direction, but he was already on me. He gripped one of my arms and I swung out with the other, attempting to hit, scratch, punch, whatever I could manage. It was like hitting a brick wall. He took my blows and grabbed the other hand, wrestling my arms behind my back. I was strong and agile, I worked out constantly for ballet, but even still I was no match for him. With what seemed like no effort at all, he had my hands secured behind my back and panic flooded me full force. *My voice, why wasn't I screaming?*

"Help! Help!" I screeched as loud as I could manage, praying that a nearby neighbor would be awoken by the commotion and do something about it. My captor grunted and I felt something sharp against the side of my neck before everything went black.

~ ~ ~

This time when my brain fought for conciseness it was like swimming through mud. Everything hurt, my head most of all, and I couldn't think straight. Where was I? Why did everything hurt? What was going on?

I tried to roll over but realized I was stuck. My hands wouldn't move from behind my back and I couldn't straighten my legs. Reality finally settled back in as I remembered waking up to someone in my bedroom. I tried to kick out again and felt something hard against my feet. I wriggled as best as I could only to find myself enclosed in some sort of box. I stopped my frantic thrashing to take in my surroundings. I felt something rough against my cheek and I could smell some type of gas. I tried to listen above the pounding in my head and finally picked up the rumble of an engine. I was in a trunk.

"Help me!" I attempted to scream again but the sound was a squeak. My throat felt like it was full of cotton. Who would have broken into my house to take me?

As soon as the question presented itself, I already knew the answer. The group I'd just had dinner with and stupidly given my name to. Ava had been right. Finn had been right. That fucking group really had nothing to do with recruiting ballerinas for free classes. I'd been trafficked.

A sob broke through my shock. Finn had told me about that ballerina who'd been taken and never heard from again. He was investigating the case but said even after all this time there were no leads. Was it truly his uncle? Was he the one who'd kidnapped me?

I tried to remember the guy who'd been in my room, but he'd been clad in all black including a ski mask. I had no idea if it was one of the people we'd met last night or somebody else.

Finn and Libby were already investigating, I reminded myself. That other ballerina had been taken, and there were no leads. But Finn and Libby were on it, already suspicious of the group. They'd find them. They had to. They'd find me.

Yeah, find you dead. Or worse.

Another sob hiccuped out of me. Why? Why had I agreed to get involved in this? It had nothing to do with me, I wasn't some savior trying to fix the world. I should have stayed in my lane, kept my head down, and gone about my business by myself.

How had I gotten on their radar? Just from the meeting? Had they followed me home and waited for Finn to leave? Were the other girls okay? Was I the only one they'd taken? Where were they taking me?

My brain spun with all the thoughts and questions. I just had to survive. Finn and Libby would find me, I just had to survive long enough for them to do that, I told myself as I closed my eyes and tried every single breathing exercise I knew to try not to spiral into a panic attack.

~ ~ ~

The vehicle finally stopped moving and I began yelling once more, hoping, praying that anyone would hear me. I heard what sounded like gravel crunching before the trunk popped open and I was met with the pitch-black sky. I blinked, willing my eyes to adjust before feeling hands roughly grab me and haul me out of the car. My knees hit the gravel below me with a thud and I cried out at the pain that shot through my body. I was in nothing but the t-shirt and underwear that I'd slept in which did nothing to shield my bare legs from the sharp rocks or the chill night air. What time was it? How long had I been out?

"Move," my captor grunted, tugging on my arm. My hands were still secured behind my back and the tugging sent pain spearing through my shoulder. I tried my best to get my feet under me and follow his commands. I stumbled forward, feeling sharp rocks dig into my feet, but managed to keep my balance. My eyes were adjusting to the dimness and I could make out a two-story house in front of us where the gravel driveway ended. There were several stars in the sky so I knew it had to be early still.

We reached the front door which my captor pushed open before yanking me inside. I blinked at the lit foyer where I stood. The house was old, it smelled like dust and mold and the inside was mostly wood. If it had been properly taken care of it probably would have been nice, but, as it was, it looked old and haunting. The door slammed behind me and I spun around to see another man standing there, leering at me. He wore no mask and his greasy blonde hair fell into his eyes.

"God, I love retrieval days," he said with a smirk, his gaze roaming over me. I tried to hunch down in my shirt but I could tell it did nothing, in fact, the act seemed to encourage him. He stepped forward, gripped my hair in his fist, and yanked my head back, almost causing me to lose my balance as my neck was wrenched painfully backward. I let out a sharp yelp and he laughed before biting hard on my throat. A sharp pain shot through me where I felt his teeth break skin and I tried to fight him but it was no use. Tears pricked my eyes before my captor's voice rang through the empty room.

"Griffith, mouth off of the merchandise."

Griffith grunted but released me after a slow lick along the side of my throat where he'd bitten me. "It's only fair that I get a taste before everyone else does."

I cowered away from him, stepping closer to the other man. He might have been the one to grab me and even sedate me, but at least he hadn't tried to touch me. I felt a tear fall and I desperately tried to hold any more back. I was in so much danger, completely defenseless against my captors.

The first man grabbed my arm again and steered me towards a large set of stairs in the middle of the room. I did my best to keep up and try not to think about Griffith who I could hear right behind me.

We reached the second floor and turned the corner, stopping in front of a large wooden door. The man before me fished out a key and unlocked the door before pushing me inside, closing and locking me in. I stumbled into the room but managed to remain on my feet. Once I had my balance I looked up in time to hear a broken sob, "Vi."

Bella stood against the far wall huddled with several other bodies.

"No, no," I said as the tears began to fall despite my best effort. I'd known it was a possibility that she was targeted as well, but I'd been trying to convince myself that wasn't the case.

She hurried towards me and I noticed that her hands were unbound and she was similarly dressed in pajamas. She pulled me into a hug, careful to avoid tugging on my restrained arms.

There was so much I wanted to ask, but no words came out as sobs wracked my body.

"Shhh, shh, it's gonna be okay, I'm right here," she murmured soothingly which just made the sobbing worse. Finally, I pulled myself together enough to step back and look behind her. Two other women sat against the wall and I was not surprised to see that it was Shelby and Julia. They'd taken us all. They'd invited us to dinner and most likely, used it as an opportunity to follow us home or however they did it. Shelby's gaze looked vacant and Julia met my gaze before leaning her head back against the wall and closing her eyes.

"Why are we here? What do they want?" I asked in a broken whisper but Bella placed her arm around me and led me towards the other girls, "Come on, let's see if we can find some way to get your hands free."

29

Finn

"So we know that the organization is a huge scam," Libby spoke from her seat across from me in the conference room. We'd met early to get a head start on this and found exactly that, none of the names or information checked out. My heart sank, remembering how excited Vi had been last night at the idea that maybe it was legit and she could do some good.

"You keep looking into it, I'm going to call her to let her know and tell the other girls not to meet with them again while we continue to investigate," I said and Libby nodded.

I stepped into another room before pulling up Vi's contact. I knew class didn't start this early so I should be able to catch her while she was still at home or on her way in. I waited, tapping my fingers on the nearest desk while the phone continued to ring. It went to voicemail and I debated whether I should leave a message or try again. She could be in the shower or something.

"Hey Vi, just wanted to let you know we got an update on the case with the information you got us. It's a total sham. I'll tell you more later, but I wanted to let you know so you could tell the others in case they try to contact you in the meantime. Okay, that's it. Let me know when you get this and I'll talk to you later. Bye."

I joined Libby again in the conference room. "She didn't pick up but I left a message. So where does this leave us?"

"Unfortunately we really don't have much to go on. We know the information they gave us was bogus, but we don't have any real names or information to work with."

"What about the suspects from Rosie's case?"

She nodded. "Yeah, I think it would be a good idea to revisit some of those." She began typing and I took a deep breath before plowing ahead.

"Before you find it yourself, I need to let you know something about Rosie's case." She looked up at me and I forced myself to continue before I lost my nerve.

"One of the suspects from Rosie's case has the same last name as I do. And yes, it is a distant relative of mine."

"How distant?"

"My uncle."

"And you were going to tell me this, when?" There was a bite to her tone.

Fuck. I'd messed up. "I realized when I first looked into it that I recognized the name. I don't have a relationship with my family, I haven't since before I graduated high school. But they do have some connections with the Irish mob." I was going to get kicked off this case. Probably kicked out of the force and blacklisted forever, if I didn't become a suspect myself.

"Does Cap know?"

"Not about my connection to one of the suspects specifically, but he did see on my background and everything that I had a relation to some people who've been on several watch lists."

She nodded thoughtfully. "This might be a conflict of

interest. I'm going to have to talk to him about it to see if he wants you off this case."

My heart sank. I had known this was coming, yet I couldn't help but hope it wouldn't end up this way. Someone needed to investigate this case and if not for me it wouldn't be on anyone's radar.

"Regardless of his decision, I will continue to look into this, Sullivan." Sweet relief washed over me at her words.

"Thank you, Libby. I understand the conflict and I don't want to do anything to jeopardize it, but I need to find out what's going on with this."

"I understand. Your friend, Victoria. She seems really nice."

I couldn't even deny it. I was one hundred percent doing this for her.

"She's amazing," I replied.

She nodded before getting up. "Come on, let's go talk to Cap."

Marcus was his usually levelheaded self.

"I can see the concern, but as he was only one of the people we talked to regarding this case, I don't think it is necessary to remove you from the case completely. I do not want you to be the one interviewing him, but there is plenty to do that does not involve him. I also want to stay updated on all of the progress made, and I want Libby to accompany you on any other interview such as with the family, but I don't feel the need to pull you just yet."

"Thank you, sir."

"I know how much this case means to you. I can tell it's really hitting you—" My phone buzzed in my pocket, interrupting him. Ava. I silenced it before turning back to him. It rang through again immediately.

"Take that if you need to." He said nodding at me.

"Thanks." I stepped out into the hall. "Hey A, what's up?"

"Have you heard from Vi recently?"

"No, not since last night, why?"

"Winnie, her ballet director called me. She didn't show up today for practice, along with several other dancers. None of them called to tell her they would be out today, and she hasn't been able to get ahold of any of them so she contacted their emergency contacts, like me."

Dread ballooned in my gut. *No, not this. Anything but this.* "I dropped her off last night, she was okay then. Maybe they're all just exhausted from last night and decided to sleep in." Even as I said it, I knew it wasn't true.

"All of them? Even when I'm blowing up her phone? I'm on my way over there right now, but I wanted to make sure you hadn't heard anything."

"No, I haven't. I'll meet you there." I hung up and all but ran back into Cap's office. "They can't get ahold of the girls from last night. The ballet director said none of them showed up to dance this morning and they can't reach them. I'm about to head to Victoria's house to check."

"I'm coming with," Libby said.

"Let me know, I'll send whoever else you need," Marcus responded.

"We're taking my car," Libby said as we jogged towards the garage. I didn't bother arguing. I knew it would be safer for her to drive at this point.

Fifteen excruciating minutes later, we pulled up at the girls' house. Ava's car was already in the driveway and I cursed myself for not telling her to stay put. This could be a crime scene and I didn't need anything disturbed.

We pulled on gloves as we went, and the door opened before we reached it.

"She's not here," Ava said in a panic.

"Okay, that doesn't mean she's not on her way to the theater."

"Her phone is still here, so is her workout bag."

Fuck.

"Have you touched anything?" Libby asked, stepping in and immediately taking charge.

"No, I mean yes but not without gloves," Ava said, motioning to her gloved hands.

"Okay, stay here, I need to take pictures. Did you move anything?"

"No, I just checked and saw her phone on her nightstand and her bag in the corner of her room."

Libby headed towards Vi's bedroom after brief directions from Ava and I tried to get my head in the case.

"Was the door unlocked when you got here?"

"No. I mean, yes. The door was closed but it was unlocked."

"Any signs of forced entry?"

"No, the door wasn't broken or anything if that's what you mean."

"Do you have a security system?"

Ava winced and I mentally berated both myself and Art. How had neither of us forced them to get something?

"We keep talking about it but no, we don't yet."

"Okay. Stay here, don't touch anything."

With that, I followed Libby into the bedroom. I was scared about what I might find, but the room looked pretty much the same as when I'd been in here last. Nothing broken, no blood. The bed was unmade as if she'd slipped out this morning, but nothing indicating signs of a struggle. Her phone was sitting on her nightstand as Ava had said and her bag was in the corner where she must have dropped it after getting home last.

"I've got pictures, let's bag the phone. I want to check the nobs for fingerprints and I'm going to call it in. We also need to go visit the other girls' houses, see if they're there or if we can find anything from them." Libby told me.

I nodded, pulling out an evidence bag to place the phone in.

"Are you going to be able to do this?" Libby said, stopping next to me.

"Yes," I said although the emotions in my voice betrayed me.

She nodded once. "I'll let you stay on for now as your insight into her might prove beneficial. But I will take you off this case the minute I think you're going to be more of a hindrance than a help."

"Understood," I replied, bagging the phone and turning towards the door.

I knew in my gut she'd been taken. And my brain was already reminding me of all the reasons I should be freaking out, like the fact that Rosie had likely been taken by this group and never found again. But I tried to drown that voice. We had more to go on now. We had eyewitnesses who'd seen this group. Had recordings of their voices, and proof of their sham organization. We'd find her. We had to. There was no other option.

30

Vi

There was nothing in this large empty room to remove my cuffs, so I sat against the wall, trying to keep the pressure off my wrists as best as I could. We exchanged murmured stories of how we'd been ambushed in our beds and brought here. Julia had been the first to arrive, followed closely by Bella, then Shelby. We'd all had someone different take us and the realization that there were that many people involved was terrifying.

"How long do you think they've been planning this?" Julia asked quietly from her spot on the wall. When no one else spoke I did.

"A long time. I don't think we're their first."

They all swung to look at me and I tried to remember what I'd told them about Finn's investigation.

"Finn, my cop friend," I said for Julia's benefit, "has been looking into the disappearances of some dancers. I think the first one goes all the way back twelve years ago."

"They've been doing this for twelve years?!" Julia gasped and my heart broke at the betrayal on Bella's face. She'd been against this idea from the very beginning. Shelby and I had talked her into it and now here we were.

"I'm so sorry," I whispered as my voice caught. Shelby looked at me blankly before closing her eyes and leaning her head against the wall again, clearly in shock.

Bella squeezed my thigh but didn't say anything. Having the other girls here should bring me some comfort, but honestly, the fact that this group had managed to take four of us filled me with so much hopelessness. This wasn't their first time. They were used to getting away with this. We'd just be one of the many missing women over the years.

Another sob hiccuped out of me as the full weight of our situation settled in on me. *Finn is looking for you*, a tiny voice in the back of my head said. *He'll find you.* How? He had nothing to go on, did he even know we were gone yet? Who would find us missing?

The door that I had been pushed through opened and we all looked up, attempting to huddle closer together somehow. A man and a woman entered and I almost gasped aloud at the man's shocking resemblance to Finn. This must be his uncle.

"Bring them to me, Pet," he said, motioning to us. The woman obediently moved towards us until she was standing above us. "Up," she said, grabbing Bella who happened to be closest to her. Bella let out a squeak but did as she was told, reaching back to help me to my feet as well. The other two stood next to us and the woman turned back to Finn's uncle, an expectant look on her face.

"Here," he said in the same tone someone would use on a dog, motioning in front of him. She ushered us forward and we moved slowly. I had no intention of being closer to this man than I already was, but I currently had little choice. Despite my friends having their hands unbound, they were no match for the man in front of us. Even if they worked together, it wouldn't take long for the other men to come in. Not to mention he was probably armed. And what of the woman following his orders?

He started a slow walk in front of us, eyes trailing over us like he was appraising a fancy car rather than looking at human beings. At least his eyes didn't hold the same lust that had been present in Griffith's.

"Release her restrains, Pet," he said and I realized he was talking about me when the woman stepped behind me and grabbed my bound hands. After a moment of twisting, I felt my hands fall free and I brought them to my front, rubbing the raw skin. He reached for me and I recoiled when his cold hand touched mine. Undeterred, he inspected my wrists and then gripped my chin, tilting my head to the side to expose the bite mark from Griffith. He tsked before taking a step back and assessing us as a group once again.

"Fine work, this time," he said and I had no idea who he was talking to. "My name is Cillian," he said to us. "You can think of me as your pilot. I will be guiding you to your destination. While you are under my care, I would prefer not to have to sedate you. I'd much rather use my energy on my Pet," he said, grabbing the woman's ass and pulling her to himself. She went willingly and giggled when he pressed a kiss to her neck. She looked back at us with what looked like pride at the attention she was getting from Cillian. Who was she and how was she okay standing by while he was kidnapping and selling woman?

"That being said," he continued. "I will not hesitate to sedate you or use whatever means necessary to keep you obedient. It would be in your best interest to lay low and not cause any trouble. You won't be here long." With that he nodded and turned towards the door, his *Pet* in tow.

"What do you want from us?" Bella asked, stepping forward defiantly.

"My dear, don't take this personally. I have no interest in you specifically. You all, however, are quite profitable and I am a businessman. It is simple math," he replied before closing the door and locking it behind them.

I heard a sob beside me and I reached out without thinking, gripping Julia's hand. She held on for dear life. There was nothing to say. Somehow we had found ourselves in the web of a man whose only concern was money, no matter the cost. We just happened to be the cost, and that idea clearly didn't keep him up at night.

"We'll get out of here," Bella said, the face-off with Cillian clearly having bolstered her courage. "There's four of us, we are smart and competent, we'll figure it out."

How I wanted to believe her, but the voice in my head was telling me that last night was the last taste of freedom we'd ever have.

31

Finn

We drove to Julia's place first as it was the closest one to us. We met several other officers there and I knew more had been dispatched to the remaining ballerinas' residences. Ava was not allowed to come with me, despite her begging me, and Art texted me as we were driving that he had picked her up and to call him as soon as I had a chance. Ava would fill him in on what she could, and there was not much I could add to this currently ongoing investigation. Plus, I didn't need his emotions concerning Vi. I was already at maximum capacity trying to ignore my own emotions.

We arrived at the apartment complex where Julia lived and double-checked our equipment before heading inside. The place was modest and clean, nothing fancy as we walked through the halls. There was already an officer inside her apartment who gave us the rundown as we entered.

"There's not a whole lot to see. The space looks lived in, but there's no signs of a break-in and nothing that I think will be helpful in proving if she was taken or by whom."

I'd figured based on Vi's place that's what we'd find, but

part of me had still clung to the hope that something, somewhere would give us a path forward. Instead, the more we found out the more obvious it was that this group knew exactly what they were doing. This was not their first time, and, unless we did something to stop them, it wouldn't be their last.

I couldn't let myself dwell on that.

Libby did her own sweep of the area while I called Marcus.

"Find anything?" He asked.

"Nothing obvious. Anything from the other two girls' place?"

"Negative. Where are we on the information from last night?"

"Beyond the fact that we know it was a sham? Nowhere. None of the names or aliases check out, the packet of information they gave us is a dead end."

"Okay. I want you guys back to the bar where the meeting took place. Gather any security videos that they might have. We will try facial recognition. In the meantime, we will send out a missing person alert on all four of them. This is an official kidnapping case. You and Libby will run point on it until I decide otherwise. Once you finish up there, I'd like you back at the station to begin."

"Yes, sir," I said hollowly.

"And Sullivan—"

I waited a beat for whatever was coming next.

"You will let me know if you need to step back from this. Your research and involvement will be extremely helpful to catch everyone up to speed, but you will let me know the minute you need to step back." The command in his voice was clear and brokered no argument.

"Yes, sir," I responded again before ending the phone call.

32

Vi

After Cillian's introduction, they seemed content to leave us alone and we huddled together, mostly quiet.

"Where do you think they're going to take us?" Julia asked in a shaky voice. Shelby continued to stare wordlessly at the closed door and I squeezed her hand but, when she gave no indication that she noticed, I began to wonder if they had given her something else to sedate her.

Bella began murmuring to Julia and I tried harder to get Shelby's attention.

"Are you okay?" I asked quietly.

Finally, she turned to look at me with glassy eyes. "No," was all she said.

My heart cracked at the pain in her eyes. I wanted desperately to help but what was I supposed to say?

"Are you hurt? Did they drug you?"

She scoffed, "I wish."

"What do you mean?"

She glanced towards the other two who were still lost in conversation before pulling up her shirt to reveal her stomach. I tried to keep my face neutral but couldn't stop the small gasp at the sight. Her dark skin was broken and scratched in multiple places almost like—

"Did someone bite you?" I whispered.

She dropped her shirt and nodded towards my neck. "I guess some of the guys here have a fetish."

I couldn't stop my shiver at the memory of my own assault."Was it Griffith?"

"He didn't feel the need to introduce himself before raping me," she said with a bitter laugh. "But if he's blond then yeah, it was probably him."

There was nothing else to say so I sat in silence, continuing to hold her hand. After a moment she spoke again.

"I woke up in the car. When it stopped I figured we were here but, well apparently, he wanted to take a detour on the way. I guess I was part of his payout for the abductions," she bit out. For the first time, I noticed the broken nails and bruises covering her normally flawless skin. With how aggressive he'd been with me in those few seconds, I could only imagine what she'd endured with no one to stop him.

"Shelby," my voice cracked.

"Don't," she pulled her hand back. "I don't need your pity."

"I'm not—"

"I'm going to get us out of here," Bella interrupted. She'd clearly begun listening to the conversation and she stood with a determined look on her face. "No one is going to touch us again. We're going to get out of here."

Shelby closed her eyes and Julia asked in a desperate voice, "How? How the hell do you propose to do that?"

"I don't know," Bella said with a shake of her dirty, blonde hair. "But I will. There's got to be something in here."

I watched as she stalked across the room, trying the locked door before spinning around and scouring the room with her eyes. I did my own sweep but, just like the first time I'd looked around, there was nothing here.

"Maybe we could dig up the floorboards," Bella pondered aloud. "Or if we can't find anything, maybe we can hide behind the door and when they come for us next we'll jump them. They can't take all four of us."

No one argued with her but we all knew her plotting was futile. Finally, she came to sit down next to us again. "If they try to move us, the first opportunity we get, everyone run in a different direction. They won't be able to chase us all, chances are one of us will get away and can go get help."

"And go where, exactly?" Julia asked. "From what it looked like when we got here, there's nothing around for miles. They'd totally catch us first."

"I don't know, Julia," Bella finally snapped. "I. Don't. Know. But what I do know is that if we don't manage to find a way to get out of here, we are all going to die or wish we had by the end of this."

"Already there," Shelby mumbled barely loud enough for me to hear.

"She's right," I said, trying to force some fake confidence into my voice. Bella shot me a grateful look so I continued. "When they go to move us, we'll try to escape. It's a straight shot back to the front door and from there maybe we can flag down a car or something. The sun is probably up by now so someone is more likely to see us."

We settled into a heavy silence.

"Do you think anyone has even noticed we're gone yet?" Julia whispered. Long gone was the haughty demeanor and bitchy tone she'd given me at the theater. In its place was a broken girl, just as scared as the rest of us. It was like seeing a completely different person. I turned my thoughts to her question. Ava might or might not be home yet to find me gone. Winnie would notice we never came to class and maybe she'd say something to someone, but Finn had made it clear he wanted to chat about the meeting last night. When he tried to get ahold of me and I didn't answer, I was confident that he'd follow up.

"I usually call my mom on the way into class," Bella said quietly. "She isn't doing too well emotionally, so I always check in with her, even if it's only for a minute or two. I'm sure she'll notice that I didn't call. I don't know if she'll tell anyone about it though."

That sent me into thoughts of my own family. My dad had finally drunk himself to death several years ago, and my mom lived alone on the poorer side of town. I visited her when I could find time between jobs which, admittedly had been less and less recently. Our relationship had also been strained ever since my dad passed and I had made it obvious that his death was a relief to me. Even still, I tried to stay in contact with her. When was the last time I'd talked to her? Had I made sure to tell her I loved her?

Emotion clogged my throat at all the things I wished I had shared with people, all the things I wished I'd been brave enough to do. From the sniffling coming from around me, I knew I wasn't the only one thinking about such things.

Footsteps outside our door snapped our attention back in that direction and we all stumbled to our feet.

"Remember, the first chance we get, we run. No playing the hero," Bella murmured. Sweat coated my hands and I wiped them on my shirt, taking deep breaths in preparation for what was about to come. The door opened and Griffith stepped through with a smarmy smile on his face.

"Breakfast time, don't want the cattle to get too thin," he said with a laugh as if it was some great joke. Both of his hands were full with several plates and I caught Bella's determined gaze. His hands were occupied and there was only one of them. We needed to try to make a break for it.

There was no telling where anyone else was, and the house had been pretty quiet, so there was a chance Griffith was the only one here with us at the moment.

He bent down to place the plates on the ground and with the most beautiful sauté I'd ever seen, Bella was in front of him and her knee came up to connect with his face right before I heard a crunch and he began to scream.

"Run!" Bella screeched. The word was an accelerant to the flames beneath our feet and it became a scramble for the still open door. I fled through the door behind Shelby, hearing steps behind me. I heard a crash and a very feminine scream of pain. Despite my self preservation, I chanced a glance behind me to see Julia behind and no sign of Bella. She hadn't made it out the door. Had she even been planning on running with us?

I cleared the stairs before hearing a loud gunshot. Julia screamed behind me and I turned to see Griffith racing down after us. Panic flooded my veins and I spun back towards the front door just in time to see it swing open and Cillian standing on the other side, holding a gun of his own.

"What. The. Fuck."

Griffith stopped behind us, panting. "I was delivering food to the bitches when that cunt fucking broke my nose," he said, spitting blood.

"And why, exactly, were you close enough to them to be hit? I told you to leave the food inside the door. You weren't by any chance trying to take advantage of my hospitality, were you?" Cillian questioned, gaze sliding over Shelby's bruised body.

"Of course not," the other man grumbled.

"And where is the blonde one?"

"She's the one who attacked me. I had to shoot her, she was trying to scratch my eyes out."

Terror clawed at me at his admission.

"Is she alive?" I croaked, fearing the answer.

"If so, she won't be for long," Griffith grunted.

Cillian cursed. "I hope you know that this mistake is costing you your payout for this run."

Griffith opened his mouth to argue but Cillian held up his hand. "You cost me thousands at least," he gritted out. "Be lucky I don't take payment with your own life."

"Bella," Shelby squeaked and I turned towards the stairs once more, expecting her to emerge at any moment.

"Get the girls in the van. Your fucking gunshot could be heard for miles. We're moving them now."

"No! Bella!" Shelby screamed, starting to run back for the stairs. Griffith grabbed her roughly and pointed the gun at her temple. "Get. In. The. Van."

Julia and I froze at the sight and Cillian motioned towards the front door. "Behave or I *will* sedate you," he said to us before ushering us out the door to the awaiting van.

33

Finn

I was running out of time. Every minute that ticked by, I could feel the chance of us getting the girls back dwindling. We were working every angle we could, and yet it wasn't enough. We'd gotten the security feed from the restaurant back, but so far had no matches. Nothing had been left at the scenes to point us in a direction, and, despite the fact that their pictures were plastered everywhere, there had been no sightings. They'd disappeared.

I pushed up from the conference table where I was working alongside the rest of the team and caught Libby's eye, nodding towards the hallway. She gave me a thumbs up and I ducked out, pulling my phone as I went.

I called Art as soon as I was alone.

"What have you found?" He asked in greeting.

"Nothing, and I'm going to lose it."

There was a beat of silence and then, "What can I do?"

"I need Toni's contact information."

"Finn—"

"I need her, Art."

"And you know I have absolutely no problem sharing that with you, but I need to be sure you understand that Toni works outside the law. I can tell her you want to chat, but she may not be willing to talk to you out of self-preservation. You might not like her methods."

"I. Don't. Care."

"I'm just trying to be straight with you, man. I don't want you to get into a situation that you're uncomfortable with."

"I have to find her, Art. Not only because I like her, which I do, but—" I took a deep breath. "It's my fault she was taken."

"No, it's not."

"It absolutely is. She wanted nothing to do with this. I never should have involved her. She only said yes because I asked her to and she was trying to be a good friend."

He didn't respond. What was he supposed to say? We both knew that I was right.

"Okay, I texted her. If she's willing to talk to you she'll reach out. In the meantime, you know anything I have is yours. Just say the word."

"I know, brother." And that's what he was. Maybe not by blood, but Art was the closest thing to family I had and even if he couldn't help find her, I appreciated his support so much. "I'll let you know. How's Ava?"

"Losing her mind."

I sighed as I pictured how harrowed she'd looked when I'd seen her last.

"I vote when we get Vi back, I buy a mansion to lock them in and never let them leave." He said, no humor in his voice.

I laughed because of course his first reaction would be to lock them away. But my throat tightened at his words. *When we get her back. Not if.* When. I would hold onto that.

~ ~ ~
* * *

We were going over the security videos for the umpteenth time when my phone buzzed from beside my computer. I flipped it over and paused when I saw a text from an unknown number.

Unknown: Got A's text. Willing to chat.

I immediately typed back. *Me: Nice to talk to you too. Can I call you?*

Unknown: I'd prefer to meet in person. I'll text you an address. How soon can you meet? A said it was time-sensitive.

Me: Depends on the location but I can leave now.

A few moments passed before another text came through with an address not far from me. *Unknown: Got a reservation for two people.*

Me: Understood, thanks. Don't bring anyone else.

I pushed up from the table and made my way to Libby's side. "Find anything?" She was looking over the fake information the girls had been given again in hopes of finding something new. We also were pursuing leads trying to find anyone who'd been a suspect in Rosie's case, but so far we couldn't find anything, even with the information my dad had provided on Cillian.

"Nothing," she said with a discouraged sigh.

"I'm going to go grab a cup of quality coffee and take a breather. I'll obviously have my phone on me, let me know the moment anyone finds something."

"Okay. I'm glad you're taking a break, get your heard right and I'll let you know."

I nodded and walked out, feeling guilt gnaw at me for what I wasn't telling her. If Toni found them or even anything that could lead to them, I would absolutely share it with her. I wasn't trying to be some hero. I just had no issues using whatever resources to give us a chance, even if they were illegal. I'd save that moral dilemma for a later date.

I pulled up to the family-run diner and exited, walking in

to greet the hostess.

"Hey Sugaa, what can I get for ya?"

"Hey, I'm meeting someone, I think she got a reservation for Toni?"

"Ahh, folla me," she said heading towards an empty corner table. I sat down, ordered a Coke, and turned to watch the door as I waited. A few minutes passed, long enough for me to wonder if Toni had bailed, when the doors opened and in rolled a petite woman in a wheelchair, her black hair styled in a bob. I was pretty sure the last time I'd seen her her hair had been a different color, but otherwise, she looked much the same.

She rolled over to the table and took the vacated spot across from me where our server had removed the chair.

"Finn, it's been a long time."

"Since graduation, right?" I asked with a smile. "You look good."

She ignored my comment but smiled at our server when she brought me my Coke. "Hey Linda,"

"Hey, Darlin. Anything else I can get you, sir?" She said, turning towards me.

"Are you going to get anything?" I asked Toni and she laughed.

"Nope." She lifted her shirt enough for me to see the feeding tube in her stomach. God, I wanted the floor to swallow me whole. *Eejit.*

"Sorry-"

"It's fine," she said cutting me off. "I'm good, but do you want anything else?"

"Nope, I'll stick with my coke."

With that, Linda sauntered off and I turned back towards Toni. "Well, I'm clearly as much of an idiot as I was in high school."

She laughed and this time it actually held humor. "No

wonder you need my help."

"Do you think you can help me?"

She nodded slowly. "It really depends on how good they are at covering their tracks but yeah, I feel pretty confident that I can help track them down."

Hope bloomed in my chest for the first day since this whole thing had started.

"What do you need from me?" I asked, desperation clinging to every word.

Toni reached into a bag attached to her wheelchair and pulled out a laptop. "Tell me everything you know."

Twenty minutes later, I'd recounted everything I could think of, answering every question she asked as best as I could.

"There's no magic 'find them' button, but, based on what you've given me so far, I do think I can get somewhere. Send me whatever evidence you can manage and I'll do my own research and get back to you as soon as I find something."

"Thank you, Toni," I said and she waved me off but I stopped her, grabbing her hand. "I mean it. I know you and Art have kept in contact and you helped save Ava's life. And now this. Seriously, you're incredible, and I appreciate it more than I can express."

She finally gave my hand a gentle squeeze. "There's too many horrible people in this world getting away with horrible things. If I can do even a little to help stop them, I'm happy."

"You are doing so much and are seriously a real-life superhero."

She scoffed and pulled her hand free. "Okay, Finnian, leave me alone to work."

"Whatever you say, Antoinette."

She glared at me and I laughed, placing a ten on the table before heading back to the station.

34

Vi

We were shoved into the back of an empty van before the vehicle took off. I immediately tried the handle, but the door was locked and the internal locking mechanism had clearly been broken and was unusable from the inside. I sat back down against the wall and looked towards the other two. Two. There were only two other girls now. Bella was gone.

"They killed her," Shelby whispered brokenly.

"We don't know that," I replied. "He—he said she was still alive."

"And what?" She snapped back. "They're going to take her to the hospital to let them patch up her up?" She scoffed. "They're going to let her bleed out on the floor. Maybe—maybe even take advantage of her before she's gone."

Julia sobbed and I shook my head. "Stop it. Stop, we can't think like that."

"We're doomed, Victoria," Shelby rasped. "I've been raped, Bella's dead, it's just a matter of time until that happens to one of you," she said motioning to Julia and me. I knew she wasn't trying to be hurtful. She was broken. And scared. And she was right. How I wanted to pretend this would all be okay, but it wouldn't. Bella had been the bravest of us all, she'd been confident we could work together, and she'd sacrificed herself so that we could get free.

A sob broke from my own mouth and I leaned my head against the wall and let my despair overtake me. We'd failed. Bella was dead, and it was only a matter of time until we joined her.

~ ~ ~

I woke to the van jerking to a stop. I hadn't even realized I had passed out. I never would have thought that was possible in this current state, but my exhaustion must have caught up to me. Shelby was staring blankly at the wall and Julia was snoring softly beside her. The back door opened and I scrambled to move backward, further away from our captor. The man who'd taken me jumped into the truck, closing the door behind himself.

At least it wasn't Griffith. Maybe we were safe from assault for the moment. He approached me first and grabbed my wrist. I thought about struggling, but what was the use? He flipped my hand over and only then did I notice the needle in his other hand. Wordlessly, he slammed it into my arm and I jerked and tried to pull free from his iron grip but then my mind went utterly blank.

The next time I awoke it was with a pounding headache. It took several tries before I was able to peel my eyelids open and, once I cleared as much of the blur from my vision as I could, I found myself lying on a thin mattress on a plain metal cot. My whole body ached and I prayed it was only from whatever they had drugged me with and not due to anyone's hands on me while I was out.

I slowly turned to look around me and found myself in a

small white room with three more identical cots beside me, spaced every few feet. Two of them were occupied by Shelby and Julia's unconscious bodies. A small amount of relief filled me at the sight of them. They might not provide any sort of protection in this horrible place, but at least I wasn't completely alone. Guilt replaced the relief as I realized that I should not be grateful that any other person was subjected to this.

A door to my right opened and Cillian's woman stepped through the door. I tried to push myself to my feet but my head swam at the action and I sat back down, leaning my weight against the wall.

"Oh good, you're awake," she said, closing the door behind her. She was alone.

"Help us," I croaked out.

She cocked her head and seemed to contemplate me. "Why would I do that?"

"They took us, they kidnapped us." I cleared my throat and tried to get through to her. "They killed our friend, we need to get out of here."

She continued to stare at me in a way that made my skin crawl. "Your friend attacked one of the guys. And anyway," she continued when I tried to interrupt. "My master wouldn't be happy with me if I helped you guys leave." She shook her head firmly. "He would be very, very mad."

"We can help you. I have friends in the police, we will keep you safe and protect you from Cillian."

"Protect me?" She asked incredulously. "I don't need protection from Master. I am his Pet and I will never leave."

This was going absolutely nowhere. I had to make her understand.

"What's your name?" I tried again. Wasn't there something about helping victims remember who they were, if they could at least recall their name? I swear I'd seen that in some TV show. She stared at me for so long that I didn't think she would answer but finally, she stepped forward.

"My name is Rosie. Now wake up your friends so that we can start your classes."

35

Finn

"I think I found them."

My heart leaped at the words. "You're sure?"

"No. If I was sure I would have said that. But based on what I've found, I'm pretty positive that this location is at least one that is used by that group. I'm sending you the information now."

My mind spun as Toni hung up. It had only been a couple of hours since I'd given her the information. She truly was incredible at her job. Now I needed to figure out how to pass the information on to the team without bringing Toni into it.

I didn't want to lie, I didn't want to keep them in the dark, but I couldn't risk sharing Toni's identity in case they decided to look into exactly how she'd gotten this information.

"Cap," I said as I entered his office. He looked up and waved me over.

"What's the update?"

"I got an anonymous tip for a possible sighting of the girls."

His eyebrows rose and I worried he was going to push for

more. "Where at?"

"It looks like it's an old farm outside the city. I haven't looked into it to see who owns it or anything yet, I came straight in here."

"Take some guys, go check it out. I'll have some people work on looking into it from here and any warrants if we need them."

I left and found Libby at the conference room table. "I got a tip about a possible sighting. Cap gave us the green light to go check it out with a team."

"Let's go."

We took my car and the rest of the group followed in a van. The ride was silent as I drove, lost in my thoughts and Libby remained glued to her phone in the passenger seat. By the time we arrived, we had the name of the person who owned the property which, unsurprisingly, was a dead end.

We parked on the dirt driveway and approached the house cautiously. There was a detached garage and no visible vehicles.

"Check out the garage, we'll try the house," I said, motioning to the group. Several officers headed that way and Libby followed me as I approached the front door. I knocked loudly. "Police."

No response. I knocked again and when there was still nothing I walked to the side to peer in the window. The room I could see appeared to be empty and dirty, the only thing visible being a set of stairs.

"We found something."

I turned at the voice. "What is it?"

The male officer held out a gloved hand. "Looks to be some kind of diamond ring. It was in the dirt by the garage door. Could possibly be from one of the women, but we'll have to bring it back and ask their families."

I grunted in response. I was sure Toni was right and if this was a place they'd taken the girls, I was not simply going to leave. I turned back to the window and strained for anything else I could possibly see.

"We can take it back to the station and see if—"

"Stop." I held up my hand to cut off the speaker as I looked again. Was that— "Blood. There's a fucking streak of blood down the stairs," I said, turning and almost running Libby over in my race for the door. I pulled my gun and pounded once more on the door.

"Police, open up," I yelled. I gave them a few seconds and when no one came to the door I kicked it open.

It took a couple of hits but it finally broke in on itself and I entered, gun drawn.

I heard several people following me in and I knew they'd cover me as I approached the stairs. "Fuck."

I'd been right. There was a streak of dark brown coming down the steps.

"Right behind you," Libby said and I took the stairs two at a time, careful to avoid stepping in the substance. There were several doors on the landing and I took the left, following the blood trail. I made eye contact with Libby briefly before kicking in the door at the end of the hall.

It opened with a crash and I half expected to hear a scream or a gunshot, but there was nothing except the sounds of my boots and the door hitting the wall.

We cleared the room and I took in the large splatter of blood in the middle of the room where the trail ended. My gut sank as my pulse pounded in my ears, panic threatening to pull me under. I stopped and took two deep breaths before crouching next to the scene.

"It looks fresh," Libby murmured next to me.

"It's way too much. Whoever it's from didn't survive." I responded.

A camera snapped as one of the officers took pictures and

another dropped down to gather some of the liquid for evidence.

"It appears to be only one body that was dragged out of here. We need to figure out who it was and where the others are."

I closed my eyes again as I tried to wrestle my skyrocketing anxiety back under control. Images flashed behind my eyelids. Vi, lying bloodied and broken, gunshots tearing through her body. A masked man dragging her out of the room and down the steps to bury her in an unmarked grave.

"Sullivan!"

I snapped my eyes open to see Libby staring at me.

"You're done."

I blinked at her and she grabbed my shoulder, pulling me up and away from the bloody scene.

"I'm making the call. You're done here. You can go over the information back at the station, but right now, you're more of a liability than you are a help in this investigation. I need you to take care of yourself, and I need to not have to worry about you passing out. Let's go."

I wanted to argue. I wanted so badly to push her off and tell her she was being ridiculous. This wasn't my first time seeing a bloody crime scene. It wasn't even my dozenth time. I wasn't squeamish, I knew how to do my job. But I couldn't argue. I could feel my emotions slowly crumbling in on myself. This was personal.

I'd always been able to distance myself, disconnecting what was happening from my emotions. But this time I couldn't, I was feeling everything, and I knew the girls needed someone better. Vi needed more.

So I let Libby lead me out to my car and I took a seat in the passenger seat while she chatted with the other officers on the scene. I rested my head against the headrest and sent a prayer to anyone who'd listen. I wasn't devout, but I'd seen enough in my life to believe that there was some higher power at work. And now I prayed with everything in me that they were watching out for Vi. She couldn't be dead. She couldn't be.

36

Vi

Rosie. Like *the* Rosie?

"Sanchez?"

She looked startled before her face went blank once more and she motioned to the girls lying on the cots. "Up. Now."

I slid from my bed, moving gingerly in an attempt to keep the dizziness at bay, and approached the other cots. I gently shook Shelby's shoulder, "Wake up," before moving to Julia. They both stirred and came to, breaking through whatever sedative we'd been given this time.

Rosie tapped her foot impatiently as if it was our fault that we'd been drugged. Could this really be the same person that Finn was searching for? Hadn't she been a normal person with a son before she was taken?

"Why are you helping them?" I asked. Getting her to realize how fucked up this was and help us was our best chance at getting out of here alive. She didn't answer and I tried again. "What is your child's name? The one who you had before they kidnapped you."

She finally met my gaze and the coldness I saw there both

saddened and scared me. "I don't know what you are talking about. I have no children. I have a Master and he wishes me to train you. We don't have much time so we must begin."

"Train us?" Julia asked from behind me. "What do you mean train us?"

"Your looks will get you far," she said matter of factly. "But Master prides himself in long-term business. You may be beautiful, yes, but you also must act appropriately. If you are not trained you will end up as an embarrassment to him." She shuddered as if the idea was abhorrent. "Thus we practice."

"What are we practicing?" I asked. "Ballet?"

She began to laugh and embarrassment warmed my face. We were all ballerinas so part of me was hoping that somehow this was some fucked up way for people to get private ballet dances. Her face told me exactly what she thought of that idea.

She abruptly stopped laughing and stepped towards me, gripping my chin between her long fingers. "You will be practicing everything that it takes to be a good whore." I flinched at her harsh words and she continued.

"You will learn to be respectful and obey. The men who buy you do not want some uneducated bitch who doesn't know the first thing about serving. You are to be whatever they wish you to be. You will bow when they say bow, kneel until they give you permission to stand, and crawl the minute they point to the floor.

"You will fulfill every sexual fantasy they can think of and only exist with their permission. You will be seen and not heard, you will be the perfect submissive servant to your master and nothing less."

As she spoke, images flashed through my mind and I couldn't help but glance towards the others. Julia had tears silently sliding down her cheeks and Shelby clenched her hands at her side.

"And how do you expect us to *practice*?" she spit out.

Rosie turned in her direction and gave her a pitiful once over. "The guys have been gracious enough to help."

With that the door opened and three men walked in. I recognized Griffith right away from his greasy hair and black eyes. Bella had really done a number on him. *Bella*. My heart squeezed and Rosie nodded towards us.

"Gentleman, take your pick, and let's begin."

37

Finn

"I'm going to drop you off at your place," Libby said, throwing me a concerned look from her side of the vehicle. I was too numb to argue, instead, I silently nodded.

"My car—" I started but she cut me off.

"I'll have someone drop it off tonight. You need to take a break, eat something, and get out of the station for a while. Take a shower, call your mom, do something."

I laughed at her comment about my mom but she wasn't that far off. I needed a break. One of the first things we learned in school was that if we couldn't take care of ourselves, we couldn't help anyone else. And despite the fact that it was the last thing I wanted right now, I knew I was currently no help to Vi or anyone else.

The rest of the drive was quiet and she pulled into my driveway where I stared out the front windshield for a moment.

"We're doing everything we can," she said quietly. I nodded because I knew she was right. I was glad that she didn't make any empty promises about how everything would be okay or how we'd find them before it was too late, because we both knew she couldn't promise that.

"I'll let you know the minute we have an update. And I'll fill Cap in about everything. Please call someone."

I nodded again before heading inside. I listened to the car reverse out of the driveway as I wandered into the kitchen. I poured myself a glass of water and stared at the inside of my refrigerator. I felt numb. I didn't know who that blood belonged to, there was a chance it wasn't Vi. But there was a chance that it was. And even if it wasn't her, someone had died while waiting for us to come help them. Maybe even because of my involvement in the case.

I wasn't a narcissist, I knew the world didn't revolve around me. And this group had been targeting the dancers before I began investigating them. But had my request to have them meet to record them sped things up? I'd never know if this would have happened without my pushing and the thought was killing me.

I grabbed a cheese stick from the fridge and walked into the living room, collapsing onto the couch. Jake was working right now and I didn't know whether to be glad or not. It might be nice to have someone else here, but I also didn't feel like I had the emotional energy to talk to anyone.

Libby had suggested I call my mom. Not happening. But maybe I should call Art. We'd already been in contact after the situation with Ava at her house, and I knew he'd be over in a second if I needed him. But what could I even say at this point?

I was just about to call him anyway, when I heard an odd sound from the back of the house. I stopped and tried to pick out what it was. We had a backdoor that we didn't use very often, but Jake swore would be perfect for a dog as if either of us had the time or energy to give to a dog right now.

There it was again. Was someone trying to open the door?

I grunted as I got up from the couch and walked towards the back of the house. I grabbed my gun from the counter as I went. It was broad daylight, there was no way someone was trying to break in at the moment, right? That would be just my luck.

I stopped at the back door, still holding my gun ready. Whoever was out there had picked the wrong day to fuck with me.

I waited a beat and then the door swung open, revealing Greg fucking Thomas holding a set that he'd just used to pick my lock.

I held up my gun and stared him down from where he stood, looking back at me in shock. "Are you fucking serious right now?" I asked him as his face began to turn a deep red. I honestly didn't even know what to say. Part of me was tempted to just close the door in his face, the other to call into the station and let them know I'd found him breaking into my house.

"What do you think you're doing here?" I asked as he continued to stare at me silently, not taking his eyes off my gun.

"Being a royal idiot," I heard from behind me at the same time as I felt the press of cold steel into the back of my head.

Fucking shit.

"Drop your gun and step back, slowly," came the voice again, and recognition hit me. Sam fucking Jenkins.

I did as he said, letting my arm fall to the side before dropping my gun and taking a step backward. I was tempted to yell in an attempt to alert the neighbors, but if these two were desperate enough to break into my house in broad daylight, I didn't put it past them to not shoot me before fleeing the scene.

"I don't have anything on you, if that's what you think," I said, my back still to Sam as Greg closed the door in front of me.

He laughed at my back. "It doesn't matter, it's already done. You've already ruined us," he said.

"So what do you want?"

"Revenge? Retribution? Take your pick. Hands, behind your back. Now."

My mind raced as I tried to think of a way out of this situation, but nothing came to mind. It was two against one. Sam was armed, Greg probably was too. I might be a great boxer, but I wasn't an idiot. I was at a severe disadvantage.

Slowly I moved my hands behind my back and Sam barked at Greg to come over to him. I stood, staring at my wall as I felt the tug and bite of cuffs being applied. My mind chose that moment to inappropriately think back to Vi and me using her pink fluffy handcuffs and I didn't know whether to laugh or cry at the thought.

I must have laughed because I felt a jerk against my bound wrists as Sam snarled, "I would love to know exactly what about this predicament is so funny to you."

I was either in shock or completely losing my mind because this time I did chuckle as I responded. "Just thinking about how these cuffs are a lot more uncomfortable than the ones my girl and I were playing around with."

I felt something hit the back of my knees and I grunted as my legs buckled and I hit the floor.

"Not in the mood for jokes, got it," I grunted.

"Keep him here while I go check out the space," Sam said before I heard his steps move away from us.

"Was our time at the bar that bad you had to break into my house?" I asked Greg who was standing behind me still. He grunted and came around to face me.

"I thought you were just being friendly, but then Sam told me what you did."

"What did I do?"

"Don't play dumb," he spat. "He explained how you traced our call and went to the captain squealing like a little bitch."

"Well maybe if you didn't want to get in trouble you shouldn't be helping out a fucking murderer?" I asked sarcastically. When he didn't respond I pressed on. "Why are you doing this, Greg? You gave up your job, your integrity, everything for what? A little money?"

"You wouldn't understand," he grunted again.

"No, I absolutely don't. You don't need to be caught up in all of this."

"Shut up, just shut up," he said turning away. I was about to continue when I heard Sam reappear. I turned to watch him approach.

"There's a basement over here. Bring him with."

"I can walk just fine," I said but they ignored me and I was yanked by my arm in the direction of our basement. I had no leverage here, but I knew if I let them take me into the basement nothing good would come out of it. The only chance that I could think of was convincing Greg that this was a bad idea and letting me go.

I didn't know his exact involvement in this, but I was pretty sure he wasn't as deep in it as Sam was. I didn't believe he was a cold killer.

I stumbled along as they steered me towards the stairs and again I debated whether I should scream and try to alert someone in the neighborhood. There was no way someone would get here in time to stop them from shooting me, but maybe they'd be able to catch them before they fled the scene. Was getting them arrested worth dying for? Absolutely not.

They were already being investigated, as far as I knew there was currently a warrant out for Sam. That clearly wasn't stopping him. He really had nothing to lose.

We made it down the steps and Sam led the way into the

middle of the living room to where he'd placed Jake's gaming chair.

"Ooh, are we gonna have a competition to see who's better at Call of Duty?" I asked. Sam responded by shoving me into the chair.

"Not one for small talk, huh? I get it, we never really hung out before so there's not a lot of common ground. Not that we have a lot in common, I spend my days trying to catch people who are breaking the law, you spend them in bed with psycho business owners. Well technically he wasn't a business owner, what was his position again? Chief management officer I think?"

Right as I finished my sentence Sam backhanded me, snapping my head to the side and sending shooting pain through my jaw. I grunted at the impact and felt tears gather at the pain.

"That was fucking mean," I said, opening and closing my throbbing jaw.

"Shut. Up." He ground out, waving his gun in my face. For once I did so, instead looking towards Greg who was staring wide-eyed at Sam. Maybe he was finally realizing what he was doing here.

"Little late to grow a conscious," I couldn't help myself from blurting out.

He looked at me and then back to Sam. "What now?"

Sam glared at him. "Don't chicken out on me now."

"I'm not, I just— I thought we were here to scare him," he said motioning to me.

"Scare him?" Sam laughed humorlessly. "Is that gonna reverse the damage he's done?"

"Well no but—"

"Finn?" A voice called from upstairs and panic instantly flooded me. No. This couldn't be happening.

"Ava, run!" I screamed as loud as I could a second before

Sam's fist collided with my stomach, knocking the air out of my lungs. I attempted to curl in on myself, fighting to get oxygen back into my body. I felt something wrap around my face from behind and Sam snarled as he tightened the gag. "Not another word."

He stepped back into my line of vision. "Go, take care of her," he commanded Greg.

"What?" The other man said, looking between us.

"Go, fucking kill whoever is upstairs." He snarled.

"I didn't sign up for this," Greg said, taking a step backward.

"I don't give a shit. If you don't go take care of whoever is upstairs, you're going to end up with a bullet in your chest when they call someone."

Greg gave me one last look before heading upstairs.

I thrashed in my chair, trying to fight the bindings. I couldn't be the reason Ava got killed. No, no I couldn't. I tried to scream against my gag but nothing came out. Maybe she'd heard me, maybe she'd already gotten out of here.

But as I squirmed in my chair I knew that I hadn't heard the front door open and she was still somewhere in this house while Greg stalked towards her with a loaded gun.

38

Vi

Griffith leered at us and then beelined straight towards me without a second look towards Shelby. Apparently, his interest had waned when he got what he wanted. I felt frustrated tears sting the back of my eyes. *Why us?* It was a shitty thing to think since no one deserved this, but I'd never imagined that this could happen to me. My life was normal and boring, how had it turned into this?

I felt his rough grip on my arm and I attempted to pull away, but it was useless, his grip was like iron.

"Let me go," I demanded, despite knowing how futile it would be.

He *tsked* and backhanded me across the face, sending a burning pain ricocheting through my face. I didn't even have time to blink the tears from my eyes before he grabbed a fistful of my hair and yanked my head backward.

"I know Rose is teaching you better than that," he snarled, his foul breath hitting me straight in the face as he leaned over me. "You are nothing. You have no say here, you obey like the little whore that you are, and when we are done with you, you say thank you, sir."

Tears streamed down my face from the pain searing through my scalp at his grip but I refused to break his stare as he spat in my face.

"Griffith, the merchandise," Rosie said calmly from her spot on the other side of the room. "Cillian does not want it broken."

"What the fuck is makeup for then?" He snarled again but loosened his grip on my hair.

"Griffith is right," she said in response. "The majority of the buyers who will be here tomorrow will not tolerate disrespect."

Her words droned on as one word began to blare in my head. Tomorrow. *Tomorrow?!*

It took everything in me not to sob and fall to the floor. Even when we'd been moved, I'd held onto the briefest hope that Finn was out there searching for us. But we were going to be sold tomorrow. He had less than a day to find us. How had they organized this so quickly? What was Finn doing right now? And how were we going to survive the next twenty-four hours?

Griffith spun me around and yanked me against him and I could feel his erection press into my ass. I felt bile creep into the back of my throat, but the fight had left me. There was nothing I could do. I was here to be used and abused and sold to the highest bidder. Rosie had been taken from her old life and turned into this shell of a woman who kissed the feet of her abusers. Is that what was going to happen to me? How long would it take until I ended up like her? Could I find a way to kill myself before that happened?

I felt Griffith's hot breath against my ear as he murmured, "So she *can* learn? Don't worry, when I'm done with you, there will be nothing left of that fighting spirit. I will pass you off to your next owner as a used and empty body to live out

the rest of your miserable life."
And as he spoke, I believed every word.

39

Finn

All I could do was sit and pull at my restraints as I listened to Greg's footsteps head up the stairs. There was no sound of scrambling or slamming doors. She had to have heard me, right? I knew sound traveled from how many times I'd been forced to listen to Jake play video games while I was upstairs. Was she hiding? Was she calling the police?

I listened as Greg's footsteps stopped at the top of the stairs before he began to move towards the kitchen. At any moment I expected to hear a gunshot, a scream, a body hitting the floor. But I heard nothing except his slow, measured steps. Had I been wrong? Had she gotten out of the house after all? I clung to that thought, desperate, praying it was true.

After what seemed like an eternity, I heard a grunt and thud. My heart threatened to pound out of my chest as I imagined all of the scenarios that could be playing out upstairs. Sam was becoming increasingly agitated as he paced in front of me, cursing under his breath. "What the hell is taking him so long?"

I mumbled under my gag and he held the gun up towards me again. "Not another fucking word."

I obeyed and kept my inner monologue to myself. Finally, the basement door opened and I sucked in a breath as well as I could behind my gag, waiting to see Greg emerge. Instead, I heard something tumble down the steps. I couldn't see what the object was from my vantage point and apparently, neither could Sam, because, with another glance towards me, he walked towards the bottom of the stairs and cursed as he picked up— a shoe? A man's shoe. Specifically— Greg's?

That fucking badass. She'd done it. I didn't know how, but it had to have been Ava. Greg would have already been back down here with her. Ava had somehow managed to incapacitate him and removed his shoe to send a message to Sam. What an idiotic, brave, human being.

"I should just fucking kill you right now," Sam snarled but I knew by his words that he wasn't going to. He was way too concerned with what was happening upstairs right now. Apparently, self-preservation did win out in his little game for revenge.

He took the stairs two at a time and dread filled me as I watched him disappear from view. I didn't know what Ava had done to Greg, but I couldn't believe that she'd be able to fight off two of them. As much as I had faith in her and Art's insistence that she begin learning to defend herself, I one hundred percent believed that it had been complete luck that she'd stopped Greg. Her luck could only run for so much longer.

Sam slammed the door as he went and I knew he didn't even consider her a threat enough to need the element of surprise. I pulled frantically at my bonds which only resulted in my chair tipping forward and me landing on the floor with a thud. My jaw took the brunt of the fall and I felt dizzy as waves of pain washed through me. I cried out behind my gag and tried to blink against the pain. I was utterly stuck, no help to Ava, and Sam was going to kill her.

A door slammed somewhere upstairs, presumably Sam again as he tried to track her down. Maybe she'd hid somewhere he wouldn't find her. My mind went to all the potential hiding spots in our house and my stomach sank further when I couldn't come up with many places she could remain hidden. Fuck houses with zero storage.

I heard a gunshot and reflexively jerked at the noise, crying out again as I thrashed on the floor. Dear god please, she couldn't be dead. Not when she'd come here to try to save me. I could not be responsible for her death. Art would never forgive me. I would never forgive myself.

The basement door opened and I craned my neck to watch Sam walk down the steps in triumph. Instead, Ava raced down the stairs, stopping at my head and placing her hand gently on my shoulder.

"Oh my god, Finn." She looked around the room and then moved behind me to tug at the back of my gag. Had she really done it? She'd shot him? How? With what?

I heard more footsteps approaching the basements just as I felt the gag fall free.

"Ava, run!" I begged but she placed her hand back on my shoulder again.

"Shhh, it's Art," she soothed just as he appeared in my vision on the steps. He stomped his way down the steps, his face set in grim determination and fierce anger. He reached my side and pulled out a key, reaching behind and unlocking my cuffs, freeing me from the chair. I fell forward with a grunt and Ava shot a menacing look at her boyfriend.

"You couldn't be a little more careful?"

Remorse crossed his face and he muttered, "Sorry."

Miracles truly did exist, Ava had managed to whip my best friend. I pushed myself to my butt and rubbed my aching jaw. "How did you guys find me?"

Art was the one to answer. "Libby called me, I'm your emergency contact, she said she was worried about you and thought I should check-in. Ava was closer and—"

"I came in to see how you were doing and heard you scream from downstairs. I knew something was wrong so I texted Art and heard that creep coming upstairs."

"And you didn't think maybe you should run when you heard me yell?"

She shrugged. "And let them kill you?"

"If they had gotten ahold of you—"

"I'm fine. I'm offended you doubted me," she said but her pale features betrayed her confident demeanor.

"How on earth did you stop him?"

"Art and I have been spending one day a week taking self-defense lessons and practicing shooting. I'm a certified badass now," she said with a smirk. "And I know this place better than him and was able to use the element of surprise."

"What on earth were they doing here anyway? Who are they?" Art asked.

"Greg and Sam. Two of the cops that were involved in helping Cain with his murder spree."

Both their faces darkened at his name but I continued. "They rightfully blamed me for them being investigated and fired."

"So they decided to come kill you?" Ava asked in disbelief. Now it was my turn to shrug.

"I guess they didn't have much to lose. They were looking at a long prison sentence for possible conspiracy to commit murder. What's one more step?"

Ava pulled me into a hug and I wrapped my own arms around her.

"I'm glad you're okay," she murmured.

"Thanks to you," I said back, giving her a gentle squeeze.

When she let me go Art pulled me into a hug too, tightening his grip but not saying anything. I understood. Words weren't needed at this point.

When we separated I asked, "Are they—"

"Alive, but currently unconscious bleeding out on your kitchen floor? Yep."Art replied. Just then I heard the front door slam and a familiar voice yell, "Police!"

I pulled myself to my feet gingerly. "Down here, Libby."

I listened to footsteps clomping upstairs before Libby appeared in the doorway, gun drawn. She took in the sight below her before slowly making her way down the steps.

"Welcome to the party, a little late," I said with a laugh.

"What the fuck, Sullivan?" She asked as several other officers joined us.

"Apparently they decided to try to get some revenge on me after I figured out their involvement in the Laurie case. Thanks for calling Art, you saved my life."

She just continued to stare at me and I pointed to a camera in the corner of the basement. "You should be able to get whatever recording you need from that."

"When I told you to do something, this wasn't exactly what I had in mind."

I laughed as she came over and clapped me on the shoulder. "I think you're gonna have a shiner."

"They say girls love black eyes," I said smirking. I immediately sobered when my mind went to one girl in particular. In all this excitement, I'd forgotten about Vi for a moment. Now, the panic and dread were back in full force.

Libby must have seen the emotions on my face but she just nodded and gave me a small smile. "That they do."

40

Our *lesson* consisted of the men having free reign to assault us while Rosie watched. They claimed it was to teach us how to be submissive, but I guessed a large part was also to keep the men happy and loyal. What better way than to offer the bodies of non-consenting women to them on a silver platter?

Afterwards, we were once again left alone in our room with our cots. My tears had all dried up and every single part of my body ached from the abuse it had just endured at the hands of Griffith. I knew the experience had been more about breaking us than it was about training us to be good little whores. And it had worked. I felt numb, dirty, and hopeless. In the midst of my pain, I wondered if it had been a blessing for Bella to have died before she was subjected to any of this.

I must have said her name aloud because the other two turned towards me. Shelby wiped at her eyes and Julia turned back towards the wall before whispering, "I was always so jealous of her."

I didn't know what to say so I stayed quiet.

"She had such natural talent. And more than that, she

somehow made friends with everyone," she continued.

My thoughts drifted back to how Bella had approached me on my very first day. I'd been overwhelmed and she'd seen that and immediately taken me under her wing. From then on, it had been the three of us. But even when she was the leader of our little pack, she'd somehow still always made time for any other dancer who she saw struggling.

"I'll never get to perform with her," I said in a broken whisper. It was stupid. Such a stupid thing to be sad over given our current situation. But it was all I could think about.

"She was an angel," Shelby said softly. "I'm still not convinced that she was human. She'd float across the stage, performing as if she was born dancing."

"Do you think her mom noticed she's gone yet?" I asked, remembering what she'd said about calling her mom every day. No one responded and we all fell into our own thoughts. Her mom had no idea that their last phone conversation would be the last ever. What were my last conversations with my friends and family?

"She was the closest thing I had to a sister," Shelby said quietly, wiping her eyes again.

I reached over and grabbed her hand, squeezing before I forced out through a too-tight throat. "I'm so glad I met you guys, even for a brief time. Ava is my best friend, but I'd never really been part of a group of girls like this until you two. I'm so glad I got to experience that."

She gave me a sad smile and squeezed my hand back.

The door opened and we all flinched, pushing ourselves closer to the wall. Rosie entered, mercifully alone, although I was sure the men were just outside if she wanted to call them in again.

"Break time is over, Cillian wants you prepped for tomorrow." I unconsciously shivered at her words. What more could they possibly have in mind for us now?

I didn't have to wonder for long as several women entered carrying supplies. I tried to determine what exactly they were planning as I read the labels. Wax, scrubs, lotions. We were about to be primped and pampered before being led to the slaughter.

I let my mind wander as the women before me treated my body as if it were not my own. I'd lived my life feeling stuck in a cage, no matter what I tried to make of myself, I always felt like I ended up back in the same box. Only now that I was physically stuck did I realize that it had mostly been self-imposed. Sure, on the outside I was outgoing and flirtatious, but it was a mask to hide the insecurities buried deep. The belief that I was nothing and would never do anything of value.

I could still hear my father's words echo in my mind like a symphony and had never taken the time to understand that by believing the things he said about me, I was building my own bars and shackles.

I was more than that. I knew in my head that the lies and insults that my father threw at me were unfair, but only now that Bella had sacrificed everything for us did I truly understand that love was the key to my emotional freedom. Love of a friend, love for myself. True love was a sacrifice. The sacrifice of a friend offering her life for a chance to get free, the sacrifice of choosing the uncomfortable path for a chance to truly live.

How many times had I been faced with a decision in life and had chosen the shackles instead of being brave and loving myself?

I thought back to my relationship with Phil. It had never been abusive or even particularly toxic, but I'd always known it wasn't right for me. Ava had told me straight to my face, and yet I had refused to move on because part of me had believed that I wasn't worth more. When had I decided to stop fighting the lies I'd been told and decided I was content in my self-imposed cage?

My eyes burned but I had no more tears left. Ava had tried to show me. Finn had done his best. And yet it took Bella to finally realize that the only way to set myself free was to accept love, to actively choose love. To stop hiding and taking the easy way out, and instead choose every day to love myself. To love the little girl who grew up too fast and too alone, and love those around me who showed me every day how much I meant to them. If only I hadn't realized it all too late.

41

Finn

The three of us went to the station with Libby. I could tell Ava was nervous, but either Sam was dumb or simply incompetent because they hadn't taken out the video and we had clear evidence of them assaulting me. There wasn't any direct video of the upstairs fights, but it was clear that my friends were stopping my assailants and I wasn't concerned they would be in any trouble.

Even still, we had to do an official interview process, give our statements, and finally, we were back together in the conference room. Libby entered and gave my shoulder a shove. "If I tell you to go home can you manage to stay out of trouble this time?"

I raised my hands in protest of my innocence. "As if I wanted them to come beat the shit out of me."

"I'm glad you're okay, Sullivan. You've got some good friends."

"Have you guys found anything else?" I asked, changing the subject. She looked towards my friends who busied themselves together, bending their heads close to talk. "I just heard back. The blood is not a match for Victoria," she said in a low voice.

Relief flooded me so strongly that I thought I might start crying. "Do we know who it was?"

"No. We're still trying to match the DNA with the others, but we know that it wasn't a match for Victoria."

"Thank you, Libby," I said, grabbing her hand. She tensed for a moment at the contact before squeezing me back.

"Go, get some rest. I'll let you know the minute I have something concrete to follow. And Sullivan, please try to stay out of trouble this time."

I could only manage a hint of a smile and then she was gone. I stood on shaky legs, feeling my adrenaline pumping through me.

"You okay?" Art said, coming up beside me. I hadn't told them about my fears that Vi was gone. They didn't know about what had seemed like gallons of blood in that house. There were certain things I couldn't— wouldn't share.

"Yeah," I said unconvincingly. "Actually, no. But Libby's right, I do need to get home."

"I'm pretty sure your house is currently a crime scene. We'll go back to my place." Art said matter of factly.

I put up no argument and we drove together towards his hotel. On the way, Art stopped at a pizza place where Ava ran in and came back carrying two large pizzas. The last thing I wanted to do right now was eat, but once we reached his suite I forced myself to do just that.

I texted Jake to warn him of the investigation taking place at our house, on the off chance he hadn't already been made aware. And then I sat in front of Art's massive TV screen and stared blankly at whatever trashy reality show Ava had chosen.

Somewhere along the way, I fell asleep and I woke up to my phone buzzing on the table next to me. I grabbed it and blinked to clear my eyes. Toni.

"Yes," I answered breathlessly.

"I found them."

For the second time in a matter of hours, the relief hit me and tears fought to explode.

"Where? Send me the address," I said, jumping to my feet.

"Slow down. You can't just go barging in there, guns blazing."

"Like fuck I can't."

"Finn. These guys aren't amateurs. The minute they catch a whiff of you, they'll be long gone. I bet you couldn't get within a hundred miles of them without setting off their alarms."

"So what the fuck do you expect me to do?" I gritted out.

"I'm working on a way in. These people know their shit, it won't be easy, but I can absolutely do it. Just give me some time."

"Who the fuck says they have any more time?" I all but yelled.

"I do. They are hosting an auction tomorrow. The girls will be kept put until then, unless they are spooked. I will find a way in, just hold tight."

I clenched my jaw so hard I felt something pop. We were so fucking close. We had an address. Why the hell shouldn't I call Libby and we head in with the calvary?

But Toni was good. She knew what she was doing. If she said that would make things worse, I had to believe her.

But what was I supposed to do? I couldn't just sit on my hands. There had to be something, anything.

My dad. The thought came to me out of nowhere. What about him? He had connections. Could he help speed up the process? Why wouldn't he just turn on me or the girls instead? Although he *had* given me information on Cillian previously.

My mind waged war with itself and before I could help myself I pulled up his previous email and typed out a reply.

Me: V was taken. When I find him, I will end him.

Less than a minute later my phone rang. I stared at the blocked number for a moment, trying to decide what to do. I knew who it was. There was no way I had emailed him and the next moment I received a blocked phone call. But what did he want? Would he help? Could he help? Would he only make things worse?

Anxiety knotted my stomach at the possibility that me involving him could worsen Vi's situation. But I had to try. I couldn't just sit here waiting for her to be sold off like cattle.

I pictured her alone, scared, beaten, and bruised and my heart threatened to stop right there in my chest.

With a deep breath, I pressed the button on my phone and wordlessly held it up to my ear.

"I can help you get her back."

42

Finn

I can help you get her back.

"How?" I asked, desperation cracking my voice.

"I told you, the relationship with my deartháir didn't end well. I will do anything I can to help you, mac."

I ignored the way that term made my heart ache for different reasons. "That doesn't answer my question of how you can help."

Art must have heard me talking to someone because he exited the bedroom where he and Ava had moved to at some point after I fell asleep. He raised his eyebrows at me in question but I just shook my head and turned my back, focusing on the conversation with my father.

"You said she was taken. I'm assuming you believe his intent is to sell her?"

My silence was answer enough.

"If you go in as a buyer under my name, he won't be able to turn you down."

"Have you fucking bought women from him?" I gritted out, anger flashing through me. I might need him right now, although that was still to be determined, but I would absolutely set my sights on him after butchering Cillian.

"Do you really think that low of me, Finn?"

Again, I didn't answer and frankly, I hoped that realization hurt him. His voice lowered when he spoke again.

"No, mac. I have never bought or sold another human being. But he's a greedy bastard. He knows I have the ability to, I can pay, and that alone, will be enough to get you access. He will never believe that there are those of us who value human life."

His words thawed a piece of my frozen heart and I tried to rebuild my walls against him.

"Fine," I replied. "If I use your name, what does that look like?"

"Meet me at the shed as soon as you can. I don't want to talk over the phone." Always his distrust of the *'authorities.'* As if I wasn't one of the very people he spent his life trying to avoid. I had no other options so I agreed and hung up.

Ava and Art were now both in the living room watching me.

"Toni found them and my dad said he can help me get inside."

Ava gasped at the same time Art responded, "Absolutely not."

"I have no other choice. If there's even a chance he can help me save her, save them, I have to take it."

"As if he won't just sell you out the moment he gets the opportunity."

I understood Art's reservations, but I was desperate. And after all the trouble my father had gone to send me information on Cillian, and the 'risk' he'd taken by talking to me on the phone, I honestly didn't believe he was attempting to sabotage me. And hell, at this point, if I found myself as a pawn in his game, it was a risk I was willing to take. If there was even a chance this could help Vi I would do it. I had to do it.

Art insisted he wanted to come with and I argued vehemently against this decision, but, in the end, he won out and now I stood watching him and Ava embrace before we left his suite. After a long hug and kiss Ava released her boyfriend, pulling me into a hug.

"Take care of yourselves. And go get Vi."

I squeezed her back. "I promise I will do everything in my power to get her back."

Suddenly I was taken back to another time when I stood in this room with Art and Vi while Art made the same promise to get Ava back. I swallowed hard. That had turned out okay. Maybe by some miracle, this would too.

We took Art's car but I drove as he didn't know where we were going. My father wanted to meet back at their shop so here I was traveling the same road that Vi and I had taken only a short time ago. Emotion clogged my throat and I swallowed against a lump as I tried not to let myself drown in my memories.

"So Daddy dearest, huh?" Art asked from beside me.

I laughed humorlessly as I turned onto the highway. "The one and only."

"I can't believe he reached out after all this time trying to make peace."

"I mean, he didn't initially. I'm the one who reached out first when I accused him of working with Cillian. But apparently he took that as a sign that I want a relationship now."

"And do you?"

My first instinct was to scoff at the question, but I let myself consider it. Did I? I held so much bitterness from them abandoning me, actively choosing their business over me. What kind of parents decided investing themselves in the mafia was more important than caring for their child?

And then my mother's words came back to me. *We only wanted the best for you, that school could provide for you in ways that we couldn't. We didn't want you stuck in the middle of this world.*

Did I believe her? Even if what she said was true, did that absolve her of guilt?

I sighed as I adjusted my grip on the steering wheel. "I honestly don't know. I mostly want to say fuck off and never let them back into my life. But another part of me says that if they truly help get Vi back, they deserve a second chance."

Art nodded like he understood. "I get that. But just because someone does something nice for you, no matter how nice, after years of shitty behavior, that doesn't mean they automatically deserve your forgiveness. I'll stand by you whichever way you decide to go, but don't feel obligated to let them back in your life just because of this. Let them back in only if you think there's a chance that you guys could rebuild a tentative relationship."

"Since when did you get so smart?" I asked, trying to change the subject from the heaviness that crept in at his words.

"I've always been this smart, you just don't choose to listen to me very often."

I snorted, shaking my head, and we made the rest of the drive in silence.

I parked in front of my parent's building and we approached the door. It swung open before we even touched it.

"Creepy," Art muttered from behind me. We reached the end of the hall where a brutish man stood, blocking our path with his arms across his chest like someone out of a mafia movie. "Hand over any weapons."

"Not a chance," Art retorted and the wall of muscle in front of us dropped his arms and took a step towards us.

"Hawke, cut it out." My father's voice rang out from behind him. We all turned to see my father standing there.

"Come on back, boys, nice to see you again, Arthur."

Art grunted as Hawke let us pass and we followed my father into his office.

"A drink?"

"Can we please just fucking get this over with so I can go save my girl?"

Brady nodded and set down the liquor bottle. "I just thought some alcohol would help with this conversation, but I understand."

I clenched my jaw to keep the, 'you have no fucking clue' response out of my mouth. I was trying to play nice here after all.

"You wanted to know how it would work to use my name. I am not going to have you pretend to be me, Cillian wouldn't believe that for a minute. But if you go in pretending to be your ceathrair Conor, he will absolutely take you seriously enough to gain entrance."

"Conor?" I asked in disbelief.

He nodded. "He often does pickups for me."

Ignored the jealousy that stabbed me out of the blue at that information. After all, I wanted nothing to do with my father's illegal activity.

"Sorry to spoil the fun, but Conor and Finn really don't look that similar."

My father nodded towards Art. "You would be correct. The most important piece would be his fingerprints rather than his facial features, but rest assured, we have the technology to alter both."

The cop in me immediately bristled at the news. My mind flashed to all of the ways that they could be using this and how I would love to get proof of this and bring them down.

On the other hand, the part of me that was only focused on saving Vi let out a sigh of relief that this could help.

"So I just go in there with a mask on pretending to be my cousin buying girls for you?" I asked in disbelief.

"Pretty much," my father said with a shrug.

"But you said that you have never been in this business before."

"Correct. And that was a major sore spot between Cillian and me. If he believes that I am finally 'coming to my senses' and willing to buy from him, his ego is going to override any suspicion or logic. Not that logic has ever been his strong suit."

"And we're supposed to believe that you're not in this with Cillian and just using this as an excuse to get rid of your son?" Art asked from beside me.

"You're a good friend, Arthur, to be so worried about my son. But no, I can assure you that I would like nothing more than to watch my brother get taken down at the knees."

His words rang true. I'm sure taking out his brother had something to do with providing him better business opportunities or selfishly taking out the competition, but for whatever reason I trusted that he was not trying to feed me to the wolves.

"I can help you get inside, but after that it's up to you on how you bring in the NYPD and anybody else," he continued.

At the mention of my department, I thought about my coworkers, about Libby. Should I share this information with her? I didn't believe Marcus would sanction a raid when the only information I had to go on was from a notorious crime lord and a hacker. I had to do this myself and bring them in once I had Vi safe.

"Okay," I said finally.

"Come with me, let's get you ready," my father replied.

I turned to follow him and Art placed a hand on my arm. "You sure about this?"

I nodded. "I'm going in and I'm going to count on you to alert the calvary once I'm inside."

Art nodded solemnly. "Alright."

43

Vi

Somehow after our pampering, I ended up falling into a fitful sleep on the too-thin cot. I woke with a start when the door opened on a bang. Griffith strode in with Rosie behind him. I scrambled to the head of the bed as he approached, trying unsuccessfully to get away. He laughed as he grabbed my arm and hauled me closer. "Nice try."

I fought him but to no avail. His iron grip held me firm, despite my attempts to kick and scratch him.

"Let her go!" Shelby yelled from my side but it made no difference. Griffith pinned me to the cot before shoving a needle into my arm. I cried out at the pain but even more, what I knew was coming. Almost immediately, my mind began to go fuzzy around the edges and my limbs felt sluggish. He laughed again as he shoved me down against the cot before moving on to Shelby beside me. I heard her scream and I turned my head in time to see Griffith plunge the syringe into her as well. In a moment, she too was pushed back to the bed and he moved on to Julia.

I slowly swung my attention to Rosie. She stood against

the far wall holding a pile of clothes. Her face was stoic and something about that triggered something in the back of my mind. I knew it should bother me but I was struggling to remember why.

Griffith stepped back with a deep exhale. "They're ready for you."

Who was ready? Us? What were we ready for? I felt like I was in a dream and couldn't quite fight my way back to reality.

Rosie stepped forward and it was like I was watching from outside my body as she began to peel off my clothes and dress me in one of the outfits. I moved and shifted when she told me to, and soon I was wearing the bra and panties that she had brought for me. I watched numbly as she moved on to Shelby and I finally laid my head back on the bed.

I think I dozed off and the next thing I knew I was being shaken awake.

"Come on," Rosie said and I swung my legs down and followed her out of the room. We walked through the building for what seemed like forever, before arriving in a small, empty room. We filed in and Rosie closed the door behind us.

"All ready," she said to no one in particular and I looked around the room. Shelby and Julia stood nearby, staring listlessly around the room, wearing similar getups to what I had been dressed in. Rosie stopped in front of each of us and one by one helped us step into high-heeled shoes. I looked down at her and blinked, trying to ask why I was wearing these. I couldn't manage to get the words to leave my mouth.

She stepped back to the wall and murmured again to herself.

"Julia," she said pulling the girl's wrist. The dancer looked at her, also silent. "You're first." With that, Rosie opened a second door in the room and pushed Julia out with some more murmurs. She closed the door behind her and now it was just the three of us.

After what could have been seconds or hours, Rosie grabbed my wrist and pulled me forward. "You're next, Victoria."

I tried to open my mouth to ask what I was next for, but again no sound came out. She pushed me towards the open door and said quietly into my ear. "You're going to walk across the stage and stop in the circle. When the light turns green, walk the rest of the way to the other end."

I didn't understand her words, but my body seemed to follow her commands without my direction and I entered the next room. I heard the door close behind me and I blinked against the sudden bright light. Before me was a stage just like Rosie had said, and bright lights illuminated a path for me. Beyond that, the space was dark and I couldn't make out anything else.

My gaze caught on the circle in front of me and my feet began to move again. My legs wobbled as I tried to walk in the tall heels I'd been given. I could feel myself sway, but somehow I kept my balance. I reached the circle where I stopped and blinked against the light again. All at once the room began to spin and I stepped forward in an attempt to catch myself. By some miracle, I stayed on my feet and I realized it wasn't the room that was spinning, but me.

Somehow, I was slowly spinning in a circle and I got a view of the space. Or I would have had I been able to see past the bright lights.

"Twenty-seven year old female dancer. Starting at five hundred thousand." Came a strange voice from somewhere in the room.

The room stopped spinning and I found myself facing the lights once more. That voice spoke again and I tried to get my brain to process through the sludge that I felt like I was under. Several moments passed before finally, the light turned green and my foot moved forward without my control. *Green. Walk.*

"Please collect your merchandise," came the voice again as I walked.

I followed the path to the end of the stage and found another door. It opened and a strange man stood on the other side, grinning at me.

"Stunning," he said grabbing my wrist and pulling me to him. My body moved without my control and in a moment, I was pressed against his body, his cold hand roaming my body. A shiver went through me, but I could do nothing to remove myself from his grip, and despair and resignation settled deep into my stomach.

44

Finn

I entered my uncle's world, anxiety churning through my gut like week-old Mexican takeout. The building looked like any other nightclub around here, but thanks to the directions from my father, I knew that the basement held his real business.

The prosthetics on my fingertips turning me into my cousin made my skin crawl, but I had been assured that they would not come off without intense scrubbing. A little sweat would be fine. I believed it, but I still hated the sensation.

I had been given a few facial prosthetics and a new hairdo and even Art admitted that I could pass for Conor. I was unarmed as I knew I would be checked for weapons before being allowed in, and walking into this cesspool with nothing to help me or the girls felt entirely hopeless.

I'd let Toni know my plans and she agreed that if I could get inside and stop them from disposing of the girls, she could get the troops to me. I wasn't sure how I was supposed to do that, but at this point I was Vi's best hope and I would do anything, including holding every single one of them down while we waited.

The security guard standing at the basement entrance paused me with an outstretched hand. I took a deep breath. Everything from here on out required me to put complete trust in my father. While I had decided I trusted him not to double-cross me, it was bizarre to be putting my life in the hands of a man whom I had been actively avoiding for years.

"Fionn Mac Cumhail," I said the keyword I'd been given.

For a second nothing happened and then the man before me nodded. "Name?"

"Conor Sullivan."

The man paused again, doing a double take. He murmured something into what I assumed was a microphone before stepping forward to pat me down. Once he was satisfied I was unarmed, he nodded towards the door. "Good luck."

Well, that wasn't ominous at all. He held the door open and I walked through into a darkened hallway that brought me to an elevator. I entered and pressed the only button on the pad. Basement.

The car began to move, and I did my best to keep my breaths steady, trying not to show how uncomfortable I was. More than likely, there were cameras in here and someone probably watching me at this very moment.

The doors opened and I stepped into a waiting room with a desk and several doors to choose from. A man sat behind the desk and motioned me forward.

"Conor Sullivan?" He asked.

"Yes," I said, trying to keep my words to a minimum.

"And why have you decided to finally grace my halls?" Came an oily voice from behind me. I had to resist the urge to shudder. Even after all this time, his voice made my skin crawl. Instead, I slowly turned and came face to face with my uncle for the first time in years. It was uncanny how similar he looked to my father, I'd forgotten how alike they appeared. I remembered hearing stories about how they would pretend to be the other one every chance they got to get out of trouble or just generally cause havoc. Looking at him now I could believe it.

"Brady sends his regards," I said.

"No the fuck he does not," he replied smoothly.

I let a smirk lift one side of my mouth as I responded, "You're right. But he is intrigued enough to see what you have to offer."

"After denying me for so long?" He asked, clearly not believing me.

I shrugged as if it didn't matter to me. "He's always been a hard-headed bastard. I have no idea what goes on in that head of his, I just know when to follow orders. And this might be one of the better assignments I've had in a while," I added with another smirk.

His expression didn't change and I cursed myself. Had I pushed it too far? I had no idea how to pretend to be Conor. And while Cillian wasn't particularly close to my cousin, he'd still seen him more recently than I had, minus the five minutes from this week.

Just when I thought he was going to deny me entrance, he nodded towards the desk. "Fingerprint, routing information."

I nodded and kept my steps even as I approached the desk. I could feel his eyes on me the whole time as I pressed my finger to the screen, praying it would work. The man in front of me didn't say anything which I took as a good sign before he passed me a tablet. I looked at the empty boxes in front of me.

This would make or break me. My father had told me I could use the company account for this as he fully intended to get it back before this was over. Even still, the fact that he was sharing this information with me told me how desperately he was trying to reconcile. Maybe I would have to give him a chance if I got out of this alive.

The screen turned green in confirmation when I finished entering the string of numbers that I had memorized. Cillian walked over to look over my shoulder at it and then nodded. "Follow me."

I took a deep breath before doing just that. So far so good. I was now in the heart of the lion's den. Cillian led me through the second door from the right and I memorized it for later. Then we stepped into a long, curving hallway.

"You will be in room 3507. The setup is self-explanatory, but the only important button is the one that says *buy*. There are three girls available tonight."

My heart began to race at the mention of the women and the knowledge that one of them was dead.

"—the competition will be fierce so if Brady wants to walk out of here with anything, I hope he came willing to spend." I tried to focus back on what he was saying.

"The announcer will let you when bidding begins and you can press buy at any time. The auction will continue until the bids stop. There is no trick bidding, as soon as you hit your button it resets the clock to give everyone else a fair chance to play."

I nodded, nausea swirling in my gut at the matter-of-fact way that he described selling human beings. We stopped in front of a large door and he opened it for me, allowing me to see the plush seat with a built-in screen facing a wall of glass.

"It is a one-way glass, you can see out, but no one can see in. The door will lock while the auction is taking place, and unlock when it is over. At that point, you will be free to either pick up your merchandise or leave, licking your wounds," he said with a laugh.

I grunted, unable to produce a laugh at his attempt at humor.

"Good luck, hopefully your experience will bring you back

again." And with that, he closed the door behind me.

Brady was right. Cillian was blinded to everything else by his pride and his need to have something that others wanted. I took several steps to the chair before taking a seat. I still didn't have a plan, but knowing that I was locked in here until the auction was over did not bring me any sort of comfort.

Everything about the room was curated to make the patron more comfortable, the seating, temperature, lighting. How much money and thought had gone into providing comfort to these monsters as they bid for another human life? Disgust and despair coursed through me in equal measures. How many times had they done this? How many times would this happen again to others?

You can't think about that now. Just focus on getting these three out. Keep it together Finn, I berated myself.

"The first offer of tonight is a twenty-eight-year-old ballerina." I saw a door on the end of the stage open and a woman stepped onto the stage. She looked familiar but wasn't one of the dancer's I'd gone out to dinner with. This must be Julia.

"Starting the bidding at five hundred thousand," the announcer said as the platform where Julia stood began to spin. She was clad in a gauzy piece of fabric that showed every inch of her body, and heels that had to be at least six inches tall. She stumbled as the platform spun and my heart broke at the confusion and fear I saw in her expression. Part of the screen held separate close-up views of different parts of her body. I kept my eyes glued to the one zooming in on her face and my blood ran hot at the glazed look I saw in her eyes. She was clearly drugged with something, and her expression reminded me of a lost child, unsure of what was going on or what she should be doing.

The announcer called out numbers as people must have

begun bidding and finally, after a few moments of silence, he called out, "Sold for one point one million dollars. Please collect your merchandise."

The stage light turned green and then Julia was stumbling to the other side of the stage where a door opened for her as she approached. I couldn't see what was on the other side and a moment later she disappeared from view. If the buyers were told to collect their purchase then maybe there was a chance the door unlocked for whoever won the bid. My heart rate picked up speed. I would need to win if I wanted a chance to get out of here before the auction was over.

The door at the other end of the stage opened again and all thoughts left me as I took in Vi stepping forward on shaky legs. She walked towards the center of the stage just as Julia had done and my chest ached at the sight. She was clothed in nothing but two pieces of black string and those same enormous heels. She stopped in the center and the circle once more began to spin, giving everyone present a view of her from all angles. The videos began to pan and zoom in on every area imaginable and white-hot anger poured through me as I stood from my chair, clenching my fist to keep myself from smashing the screen in front of me. The knowledge that there were men memorizing every inch of her without her consent. The things they were imagining doing to her—

"Starting the bidding at five hundred thousand," the announcer said.

Before the announcer could finish speaking I hit the *buy* button on my screen.

"Six hundred thousand."

Barely a second went by before he was announcing again, "Seven hundred thousand."

I immediately smashed the button again. "Eight hundred thousand."

My heart felt like it was going to pound out of my chest. I

didn't know how much money Brady had in his account, but I would use every single cent to get to Victoria. The bidding continued until we passed one million and I waited with bated breath for my button to stop working every time I hit it. Finally, we reached one point five million dollars and I felt lightheaded as I waited in the silence that followed.

After what felt like an eternity the announcer said, "Sold for one point five million dollars. Please collect your merchandise."

I was already standing and as soon as I heard my door click I was bolting out, jogging in the opposite direction from where I'd entered with Cillian.

I followed the curved hallway, passing door after door as I went, and finally, I reached what looked like the end of the hall. A man stood at the last door with his back to me. As I approached, I saw he was holding something. *Someone.*

My blood boiled as I realized who he was pressing tight into his body.

"Get your fucking hands off of her," I growled in a voice I didn't recognize.

45

Vi

"Get your fucking hands off of her," snarled a voice behind the man clutching me and he immediately released me, moving back a step.

"Oh, sorry I was going to bring her to you—"

Before he could finish talking, a hand was flying towards him and as it connected with his throat, he wordlessly crumpled to the floor. I blinked at the man now lying at my feet. *What the fuck?*

"Baby, come here," a voice said and I glanced up to see someone who looked familiar, even though my mind was having trouble recognizing how I knew him. Regardless, my legs carried me forward as if controlled by someone else. He wrapped his arms around me, holding me to himself but, unlike the man at my feet, his touch was gentle and he smelled like safety, whatever that meant.

He stepped back from me and placed a gentle hand on my jaw. I continued to stare back at him, trying to make my muddled brain work and figure out who he was.

"Shit, I'm sorry." He said, pulling his shirt over his head.

Then he placed it over my head and helped pull my arms through where it fell to the tops of my thighs. It felt nice and smelled good, like him.

"Come on Vi, we've gotta go," he murmured, pulling my hand. I blinked at his words. They triggered something in my brain. Deep, deep, down. But for the life of me, I couldn't figure out what it was.

He reached into his mouth and pulled out something, rubbing it against his pants before placing it in his ear.

"You there, Toni?" He asked as he continued to pull me along with him down the hallway.

I didn't hear anything but apparently he did because he continued, "I've got Vi." A pause. "No," he grunted. "Well, as much as I'd like to save every last human fucking trafficked woman my priority is Vi, and if that's all I can do—"

My ears worked just fine, but there was something wrong with my ability to comprehend what I was hearing. It all felt jumbled and disconnected.

"One of the girls was already sold, I'm not sure if she's still in the building." As he talked he tugged me towards a door. He opened it and pulled me inside where I noticed a single chair and a glass wall. I looked through the glass to see Shelby exiting the stage. Concern tickled the edge of my brain.

"The last girl is walking now. Send in the troops."

I turned towards the man before me, Finn I remembered his name was, and finally fought the fog blanketing my brain to murmur, "Shelby."

He looked back towards the stage and nodded before pulling me against his chest where I stood stiffly. "They're coming in, they'll get her."

The words meant nothing to me, but I knew I needed to get to her so I managed to step out of his embrace and walk towards the door.

"Where are you going?" He asked, panic edging his voice.

"Shelby," I said again.

I could see a war rage behind his eyes before he nodded, grabbing my hand and lifting a gun I hadn't noticed before into his other hand.

"We're going after Shelby," he told whoever he had been talking to. And then he pushed the door open and we were moving back the way we had come.

As we walked, a door opened to the right of us, and a man stepped out of the room. Finn shoved me behind him and waved the gun in his face. "Go, that way, now."

The man gave us a wide-eyed look before obeying and heading in the opposite direction. Finn cursed under his breath and tugged me along again.

Another man stepped out but this time when Finn gave him the same command to leave, he stepped towards us instead, eyes roaming over my body. "Lucky man, I'll give you fifty right now if you let me take her for a spin."

"Get the fuck out, now." Finn gritted out.

"Come on now, don't be selfish. There's more than enough to go around," he said, daring to take a step closer. Before I had time to react, Finn shot the man in the knee. The guy went down with a scream and Finn pulled me hard after him.

"Where the fuck are they?" He growled. I didn't answer and he continued talking as if to the air around us. "Yes, I just shot a man who wouldn't take no for an answer. No, just the leg."

We finally made it to the end of a hallway where a couple stood embracing in the corner. Except it wasn't a couple, and they weren't embracing. It was Shelby with her back pressed up against the wall as a man in front of us groped her.

All of a sudden, an alarm began blaring throughout the building and red lights began to flash. The man spun around just as Finn's fist collided with his face. The man fell to one knee and before he could struggle to his feet again, Finn hit him in the head with the butt of his gun.

"We've got to get out of here," he said reaching for Shelby. She stared at him with a blank expression and he grabbed her wrist, tugging her towards me.

"I've got two of them. Not sure where the other is." A pause. "The alarms are going off, if I had to guess the exits are going to be locked." He grunted and I continued to stare at Shelby as my mind continued to spin like tires caught in slush. I knew I should be doing something, but for the life of me, I couldn't figure out what.

Finally, Finn began to move again, grabbing Shelby and me both by the wrists and tugging us along after him. I had no idea where we were going and wondered if he had any idea either. The way he was talking didn't sound like it.

We reached a door and he again continued to carry on a one-sided conversation that didn't mean much to me. Then he reached for the handle and gave a sharp twist. The door opened to reveal a set of stairs.

"We've got to go," Finn said but then he stopped and dropped to one knee in front of me. I had no idea what he was going to do until I felt my foot lifted and Finn removed the heel I was wearing. He repeated the process with my other foot and then helped Shelby remove hers. When we were both barefoot he grabbed our hands again and gently pulled us towards the steps.

We reached the top of the stairs to find another door which Finn reached for. The door opened without any resistance and I blinked at the sudden blinding light coming from outside.

Finn didn't waste any time pulling both of us out of the building and pushing us lightly against the wall where he stood protectively in front of us, gun hung loosely in his hands. He continued to talk and I turned to look at Shelby.

The material she had been wearing hung in tatters and she wrapped her arms around her chest, silent, eyes glazed.

A siren pierced the otherwise quiet street we stood on and I flinched, attempting to tuck myself closer into the side of the building. Finn placed a hand on my shoulder. "It's okay, they're coming to help."

A moment later a police car parked in front of us, an ambulance right behind it. Someone jumped from the cop car and came towards Finn. "Anybody else out here?"

"Not that I know of. Just us."

The cop glanced toward Shelby and me. "These are two of the women who were taken?"

"Yeah. Victoria and Shelby. I'm not sure where the third girl is."

The guy spoke into his microphone and then the ambulance doors opened, two women stepping out. They approached us and I watched them curiously. Finn stiffened beside me when they stopped in front of us.

"You guys can come with us." They held up several blankets for us and when I didn't make a move towards it, Finn grabbed one, wrapping it around my shoulders, over his shirt that I still wore. He then turned towards Shelby and similarly wrapped her. "Come on, let's get into the ambulance."

Another police car parked as we made our way towards the vehicle and filed into the back, where I took a seat on the bench. I looked around the area, having never been inside of an ambulance before. There were shelves and cupboards covering the whole interior, some familiar and lots of unfamiliar medical equipment tucked in every inch. A gurney sat in the middle and one of the women motioned for me to take a seat.

"If you're okay with it, I would like to get your blood pressure and heart rate," she said soothingly. I looked towards Finn in question and he nodded so I obliged. I didn't know why my first instinct was to turn to him for direction, but he was giving me stability in a time when I felt my mind and world spinning out of control so I would take it.

"Will they be okay if I step outside real quick?" Finn asked one of the women. She nodded, "Just knock on the door when you want to come back in."

He placed a hand on my leg, "I'll be right back," he said before exiting the back doors. I watched the monitor beep as they took my blood pressure and then glanced back to Shelby where she sat staring blankly at the wall. After minutes or maybe hours, I heard a knock on the door again and one of the women opened the door for Finn. The other woman had moved to check on Shelby and she glanced his way. "We're going to be leaving now. Are you coming with?"

He looked between us and I could see indecision in his gaze.

"If it makes the decision easier, once we get to the hospital they're not going to allow you back with them. You'll have to wait in the waiting room." One of the women told him.

He nodded at this. "And you're sure they'll be okay on the way there?"

"Yes. We will have a police escort," she replied.

He nodded again before grabbing my hand. "They're going to take care of you. I'm going to come see you as soon as I can. I'll let Ava know where you're going."

I squeezed his hand back. "Okay," I managed to say and a smile tipped up his lips.

"Okay," he echoed.

46

Finn

Cillian had fucking escaped. I'd known there was a good chance he'd run the minute I turned on my transmitter to call Toni, but I'd had no choice. The minute I'd seen Vi on that stage, nothing else had mattered except getting to her. And now that I knew she was safe, a weight had been lifted off of my shoulders and I could turn to the next most pressing matter. Catching that piece of shit.

Libby had arrived with the cavalry, something I would have to hear about from her later, and the place was swarming with cops and SWAT. They'd apprehended Shelby's buyer from where I'd knocked him out. There were also several other wannabe buyers and Cillian's employees now in custody, including the man I'd found groping Vi. But Cillian was nowhere to be found.

"But you saw him here at one point?" Libby asked while she continued to scan the video feed we had found in one of the back offices.

"Yeah, he was here to *welcome* me when I came in." I replied.

"And he didn't recognize you?"

"No," I gritted out, hating to repeat myself. I knew the story didn't make much sense considering the fact that I couldn't tell her that I'd used my dad's name and my cousin's fingerprints to gain access, but that didn't mean I liked being questioned.

"And you were here because you got a random tip from someone?"

"Yes."

She looked at me suspiciously, clearly not believing me, and for a moment I worried she would arrest me for conspiracy or not cooperating with an investigation. Instead, she nodded slowly. "We've got a lot of things to discuss, Sullivan."

I was about to argue when she raised a hand to stop me. "But for the moment I'm most concerned with finding Cillian. His name and picture are going to be flashed over every news site and media page. We'll be monitoring every known alias and, while we hunt for him, we'll see if we can get any of his cronies to talk."

"Are you taking them back to the station now?"

"Yes. Are you coming?"

I thought about Vi in that ambulance after sending her off to the hospital. A huge part of me wanted to leave right then and stand outside her door if they didn't let me in. But I'd already sent Ava in her direction and I knew there would be multiple officers watching her and Shelby. There was no way Cillian would get to them.

Not that he'd want to. They'd only been good for selling, beyond that he didn't care and had no interest in them.

"We found someone," an officer said as he came through the door.

"Who?" Libby asked.

"She says her name is Rosie."

"Sanchez?" I asked in disbelief. He shot a glance towards me and then back towards Libby. "She didn't give us a last name."

"You think it's her?" I asked Libby. "That would be crazy, right?"

"Let's go find out."

I followed her out of the space into a smaller room where a female officer stood with an olive-skinned woman. She was fully dressed in pants and a long shirt, unlike the woman who'd been auctioned, but she had the same lifeless look in her eyes.

"Rosie?" Libby asked, approaching her cautiously. She looked at us suspiciously, wrapping her arms around her middle.

"Where's Cillian?" She asked.

"We're not sure, that's what we were hoping to ask you," Libby responded, clearly going for the truth.

"What did you do to him?" The woman accused.

"Nothing, he left before I got here. We're hoping to talk to him."

"You don't want to talk to him. You want to arrest him."

"Why would we arrest him? Has he done something wrong?" Libby asked.

"I don't want to talk to you. I want to see Cillian."

"Is your last name Sanchez?" I interrupted.

She turned sharply to me. "Who are you?"

"My name is Finn, I'm here trying to make sure everyone is safe. We've been looking for a Rosie Sanchez who went missing several years ago." She continued to stare at me wordlessly.

"If you're her, we just want to make sure you're okay. Your family is worried about you. Your son."

"I don't have a son." She said angrily. But I knew I was right. We had just gotten confirmation through our earpieces that this indeed was the Rosie Sanchez who'd been missing for years after being last seen with Cillian.

"He can't hurt you anymore, we're going to protect you." Libby tried again.

"Get away from me," Rosie said, taking another step back. "He said you'd try to find him. Try to separate us. I don't want to talk to you. I just want Cillian."

Fuck. I had been hoping for a tearful release as she realized she was safe. Maybe some confusion, but not this.

"Stockholm syndrome," Libby murmured from where she had stepped back to stand beside me. "Let's get her to a hospital. There's nothing else we can do for her at the moment."

I nodded, wanting to scream as every minute ticked by and I feared Cillian slipped further and further out of our reach.

"I'll come with you," I said, answering her earlier question. "The best thing I can do for Vi now is help try to get Cillian's whereabouts out of the men here."

She nodded. "Come on then, let's get back to the station."

47

Vi

I awoke in a strange room to the sound of beeping. I blinked in an attempt to clear my blurry vision. The ceiling above me was white and I caught the sight of a clear bag full of fluids in my periphery. I looked up and followed the line to my arm where it was administering the liquid.

"Hey," came a familiar voice beside me. I turned to find Ava approaching the bed from a chair where she'd been presumably sitting.

"Hey," I croaked back.

"Shh, don't talk," she said, reaching for a red button sitting on my bed. A voice came through the intercom.

"Can I help you?"

"Yeah, Vi's awake," Ava responded.

"The nurse will be right in," replied the voice.

Ava sat on the edge of my bed and grabbed my hand tightly in hers. "Fuck, Vi I'm so fucking sorry."

"What for?" I managed to say past my dry throat.

She shushed me again before squeezing my hand and I saw a tear slip down her cheek. "I should have been at the house. If I'd been at the house that night they might not have been able to get to you." She said with a quiet sob.

A nurse entering my room interrupted my reply as she stopped at my bedside, immediately fiddling with the monitors next to me. I felt the blood pressure cuff on my arm squeeze and she checked some numbers before turning to face me. "How are you feeling?"

"My head hurts," I rasped. "And my throat is dry."

"Can she get some water?" Ava piped up from beside me.

"I'll check with the doc, but I think it should be okay for her to have some ice chips. I'll be right back."

She left and I turned back to Ava. I tried to work up some spit to moisten my throat before I tried again. "It's not your fault. And I'm glad you weren't there, or you probably would have been killed or taken too." My mind went to Bella and a pang went through me at the reminder. "Are Shelby and Julia okay?"

"Shelby is in the room next door, as far as I know, she's still out. And I haven't heard anything about Julia," she said giving my hand another gentle squeeze.

I tried to think back to the last time I'd seen them but my mind was fuzzy. I only had flashes of memories, pictures of moments like standing in a room with the two of them while Rosie undressed us.

I glanced down at myself to see a hospital gown over me, and I pulled the blankets up tighter to cover my chest. Ava moved, helping me shift the blankets until I was comfortable. Then she pulled the chair closer to the bed and took a seat, her hand finding mine again.

"I'm starting to really hate hospitals," Ava said breaking the silence.

I laughed which sent me into a coughing fit. Ava's eyes turned worried as she turned to press the call button again, but just then my nurse returned with a cup.

"Ice," she said setting it down on the table next to me as I managed to catch my breath. She pulled out a stethoscope and listened to me while I breathed. "Lungs sound clear," she reported.

"I think my throat is just really dry," I said, taking one of the ice chips into my mouth and savoring the feeling of it melting on my tongue.

"The doc will be in shortly, in the meantime, how is your pain?"

"My head is killing me," I admitted.

"Anything else?"

Embarrassment and shame coursed through me at the question. "Would you rather be alone?" The nurse asked, motioning to Ava.

"No!" I exclaimed, clutching her hand.

"Alright," she said with a patient nod.

"My neck hurts," I said quietly. "And, down here," I said, motioning to my crotch. I wasn't normally shy when it came to my body, but for some reason, the words got stuck in my throat. Like saying them aloud was admitting something that I didn't want to think about right now.

"Okay. Would you like something for the pain?"

"Maybe some ibuprofen or something? I don't want anything that's going to make me feel woozy."

"Okay, I can get that for you." She paused and I braced myself for what was coming next. "There is no obligation, but I wanted to let you know that we can perform a sexual assault forensic exam prior to you bathing if you would like."

I could feel myself physically recoil at the idea and my first instinct was to say absolutely not. The answer must have been clear on my face because the nurse spoke again. "You do not have to by any means, I just wanted to give you the option before you bathe and lose the opportunity."

Her soothing tone calmed my nerves the slightest and I

took a deep breath. "Would it help with the investigation?"

"If we were to find DNA it could help to bring chargers to some of the people involved, yes."

"And what do I have to do?"

"We have special nurses, all female, who will come and assist you with performing the exam. If you would like, I can get one to come speak with you."

"Okay," I whispered, forcing the word out of my too tight throat.

"Anything else you need while I'm out?" She asked, her tone so extremely gentle.

"No, thanks. Actually," I stopped her as she started to exit. I took a breath and tried to move past the terror gripping me. "Can I get a warm blanket? You have those, right? The movies always say you do," I went on sheepishly.

She laughed. "Yes we do, and yes I can get one for you. I'll be right back. Press the call button again in the meantime if you need anything else."

She exited and I couldn't look at Ava, not wanting to see the pity in her gaze. As if she knew how I was feeling she stayed quiet, simply holding my hand as my thoughts swirled. I laid my head back on the pillow and closed my eyes, anchoring myself with her touch.

I woke several hours later feeling disoriented but more comfortable. Ava was napping in the chair next to me and I winced at how painful her sleeping position looked. I glanced up to see my nurse entering. She kept her voice low as she spoke, "Sorry if I woke you, just time to recheck your vitals."

I nodded, using one hand to cover a yawn as I offered her my other arm for my blood pressure. "How is Shelby?" I asked, unsure if she was willing or able to give me any information on her.

"She's okay," came her vague response.

"Would it be possible for me to see her? I'm feeling good

and I could just go into her room."

She looked between me and my chart on her computer. "Let me ask my charge nurse okay?"

It was better than no so I took it as a good sign. After assessing me she left to go talk to someone. Ava continued to sleep and I wondered just how little sleep she'd gotten while I was gone. It brought back way too familiar feelings from her being kidnapped not too long ago and I shivered at the memories.

In a few minutes, my nurse was back. "They said it should be okay if you go visit her. I talked to her nurse and she's okay with you coming over."

She helped disconnect me from the chords that were attached to me and did something to keep my IV in my arm but disconnected it from the bag. I stood slowly, letting my legs get used to my weight again. I hadn't been in bed for long, I hadn't even been taken for that long, but my whole body felt so incredibly weary.

After reassuring both myself and my nurse that I wasn't going to fall, I used the bathroom before following her out of my room and down the hall. I noted the security guard who stood outside my hospital room and another outside what I assumed was Shelby's room.

We entered and I found Shelby awake, sitting up in a hospital bed that looked just like mine. I made my way to the chair next to her and took a seat, grateful for the support even after that brief walk. She gave me a small smile and held out her hand which I took gratefully.

"Hey, Shel."

She squeezed my hand and murmured back, "Hey."

"How are you?" I asked, even though we both knew the answer. She shrugged. "Excited to see my parents. They're on their way but it'll still be a little while."

My thoughts went to my own mother. Had anyone notified

her yet? Would she be able to come down?

"I'm glad they're coming," I said instead.

We fell into a heavy silence and she sighed. "I hate hospitals."

"Doesn't everybody?" I asked with a small laugh.

"Yeah, well they remind me of all the times I was in-patient while in foster care."

I sobered. "Oh wow, I didn't even think about that."

"How are you dealing with everything?" She asked after a moment.

Now it was my turn to shrug. "I don't know. I feel like I haven't really thought about or processed anything. Like I'm purposefully trying to block it out." I swallowed and touched the bruise on my neck. Her gaze followed the movement and she nodded.

"Yeah," she said in a squeaky voice. Another long moment passed before she spoke. "I'm moving out of state," she said.

I blinked at her sudden words. "Really? Where are you going?"

"Vermont. My parents have been trying to convince me to move closer to them for a while and this is the push I needed."

"So you're done dancing," I said softly.

"Yeah. I don't want anything to do with dancing again. I don't think I could even put on a leotard without breaking out in hives."

"I'm so sorry about Bella," I said brokenly. "I know I didn't know her long, but she was amazing."

Shelby smiled as tears began to slide down her cheeks. "Yeah, she was. I've never loved someone so much and yet been irritated by them in equal measures."

"I'm pretty sure that sums up what it's like to have a sibling," I said, thinking about Ava.

We fell into a comfortable silence and then she squeezed

my hand again. "She loved you. We'd go home and she'd talk about how great you were and how much potential you had."

Her words broke the dam and my tears began to flow as I let out a sob. The last few weeks played on repeat in my head: meeting Bella on the first day at the theater, her giving me a tour, introducing me to Shelby and some of the other dancers, watching her practice her solos, going out for dinner after long days of rehearsal, her corny jokes, her boldness when she confronted me about my feelings for Finn, the way she stood up to Cillian and Griffith, and her ultimate sacrifice.

"I'm glad I got to meet you and I know she was too." The words were so sweet, so heavy, and carried the weight of goodbye.

"You'll text me updates of your life?" I asked between tears.

"Of course. As long as you do too," she replied. There wasn't much else to say and when my nurse came back to get me I stood up and gave her one last hug.

"You take care of yourself, okay?" I whispered.

"You too. And thank Finn for me, will you?"

"I will," I choked out. I gave her one last watery smile before I walked with my nurse back to my room, letting my tears fall and fill the broken pieces of my soul.

48

Finn

He was in the wind. Within an hour of being booked, two of the men who'd worked for him at the club had taken plea deals and spilled everything they had on him. Apparently, his leadership was not one that instilled much loyalty. We had names, addresses, contacts, but so far nothing had led to him.

We'd frozen every asset we could get our hands on, but knowing how deep this operation went there was a good chance he had money stashed for a time such as this. It was going to be really hard for him to get anywhere and the moment he tried to access any of the considerable wealth he'd left behind, we'd get him. But for the time being he was gone without a trace.

Less than twelve hours later, I sat in Marcus' office, Libby at my side as we sat across from my boss. He had his fingers steepled together as he stared at me over his desk. I was itching to get out of here and go see Vi, but I was getting regular updates from Ava and I knew that my time was better spent here trying to catch her kidnapper. But after hours of fruitless searching, it was now time to pay the piper.

"So you were at your friend's house after your break-in. You received an address from an unknown number alerting you that they had the girls?" He asked.

I nodded, not trusting myself to speak.

"And you chose not to call it in because—?"

"They said they would know if I contacted the police." I wasn't lying, well not really. Toni had told me that Cillian would be alerted if the cops were to get involved. Not that he hadn't managed to escape anyway, but if I'd let them know beforehand he might have taken off with the girls or killed them before we had the chance to reach them.

"And we will find evidence of this in your phone records?"

Here was the hard part. I was either about to save myself or damn myself based on my answer. "Yes," I said, having to put all of my trust in Toni that she would be able to alter my phone records to match the story.

He nodded at me again. "Alright. I will look into it. For the moment you are being placed on administrative leave."

I nodded, again not having much to say. I stood but halted when he spoke again. "And Sullivan?"

"Yes, Sir."

"I'm glad we got your friend back alive. That's all thanks to you."

I dipped my head with a quiet, "Thank you, Sir."

I was heading towards my locker when Libby caught up to me.

"Hey, Sully." I stopped and turned to her. "For what it's worth, I think Cap and I both agree that you made the right call. Regardless of the sketchy ways you might have gone about it."

I laughed but the sound held no humor. "If he decides to can me over this, I understand. I stand by my actions and I'd do it again in a heartbeat if faced with the same situation though."

"I know. Now, enjoy your time off, and go get your girl."

"I plan to," I said with my first genuine smile since I had heard about her kidnapping.

I exited the station to find Art idling outside. "You okay?" He asked as I slid into the passenger seat.

"No. Do I still have a job? Yet to be determined."

Art pulled out of the parking lot and headed toward the hospital. "Well, you know you always have a job at my hotel chain. I'm sure you'd make a great bartender. Or maybe housekeeping would be better?"

I punched his thigh and he laughed.

"I have said before and I'll say it again, I would rather dance naked in Times Square than work for you," I replied.

"I'm guessing that can be arranged," he said with a grin. Silence settled between us and he sobered. "Seriously man, that was some fucked up shit you walked into."

"Yeah." My mind drifted back to the stage where I had watched the girls walk while drugged out of their minds. The sound of the announcer over the loudspeaker and the look the man gave me when he asked for a taste.

My fist clenched involuntarily and I practiced some breathing exercises in an attempt to calm down, trying to think of anything else.

"What do you think he's going to decide?" Art asked, apparently sensing my need for a distraction.

"Not sure. He's a level-headed guy, I like him. And I wouldn't blame him in the slightest if he decides he has to let me go."

"Toni is going to get everything squared away. I'm sure she already has."

"Yeah, but I don't know if it'll be enough. The fact that I went rogue without telling them. That's a big deal."

We road in silence for a few more minutes. "I don't know what I'll do if I lose the position. If I get fired, I'll never work in this field again. That thought scares the hell out of me. This is all I've ever wanted."

"Except when you wanted to be an NBA player," Art chuckled.

I glared at him. "I was eight. I didn't understand you needed to be tall and coordinated to do so."

Another moment of silence. "If he fires me I'll be sad, but I'll figure something out. Nothing scares me more than the idea of losing Vi."

He gave me a sideways look as he pulled into the hospital parking lot. "You've got it bad."

Part of me wanted to argue, to throw shade at him about how whipped he was. But I didn't. It was true. I had it bad for Vi. Since the moment I'd met her I'd been awestruck. I'd been pining over her before and even after I knew she had a boyfriend. And then all those moments we'd spent together since—

She was everything.

"Go get your girl," I was told for the second time this evening. I didn't need any more encouragement.

Art dropped me off at the door and I stopped at the front desk.

"I'm here to see Victoria Garcia."

"We don't have anyone by that name, I'm afraid," the front desk worker said without missing a beat.

"My name is Finn Sullivan. I can call her if that would be helpful."

Just when I thought she would deny me again, Ava stepped through the ER doors, coming up to me to give me a hug. "Hey, you made it."

I hugged her back and she turned to the lady at the desk, showing her badge. The receptionist nodded before asking for my ID which I handed over.

"Is she awake?" I asked Ava.

"She's been dozing on and off."

I was given my ID back and a badge with my picture on it.

"I'll show you where to go," Ava said and I followed her through the double doors. When we reached a room with a police officer who I didn't recognize we showed our badges and IDs and then Ava pushed the door open for me. "I'm gonna go find Art, I'll be right outside if you need me."

"Thanks, Ava," I said before stepping inside.

The sight before me took my breath away. Vi looked so fragile yet perfect, broken yet beautiful. She didn't have many obvious injuries aside from a nasty-looking bite mark on her neck that sent red-hot fury through me. I closed my eyes and counted to ten, taking deep measured breaths in an attempt to calm myself. When I finally felt more in control I opened my eyes to find her watching me.

"Hey," I said softly as I came to sit down beside her.

"Hey," she said with a small smile.

"You look good. Beautiful."

"So do you. Even with this," she said, touching the side of my face where I knew it was black and blue.

I winced, "Yeah, I might have been jumped by a couple of my ex coworkers after they broke into my house."

"Are you serious?" She asked, her mouth popping open in shock.

"Yeah, but that's a story for another time," I said with a laugh, leaning forward to press a kiss to her cheek. She shuddered and I pulled back, instantly regretting the move.

"I'm sorry, I shouldn't have—"

"It's okay. Really." She said when I clearly didn't believe her. She held out her hand, palm facing up and I laced my fingers through hers.

"I can't believe you found me," she whispered.

"There's nothing that could have stopped me from finding you, Beour. I would have torn apart the world brick by brick if that's what it took to find you." Silence settled between us and I stroked my thumb over her hand. "How are you feeling?"

"I'm okay," she said. "A little sore but the meds they're giving me help."

I nodded, not knowing how to ask about her emotions. After a few more beats of silence, she looked up at me and I steeled myself for whatever she was about to say.

"Did you guys find her body?"

I guessed who she was talking about but wanted to be sure. "Bella?" I asked softly. She nodded, emotion twisting her features.

"We haven't found her body yet, but we did get her DNA from the crime scene."

"From her blood?"

"Yeah."

She stared past me to the shade that was drawn on the window. "I can't believe she's gone," she said, her voice broken.

"I'm so sorry," I replied. "For her. For not finding you sooner. For everything."

"Did you catch him?" She asked, the question piercing my heart and making guilt flood through me.

"No. He must have been tipped off before we could get to him."

She nodded as if she wasn't surprised.

"We do have everything on him though. There were quite a few people who didn't escape and several of them turned on him. If he so much as pisses in the wind we'll have him."

She didn't say anything and I squeezed her hand gently. "He's not going to hurt you again, Vi. No one will. I promise."

She gave me a shaky smile that was clearly unconvinced. "Did you guys find Julia? Ava said Shelby was here but didn't know anything about Julia."

"Yeah, her captor was caught trying to flee town with her. I think she ended up at a different hospital, but she's okay." As okay as any of them could be right now.

Another nod. "Did— did you guys find someone named Griffith?"

I clenched my jaw at the fear in her voice but I tried to think of the people we had at the station. "Yeah, he was one of the guys who flipped on Cillian for a plea deal."

"So— so he's going to get off with a fine or something?" She asked, her voice trembling.

"No baby, he's getting locked away, he might just get cushier accommodations."

She didn't say anything at that so I asked. "Why, Vi? Why ask about him?"

"Nothing," she said, but the war waging on her face said otherwise.

"Victoria," I said, sitting forward, my voice coming out in a growl. "I don't want to push you, but if there's something you need to tell me, please tell me. Why are you asking about him in particular?"

She wouldn't look at me as she answered. "He's the one who did this," she said motioning to her neck and the welt there. I ground my molars so hard I worried they would crack under the pressure.

"He will never lay a finger on you or anyone else, I swear it on my life."

She finally looked back at me and tears welled in her eyes. "I fought him. I tried so hard to fight him," she sobbed.

"Baby—" I said as I gently shifted her and climbed into bed beside her, tucking her into my chest. Her sobs came harder and it was like a damn had released as she shook and cried into me.

"I'm right here, I'm right here. I'm never letting you go.

You're the strongest, most amazing woman in the world." I murmured into her hair as she cried, unsure how much she heard but desperately needing to say something.

After several minutes her sobbing turned to sniffles and she quieted as I continued to hold her.

"I don't remember much from today," she finally said. "They tried to ask me questions about how we got out and everything, but I don't remember much besides seeing you there at some point. I know they drugged us and I can't seem to remember much after that."

"You don't have to. It's not your job to put the pieces together for them. Don't worry about it," I said, rubbing her arm. "It's probably best that you don't remember everything clearly anyway."

She nodded and then her face split into a huge yawn. Before I could suggest I move so she could get more comfortable in bed, she snuggled deeper into me. Okay. Not moving, got it.

"You'll stay here if I fall asleep?" She asked sleepily.

"Honey, the entirety of the NYPD couldn't drag me away from you. Yes, I'll be here."

49

Vi

True to his word, Finn stayed with me the entire night. Every time I woke to nurses coming in for meds or vitals, I'd look over to find him slumped in what had to be the most uncomfortable sleeping position and it would bring a small smile to my face. The next morning I had a hospital breakfast of oatmeal and fruit before the doctor came by to give me the okay to discharge.

Physically, I was in pretty good shape considering everything that had happened. I was bruised, sore, and ordered to take it easy. But most of my wounds were not something that the hospital could fix, so there was no reason to stay longer than necessary.

Part of me wanted to stop in and see Shelby again before I left, but I found out that her parents had made it and I decided to leave the goodbye at our conversation yesterday. So instead, with Finn, Ava, and Art by my side, along with a security escort, I finally left the hospital.

"Okay, just confirming, we're going back to my hotel, right?" Art asked from behind the wheel. Ava turned from the front to stare at me expectantly and I nodded.

"Yeah, I don't feel ready to face my house just yet."

"You don't need to explain, I just want to make sure we're all on the same page," he replied.

"I've already packed up the important stuff from the house and anything else you need we can always send someone to get or just replace," Ava said with a smile.

"Thanks," I said, feeling my heart squeeze at their care.

"We do need to figure out the sleeping situation, however," Art said as he pulled out of the parking lot. "Obviously I can book out as many rooms as we want, but if all four of us want to stay in the loft we need to figure out how to split it."

"You're staying at the Laurie too?" I asked Finn who sat beside me in the backseat, holding my hand.

"Yeah, my house doesn't feel the greatest after my break-in either."

"You sure it has nothing to do with not being willing to leave my side?" I asked with a raised brow. He just grinned and pulled me into him. I definitely wasn't going to argue with his desire to stay close to me.

"Anyway, back to the rooming situation, I've got two rooms so we could split it boys and girls if we want?" Art continued.

Finn and I shared a look and I shook my head. "I don't want to kick Ava out of your bed," I replied.

"Yeah, I have no problem sleeping on the couch," Finn said and I rolled my eyes at him.

"That's entirely unnecessary. You and I can share a room and the love birds can still share. It's not like we haven't already slept together," I said with a pointed look.

"Well if you're offering, then absolutely I'm staying in the room with you, I was just trying to be a gentleman," he said with a smirk.

"I thought we already talked about you being a

gentleman?" I asked with a raised brow. He appeared confused for a second before his eyes heated as he too must have remembered our first time together. His head dropped lower and just as his lips pressed to mine Art's voice rang out, "Hey, y'all are in my car, watch it."

Finn continued the kiss for a moment longer before pulling away and giving Art the middle finger. I laughed as I leaned my head against him. These next couple of weeks were going to be quite interesting.

50

Finn

I was *this* close to being charged with murder. When Vi had first told me about what Griffith had done to her I had tried to keep myself calm for her sake but internally I was ready to walk right into his cell and put a bullet through his head. I had been disgusted by him and everyone else we'd apprehended already, but now knowing that it was him who was responsible for so many of her wounds, both physically and emotionally, the thought was almost too much. His DNA had been found on Vi and that should be more than enough to put him away. In the off chance that he got out, I had reached out to my father with his information and he promised me the monster wouldn't make it off of the premises alive. I was still contemplating whether I wanted him to take him out now, my dad had made it very clear that he was willing and able to remove him for me if I wanted.

My thoughts were interrupted by my phone vibrating. As if he had sensed me thinking of him, I had a text from an unknown number.

Unknown: How's V? Call me when you get a chance.

I pocketed my phone without responding, noticing Vi watching me out of the corner of my eye. We sat snuggling on one of Art's ridiculously expensive couches watching some movie that I had not been paying the least bit of attention to. Art and Ava were wrapped up in each other on the other couch and I spoke low enough so they couldn't hear, "My dad."

"Have you talked to them since— since you found me?" She asked, stumbling a little over her words.

I wrapped my arm tighter around her in an attempt to squeeze the bad memories away. "Briefly. They want us to come over for dinner sometime." I didn't feel like explaining the fact that I had requested my dad's help in murdering her rapist. That was a conversation for another day, if I ever shared.

She let the movie play for a bit before asking softly, "Are you going to? Have dinner with them?"

I sighed as my hand traced idle circles on her arm. "I don't know," I answered truthfully. "I'm grateful for the part they played in helping me get to you, but— I don't know."

She reached down, intertwining our fingers. "I don't want you to feel obligated to talk to them just because they helped you find me. I'd feel like shit if that was the case."

"It's not just that. When I saw my mom and, even hearing their flimsy excuses, I don't know, it still kind of woke something in me that I thought I'd buried." She didn't push me and after gathering my thoughts I went on. "I miss them. Or what they could have been in my life."

"You don't owe them anything. But if you do want to pursue this, I will be right there with you. I've already met them once, so it's just kind of natural," she said with a shrug. I knew she was trying to make light of our first very uncomfortable meeting with them, but I was extremely grateful for her attempt and the support she offered.

"You want to go have dinner with a couple mobsters?" I asked, raising an eyebrow.

"If it means spending more time with you and making you feel less alone then I would love to," she said, the truth shining in her eyes.

"You're amazing, you know that right?" I said, placing a kiss against her forehead. She sighed and snuggled deeper into my chest. "You've mentioned it before, but I don't think you say it nearly enough."

I rolled my eyes as I reached down to gently tickle her side. She giggled and squirmed in my arms in a halfhearted attempt to escape.

"You deserve to hear it every day, all day long, but keep up that smart mouth of yours and you'll have to face the consequences."

She immediately sat up in my arms. "Is that a promise?"

I laughed as I pulled her against me once more and turned towards the movie, "You bet your sweet ass it is, a mhuirnín."

51

Vi

You'd think someone had won the lottery with how ecstatic Finn was. Nope, I was just finally moving in with him.

After playing house with him for the last couple of weeks in Art's hotel, he'd asked me to move in with him instead of my own space when I'd admitted to him that I was going stir-crazy and needed to get out of the dorm-like environment that we were in. I'd had my reservations about moving in together so soon, but he'd been insistent during the first and last conversation we'd had about it.

"Finn, I need to get out of here. I feel like I'm suffocating on their love."

"Absolutely, and I'll go wherever you need to."

"Finn, you're not coming to babysit me."

"I'm moving in," he said in that end-of-argument tone he liked to use. "It's fine if you want me to stay in a separate bedroom or even a separate floor of the house, but there's no way in hell that I'm letting you live alone, and now that Ava has all but moved in with Art, that's way too much time by yourself even if she were to pretend to share the address."

He was right, Ava had already practically been living with Art, and I had no desire to move back to our old place and face those demons. So I'd agreed to move in with him, listed my old place, and found a cozy condo to share. I hated to admit it, but I *was* terrified to live alone. I was still having nightmares and despite weekly, and sometimes more frequent, therapy appointments, I knew I had a long way to go. We all did.

Shelby, Julia, and I had been texting over the last couple of weeks, and it was nice to hear updates about how Shelby's move had gone as Julia and I took an undetermined amount of time away from the ballet. Winnie was more than willing to accommodate us and, despite going back and forth daily about it, I hadn't yet decided if I wanted to try again. The thought of stepping through those doors without Bella or Shelby made me want to curl inside myself and cry forever. But I also felt like I was letting Cillian and every other person involved win if I let them take ballet from me. So I remained torn. Last I heard Julia also hadn't decided if she was going to return yet or not.

Bella's body had been found and, even though I had purposefully avoided asking for details, I was glad that her family had something to bury. Maybe that would help with closure.

Cillian was still in the wind, but Finn had said that they had several ideas where he'd gone and Toni was continuing to search for him. I had no doubt that despite whatever resources and connections he had, she would find him. I was starting to believe she was capable of finding anybody and anything.

The people who'd been arrested in the raid, including Griffith, were currently awaiting their trial. Finn assured me they would not be out of prison for a very long time, if ever. I had found the courage to have the rape kit performed at the hospital, and the fact that they had found Griffith's DNA in me gave me hope that at least one monster would be held accountable.

Rosie had been arrested as an accomplice despite multiple people arguing that she was a victim. Her complete devotion to Cillian definitely did not help her case, but Finn said they were going to try to work on some sort of insanity plea deal as far as he'd heard.

"You got everything?" Finn asked, pulling me from my musings.

"I think so, I didn't accumulate *that much* here in the last couple weeks."

He raised an eyebrow at me as if that was utter bullshit and I looked at my luggage and winced. Okay, maybe I had been using shopping therapy a little too frequently. Especially given the fact that I wasn't currently getting a paycheck. But come on, what was having a best friend's rich boyfriend for if not to use his credit card?

"You sure you don't want me to come with you?" Ava asked for the umpteenth time.

"Babe, I promise you the house hasn't changed in the day since you last saw it. This is the only stuff left to unpack, we'll be good."

"Alright, alright. I just miss you already," Ava said, pulling me into a tight hug. "It's been so amazing to have all of us here all the time. It's like a permanent sleepover."

"Yeah if your roommates are on their fucking honeymoon," I replied sarcastically. Ava looked sheepish but Art grinned, not the least bit embarrassed.

"I'm sorry that my girlfriend has a healthy sexual appetite and I must satisfy her—"

"Enough!" I said, covering my ears. Ava slapped Art playfully and he held up his hands in surrender.

"Goodbye freaks, we'll see you for supper tomorrow."

"Okay, call me if you miss me and I'll have Art send a car," Ava said pulling me into one last hug.

When we reached Finn's car out front I sank into the seat with a groan.

"They're utterly exhausting," Finn said, clearly enjoying the silence as much as I was.

"I never want to share the same roof with them again," I agreed and he laughed before pulling out of the circular drive.

"You really don't think this is a bad idea?" I asked him as he drove.

"I thought we just established that this was extremely necessary."

"Yes, leaving, but I'm saying moving in together. We haven't been seeing each other for that long—"

"I told you, I'll stay on the opposite side of the house if that makes you more comfortable."

"Okay, but what happens if we break up? Realize we don't like each other? That's going to be so awkward."

"First off, I will never not like you," he said with a dimpled grin. "And in the case that you get sick of me, we'll just make Art buy out the lease and we'll figure out other arrangements. Seriously Vi, don't borrow trouble."

I sank into my seat, grumbling. Of course, he was right, but I was loathe to admit it.

We arrived at the condo and I smiled as I looked at it. It was just as cute as the first time I'd seen it and fallen in love. With three beds and two baths, there was plenty of space if Finn and I didn't want to live on top of each other.

It took a couple of trips to get the rest of my luggage inside and finally, we were all moved in. I sighed as I looked around the space. Home. Ours. A new beginning.

"It feels good, doesn't it?" He asked, coming up behind me and resting his chin on my shoulder.

"Yeah, it does."

So much had changed in these last few weeks. Our housing situation, our jobs. Finn had been cleared from the investigation and was going to be reinstated as a detective once he told them he was ready to come back.

My thoughts moved to Cillian and, like every time I thought of him, my stomach twisted into a knot and I began to sweat. He was the main reason I hadn't put up a fight about Finn moving in. Art had purchased the best security system you could find, to be honest, I was pretty sure it wasn't even legally obtained, and the authorities were pretty sure Cillian had fled to some small island. But even still, I couldn't help the terror that plagued me at the thought of him finding me again and coming back to exact revenge.

"Wanna order pizza or something?" Finn asked, pulling me from my thoughts.

"Not really," I said, turning in his hold, needing him to distract me from my thoughts. He placed his arms around me to hold my lower back. "Chinese takeout? Italian?"

I continued to shake my head at his suggestions. He shook his mop of curls. "Okay, well then what *do* you want?"

I rested my hand on his chest and then began to slide it down his chest towards his crotch. Surprise filled his eyes. "Vi—"

"Shh," I said, silencing him with a finger to his lips before tugging him towards the room that I had claimed as my own, not that I thought we'd be sleeping in separate rooms very often. He followed me to the bedroom and once inside I pressed a kiss to his lips.

"We don't have to do this—" he began again and I stepped back, putting my hand on my hip. "Are you saying you don't want to?"

"Fuck no. Of course, I want to, I've been dying to touch you but—"

"*I* want this Finn. I do. On my terms." He stared at me for a moment and I swore he could see all the way to my soul.

Despite sleeping cuddled together every night since I'd left the hospital, we hadn't done anything more than kiss. I'd still been healing from the physical trauma I had endured, but emotionally and mentally I hadn't wanted to do anything else either. And he had not once pushed me. But I was sick of letting people take things from me. I wanted to take back control of my life. Starting with this.

"What do you need from me?" He finally asked.

"On the bed," I commanded and his eyes flashed with hunger. He reached for his shirt, waiting for my nod before removing it, followed by his pants.

"Leave the underwear," I said and he complied, sliding onto his back on the bed. I sauntered over to the dresser and opened the top drawer, pulling out several pairs of fluffy handcuffs. His eyes went round as he looked at them. "Is there a reason you need so many?"

"Because I don't think one would be enough to keep you on the bed?" I replied smoothly as I approached him. He gave me his foot willingly and I secured the first cuff to his ankle and then the bedpost.

"Did you wonder why I wanted a four-post bed frame?" I asked as I repeated the process to his other ankle.

"No, I figured you purchased your furniture based on things like appearance like everyone else, you freaky woman."

"I did. I imagined how you'd look splayed out on my bed quite a few times before deciding on this one."

He choked on a laugh and I finished the process by securing each wrist. Satisfied, I sat back to enjoy my work. And enjoy I did. His erection was all but bursting out of his underwear and I licked my lips at the sight, eliciting a moan from the man before me.

"Safe word?" I asked as I stepped towards him.

"Fuck me," he groaned.

"That sounds like the worst safe word you could have chosen but okay," I said, stopping at the edge of the bed. I slowly stepped out of my leggings, his eyes devouring me the entire time. Then I grabbed my hair and twisted it into a bun on the top of my head.

"Vi—" he groaned again and I looked down at him. "Shush, unless you want me to find a gag." His body jerked involuntarily at that and I tucked that tidbit away for another time. Finally, I climbed onto the bed and crawled towards him. I traced a manicured nail across the band of his underwear and he attempted to thrust himself upwards, although with the restrains he was unable to move very far.

"So fucking needy," I said before I pulled the underwear down, exposing his pierced cock. "I've missed this," I said, rubbing a finger over the head of his dick, spreading the precum and enjoying the friction from the piercing.

"Baby, you have no fucking idea how much it's missed you."

"Umm given the fact I wake up to your dick pressed into my ass every morning, I would say I do." I ran my hand down the length of him and gave a gentle jerk. His eyes closed as his mouth opened on a moan and I marveled at the look of my man so utterly undone by me.

Seeing how turned on I made him definitely heightened my own arousal. I leaned down and with one long suck, he was in my mouth. He again tried to thrust into me but I kept a hand on his hip, and the restraints did the rest.

I didn't associate him with the men who had abused me, but still, the added protection of him restrained made me feel completely in control and kept the lingering anxieties at bay about opening up to someone in this way again.

I sucked him deep, using my hand to grip his base, and

then move to his balls.

"Vic, holy shit, oh my god, yes," he moaned and I felt myself dampen at his words. I continued like that, bobbing up and down on him as I felt him shudder beneath me. Finally, I let his cock go with a *pop* and I crawled up him.

"Yes, fuck yes, please," he murmured as I lifted my shirt over my head, exposing my breasts. Next, I slid my panties off and we were both naked. Well except for his underwear that was now in the way. I hadn't thought that part through.

"Be right back," I said as I slid off the bed, making my way to the kitchen. I came back carrying scissors and he looked between my face and the item in my hand.

"Baby, I trust you and all and as much as I love giving up control to you, I think now might be a good time to remind you that I don't like knife play and I might need to pull out my safe word."

"Relax, you big baby," I said as I brought the scissors to his underwear and cut them off in one smooth motion.

"Fuck, Vi. You could have just untied me."

"Now where would be the fun in that?" I asked before dropping the scissors on my nightstand and crawling back up to him.

"Don't lie, you love being at my mercy," I whispered as I straddled him.

"You scare the shit out of me, but yeah," he whispered back and I laughed before leaning down and capturing his lips with my own. Our tongues clashed and it was delicious, and sexy, and beautiful. I kissed him, pouring every bit of my broken soul into him and he kissed me back like he accepted every piece and was the only thing that could make me whole.

I pulled away just enough to sink myself down on his cock. I paused before I was fully seated, cautiously waiting for any pain.

"You okay?" He asked at my pause. I nodded, biting my lip and sinking the last bit slowly.

"Fuckkk," he swore, drawing out the word as I drew out the descent. "You promise you're okay?" He asked again and my heart squeezed at the care in his eyes.

"I'm okay, I promise," I whispered back.

"Good, 'cause I have absolutely zero leverage at this angle and I'm going to need you to fuck me like now."

"Always the charmer," I said with a laugh as I slid up and then back down on him. We moaned in unison and I began to pick up my pace, setting a rhythm that had my toes curling as he hit every perfect spot inside of me. I leaned down and began trailing kisses over one side of his neck towards the other in a way that I knew made him crazy.

"Fuck, Vi, yes just like that." I picked up my pace, riding him like my very soul depended on it. And maybe it did. He was my protector, my lover, my savior. He'd shown me how far he was willing to go to save me. And once he'd saved me, he treasured me. Held me as I broke, gave me the space to just be. No one had ever done for me what he had. No one had ever meant to me what he did.

"I love you, Finn," I said, emotion clogging my throat before slamming down on him once more.

He grunted and I felt him jerk inside me as he emptied himself. He felt amazing and I was so fucking close. I reached down and circled my clit, imagining it was his fingers instead and then I too was coming.

Finally, I collapsed onto his chest and he pulled at one of the restraints. "Get it off."

I reached for the key on the nightstand and unlocked one then both of his wrists. Immediately, he grabbed me, pulling me into his chest so tight I struggled to take a deep breath.

"I love you so fucking much, Vic. From the moment, I laid eyes on you in Art's apartment, I knew you were the one for me. You're stunning and smart. You're funny and charismatic. You've everything my soul has searched for, the very thing my heart has craved. I love you so goddamn much."

Tears sprang to my eyes at his words and I clutched him like he was my only lifeline.

"When you told me you were in a relationship, you have no idea how much my heart broke. It was like I knew in my very essence that you were a piece of me and I couldn't understand how the universe had gotten it so wrong. And then the night you told me you'd broken up with him, I hated myself for how incredibly happy that made me. I tried so hard to think of him and how it must feel to lose you, but all I could think of was the fact that he'd had you and had never treated you right. He didn't deserve you, and neither do I, but damn if I won't try to earn it."

"Shut the fuck up with all that martyr shit," I said, silencing him with a kiss. "You have shown me in a million different ways how deserving you are."

He nuzzled into my neck. "Fine, I'll shut the fuck up but can you please release my legs? I'd really like to hold you properly."

I laughed as I climbed off of him to release him. The minute he was free he scooped me up in his arms and pulled me into his lap, arms wrapped around me like he never wanted to let go.

"You're the best thing to ever happen to me, Victoria Garcia."

"And you, Finnian Sullivan, are the very reason for my existence," I responded, kissing him deeply. My entire life I'd been terrified to truly be happy, to truly settle in for fear of losing it all. But now, here with him, I knew I was safe, and treasured. And more than that, I was home.

Epilogue

Toni

I hated when I couldn't wrap everything up into a neat little bow.

I sat at my desk typing on my computer as I entered the final information from my last case into an encrypted file for my own personal records. A lot of the jobs I worked either skated the edge of the law, or were flat-out prison time so no one would ever see this information, but for whatever reason I had to keep a copy for myself. I wasn't sure why, I'd never gone and looked back at a previous case. Maybe so one day if I felt really depressed I could go look at my successes?

Today, however, I just felt discouraged. Yes, I'd managed to track down a sex trafficking ring, however, the fact that the one who ran it had gotten away ate at me.

I usually loved what I did, computer jargon had always been as easy for me as breathing. Coding was a second language and one I was perfectly fluent in. The pay didn't hurt either. Not that I only did it for the money, I wasn't completely heartless.

In this last case, for example, Finn had nothing to offer me when he reached out. True, I figured Art would compensate me for his friend, but I'm sure I would have helped from the kindness of my heart anyway. Maybe.

My phone rang and I ignored it while I finished up what I was doing. I exited out of the program and it rang again. Sighing I picked it up to see Maggie's face on my screen. I clicked the answer button and her smiling face filled my phone.

"Hey, hope I'm not interrupting anything."

"Just finishing up," I said as I rolled my neck. She knew I wouldn't stop if I was in the middle of something important.

"Okay perfect, do you have a second?"

"Yeah, sure."

"Okay. Promise me you won't get mad."

"Not a chance."

"Not a chance you won't get mad?"

"No. Not a chance that I'll promise you that."

She winced. "I thought as much. Okay, well you know I'm leaving next week," she continued as if I had agreed.

"Yeah, you've only been planning your European escapades for a year now," I replied sarcastically.

"Yes, well. Do you remember Bryce?"

"Honestly Mags, I'm struggling to keep up with you right now. And no, I don't think I know a Bryce."

"He's my cousin, I think you've met him before. Regardless, I've definitely talked about him."

"Okay, and?"

She took a breath, seeming to gather her courage before plowing on. "So he's a travel nurse and just took a gig here in Minnesota and needs a place to crash for a minute while he gets his life together and I told him that I was going to be gone and he could use my bedroom if he agrees to pay rent."

"Absolutely not."

"Toni."

"No, I don't need the money. I will cover your half of the rent just fine while you're gone."

"I know but I promised him—"

"Then unpromise him," I said dismissively.

She took another deep breath. "Cancun."

"Excuse me?"

"Cancun. You got Norovirus and I nursed you back to health, forgoing my vacation to make sure you didn't die of dehydration."

The memory hit me like a ton of bricks and I scowled at her. "That's low, Mags. Even for you."

She stared at me and I saw no humor reflected there.

I sighed. "This is really important to you."

She nodded. "I promised him, Toni. He's done a lot for me. I owe him. He's super nice, clean, he works with cancer kids, and…" she trailed off.

I cocked a brow as I waited for her to continue.

"He's a man." She finally said.

"And?"

"And I would feel a lot better leaving knowing there was a guy around here to help deter your stalker.

I grunted. "First off, not to be a cliche, but I do *not* need a man to protect me." She opened her mouth to speak but I continued. "And, I told you whatever is going on is harmless. Give me more credit than that, no one is going to get through my security."

She nodded. "I know, and I do trust you. You're the best. And I don't think you need a man to protect you, but it's a fact of life that guys, especially the creepy non-consensual ones, are scared off or at least reconsider if they see another man around. It's all that misogyny."

I couldn't argue with that. "And he's planning on being here the whole time you're gone?"

"Until he can get a place of his own. If you're lucky, it'll only be a couple days and he'll be out of your hair."

I groaned as I rubbed my temples. I owed her. Cancun had

been horrible. I can't say I would have necessarily done what she had done if the situation had been reversed. She was an angel and I could do this for her.

"Last name and birthday," I finally responded and she full-out belly laughed.

"I really don't know how you're still surprising me at this point. Of course, you're going to stalk him."

"Hey, you're the one throwing a rando on me as a housemate with a week's notice."

"Be my guest, go check him out. But I promise he'll be a good housemate. You might even miss him when I get back," she said with a wink.

I stared at her with a frown and she laughed again. "Okay, glad we got that cleared up. I'll see you after work, and I'll grab you your favorite smokes as a thank you."

I nodded before hanging up and turning to my search. I truly hated the idea of someone else sharing this space. It had taken a while before I'd warmed up to having Maggie in my personal bubble and now to have to be thrown in with a complete stranger—

Maybe Maggie was right and he'd be a perfect housemate who'd clean up after himself and stay in his room, out of sight, out of mind.

I sighed. For some reason, I had a bad feeling that the next month was going to be an utter shitshow.

Acknowledgements

For everyone who took a chance on me with my debut novel, Love and Bruises, I hope your pillow is always cool and you hit every single green light.

Seriously, I have done an embarrassing amount of giggling and jumping up and down while reading your reviews. I am still in awe that other people love these characters and stories as much as I do.

For my beta readers, Jasmine, Becky, and Megan, thank you for your invaluable help in smoothing out the rough edges of this book.

For Kay, thanks for double checking my Irish and making sure I didn't write about temples haha.

And for anyone who is reading this as their first exposure, thank you, thank you. Seriously, you all are the reason why I continue to put myself out there.

As always, I couldn't do this without my soulmate and best friend. Thanks for encouraging me at every step of the process, and being my muse in so many ways.

About the Author

K.J. is a Midwest native who has been obsessed with the written word ever since consuming the entirety of the Nancy Drew collection. Her favorite genre is anything romance: fantasy, mystery, cozy and dark. She lives in Minnesota with her husband, two kids, and their pitbull rescue.

You can learn more by following her on Instagram @kj_ersti, TikTok @kjersti_writes or Facebook K.J. Ersti